ONE WAY TICKET

PETER SARDA

Cover design by Phil Poole.

ISBN 978-3-9822665-2-7

 Highway 99 Press

Contents

Prologue

Lars felt the giant shadow before he saw it looming behind him in the bulletproof glass.

"Game time is over," the giant said.

Lars spun around and looked up into two steel eyes embedded in a beefy skull under a single eyebrow. "What the fuck?" he said. Hasani's enforcer didn't normally work indoors.

"He wants to see you."

Lars smelled garlic. "Let me cash in my chips." He turned back to the window. The cashier was nowhere to be seen.

"Now," the giant said.

Lars shifted his weight, keeping his phone hand out of view. His thumb felt around desperately for the SOS button. Holding it down for three seconds activated a GPS alert. *Officer in trouble.*

"Let's go," the giant said.

The button vibrated confirmation.

Lars nodded and put the phone away. Then he pivoted, took a half-step, and put his full weight into the kick.

The giant's eyes went wide. He went down clutching his groin.

At the blackjack table, bettors looked at them with open mouths. The *chef de table* was frozen mid-motion, a card in his hand.

Lars slammed into the emergency exit and flew down the steps, using the railing like a sled, bumping into walls at each turn. A herd of buffalos pounded the stairways above his head. Round and round they went. Third floor, second floor, first floor, lobby.

As Lars crashed out of the stairwell, he saw a guard at the front desk talking into his sleeve and staring right at him. Lars flashed his P6 and cleared the turnstile in one fluid motion. Then he blasted through the double glass doors and raced to his Harley. It took him two frantic attempts to jump-start the beast. As it fishtailed out onto the street, he felt rain in his hair.

He made a hard right through a red at Alsterglacis. A double-articulated bus packed with commuters skidded sideways across the intersection. Up ahead was a sea of cars on Kennedybrücke.

A black van crashed through the brush of Gustav Mahler Park and accelerated into his path, its battering ram nearly grazing his right leg.

Lars gunned the chopper onto the frontage road below the bridge and through the underpass. He made a hard left onto Lombardbrücke, somehow bouncing onto the sidewalk without hitting the steel railing.

Needles of rain pelted his face as he weaved in and out of bike paths and around posts. The Alster River flew by on his right, and he kept pace with the InterCity train to his left. A kid waved at him from one of the windows.

Halfway across the bridge, the headlights were gone from his mirror. He almost laughed. Oversized black vans with snatch teams didn't fit on sidewalks.

He slowed the chopper as the path curved into a wooded area. Wet oak leaves slapped his face as broken cement rattled his spine. The chopper made a looping left at Ferdinandstor and followed the path under a second low bridge. The InterCity screeched above.

A wall of light blinded Lars. He screamed as the railing shattered his knee, flipping the chopper sideways and slamming him into an I-beam. He clawed rusty iron on his way down.

The headlights backed up through the moving spokes of his front wheel. As the van gurgled away, everything went black.

■ ■ ■

Lars woke up to a nightmare. He was buried under tons of black oily water, trying to reach the surface. He screamed and screamed, but nothing came out.

"Goddamn it, Lars, wake up!" someone said from far away. A beefy hand slapped his face.

Lars screamed bubbles at the familiar voice. It was Motz! He got the SOS.

"Lars! Don't you die on me!"

Die? Nobody was going to die, Lars thought. Except maybe Hasani. His badass buddy Motz would rip the Albanian apart at the joints. Lars laughed more bubbles.

"You're back!" Motz yelled. "You scared the shit out of me, you bastard."

"Ma—" Lars said.

"Yeah, it's me, partner," Motz said. "We'll get you out of here."

Lars shook himself free of the mask. "Mar-mal!" he screamed. Hasani's real shipment was coming from Mazar-i-Sharif.

"What?" Motz yelled back.

Lars coughed up something thick and warm.

"Stay with me, Lars!"

"An—" He couldn't get it all the way out.

"Save your breath, Lars!"

"An–ton!" Lars screamed, spitting out all that slimy warmth. His teeth began to chatter. Damn, was it cold out there.

"Antonov?"

Lars smiled and let go. Motz got it. Hasani was shipping under a Russian flag. They would catch him red-handed this time.

Delicious warmth filled Lars' mouth. No more of that chattering bullshit, he thought.

"Lars!" Motz yelled. "Stay with me! You hear me, Lars? I mean it, Goddamn it! Lars, you fucking stay with me!"

Lars chewed the thick warmth. Twenty bites before you swallow, like Grandpa Hanson always said.

Motz was drifting up and away. Lars wondered what he was doing up there in all that water. When Motz opened his mouth, he made a *woah-woah-woah* sound. Then he was just a swaying light that got further and further away. Then he was gone.

A warm wave brushed Lars' cheek with a gentle *whoosh*. He snuggled into the delicious dream. He was almost home.

ONE

Undercover

The InterCity Express veered left with a protracted sparking screech. Ritter flexed his gun hand, but the tingling didn't let go.

Outside the double-paned window, needles of sunlight bounced off yellow cranes reaching into purple sky above HafenCity. Concrete penthouses for plastic people. Behind that were the green slate roofs, ornate orange bricks, and shimmering mirrored windows of the Speicherstadt, the old warehouse district. The postcard picture put his teeth on edge.

Coming up on the right were squat brick warehouses covered with gang-like graffiti. Now that was more like it. Three punks in baggy black shorts and lace-up boots were teeing off next to beach chairs and a short case of Astra on the flat roof. It was the kind of thing the *Amis* used to do on Bagram Air Base.

Something banged the back of Ritter's seat. His hand went to his hip. Then his mind caught up. His H&K was in the duffel bag in the overhead compartment. Turning, he saw an overly tan retiree struggling with two oversized burgundy suitcases, both marked with yellow ribbons. The square-shaped wife with the "blonde" buzzcut looked on disdainfully.

The other passengers were on their feet, grabbing identical trolley bags from overhead compartments and clogging the aisle with zero regard for one another. The kind of self-righteous civilians who condemned police brutality under *any* circumstance. *The law is the law*, they would say sternly over their red wine, then move on to the weather.

None would approve of the short trigger reset on Ritter's

ambidextrous Heckler & Koch SFP9-SF. Unless, of course, a two-time kiddie rapist named Mathias Lemke had kidnapped their seven-year-old and put him in an underground box with a short oxygen supply. Then it would be: *Do whatever it takes, Herr Kriminalhauptkommissar. Just bring our little boy back home safe and sound.*

The train went dark for a moment in the shadows of sooty brick buildings and even less friendly black-and-white graffiti signed by "Oz." Ritter leaned back in his seat. That fucker sure got around. A few years back, the notorious sprayer contracted AIDS. Since then, his messages got a lot darker. Life-saving medication hadn't improved his mood.

Up ahead was a nineteenth-century structure that looked like a smaller version of the Frankfurt central station. It had one hump instead of three. Heavy steel beams bent to support the frosted glass roof high above. Somehow, they managed to look baroque. Except for the "PHILIPS" sign in the paned windows spanning the tracks.

After the train pulled to a bumpy stop, the passengers shuffled toward the doors like sludge. Two minutes later, the stale air was swept away by a fresh breeze from outside. A muffled loudspeaker on the platform reminded travelers not to leave their luggage unattended. Anything to give registered voters a false sense of security, while guys like Ritter did the dirty work in the shadows.

Ritter waited for the grizzled old guy with the filthy backpack to load up empty plastic bottles and drag it to the next car. Then he grabbed his bag and headed for the door.

On the platform, thousands of voices echoed against the dome-like roof, filling the hall with a cold, comfortable din. The station was wall-to-wall humanity, like Frankfurt four hours earlier.

Ritter went with the flow to the wide cement stairway. In the shadows underneath, two young thieves closed in on a businessman dozing on a wooden bench. They pocketed his wallet and phone before he snorted awake. You snooze, you lose, asshole.

The stairway went sideways for a moment with an electric *zap-zap*. Ritter held onto the rail until the ground righted itself. The dizzy spell never lasted long, but it was hard to get used to. It always came out of nowhere, like a sucker punch.

The first time it happened, he found himself on his hands and knees, panting like a dog on the cold cement of a crowded S-Bahn station. The Bundeswehr doctors called it "cervical vertebra syndrome," probably caused by that helicopter accident in Kandahar. The *Amis* called it "whiplash." Commuters just thought he was drunk.

This was nothing in comparison. It didn't even knock him down. He hitched the duffel bag over his shoulder and headed up the stairs.

The ground floor reeked of buttered popcorn and reefer. Arcade music was playing nearby. He walked through a wide, windy doorway, past the inevitable pale junkies clustered on the U-Bahn stairwell, and over to the front taxi in the long line at the curb. He opened the back door, threw his bag onto the seat, and said, "Alsterdorf."

The fortyish driver looked like a failed sociology grad student. He put the cream-colored Mercedes in gear without a word. A heated political debate was blaring on the radio. It sounded local.

Next to the driver was a pint-sized rag called *MOPO*. As in *Hamburger Morgenpost*. Its screaming headline: "Whores vs. Yuppies!" A tasseled brown-and-white FC St. Pauli flag swung from the mirror, in open violation of traffic regulations.

Ritter leaned over the front seat. "Who's winning?" he said.

The driver punched it through a stale yellow. "What's that?"

"The whores or the yuppies?" Ritter motioned to the newspaper.

"Oh, that," the driver said. "Don't get me started. Fucking Christian Democrats want to gentrify St. Pauli! Tear down Herbertstrasse and build one of those business parks. You believe that shit? Nothing is sacred in this town." He looked in the rearview. "Where you from?"

"Frankfurt," Ritter said, all innocent civilian. "Is Herbertstrasse near the Reeperbahn?" Like he wanted tips about the red-light district. Or "Davidwache," the smallest—and busiest—police precinct in Hamburg.

"The Herbert is the heart of St. Pauli! The *Sozis* will show those fascist bankers!" The driver slapped the wheel for emphasis. The flag fluttered approval.

Ritter gave the rage addict what he wanted. "Social Democrats run this town?"

The driver turned around completely. "Goddamn right! Mertens is going to turn the Herbert into a national monument. That'll stop those real estate sharks."

"Mertens? Who's that?" Ritter kept one eye on the right blinker of the bus looming on their left. The side was covered with a semi-transparent advertisement for a zoo. The passenger nearest him was a giraffe.

"The Innensenator, but he's okay," the driver assured him, shooting ahead of the bus, which then veered into the lane behind them.

"That the top cop?" Ritter said, settling back in his seat. The driver looked like somebody who donned a black mask and threw Molotov cocktails at riot cops on May Day. He wondered how the antifa type would square the circle.

"Yeah, but he's a *Sozi*," the driver said, like that made Mertens some kind of double agent. "The senate votes at the end of the week. Then we'll see who owns the streets."

"That we will," Ritter said. Wherever you were in the world, the locals always knew what time it was. All you had to do was ask.

．．．

After checking into Best Western under his own name, Ritter changed into sweats and went down to the basement for his Green Beret exercises. No equipment, just fifteen minutes of running in place, mid-air toe touches, and off-ground clap pushups to make up for the train ride. The only other guy in the room was a heart attack candidate on a treadmill engrossed in an overhead TV special called "Herbertstrasse: The New Silicon Alley?" Clever.

After a cold shower upstairs, Ritter was a new man. He grabbed a *MOPO* from the front desk and hit the street. Outside, he stood with all the hardworking losers on the sidewalk. The red light turned green, and the herd stepped onto the street. Ritter held his ground. It was more instinct than anything, like when walking point in Hindu Kush. Civilians didn't get it. *You listen to your gut, you might stay alive.*

Out of nowhere, an unmarked brown Opel station wagon shot past his nose, driving on the wrong side with flashing front lights but no siren, and nearly took out a dozen cursing pedestrians. At the nearby intersection, it slid to a stop, only to lurch forward a meter at a time. Ritter smiled. The two plainclothes inside weren't afraid to bend a few corners hunting bad guys.

Sure as shit, the driver craned his neck until he saw what he was chasing on a parallel street. The Opel lurched forward to the next intersection, where it did a smoking brodie and disappeared. Ritter was smiling so hard it hurt. The light had turned red again. He waved off a honking metallic gold Porsche SUV.

Two blocks later, Ritter's nose led him to a restaurant serving fresh seafood next to a canal. It looked like a former boat dock. The place was packed under the huge umbrellas. They didn't call Hamburg natives "fish-heads" for nothing.

Storm clouds hung over the canals like one big flying saucer. Underneath was purple sky streaked through with orange.

The combination made the restaurant look like a living painting.

Ritter was searching for a free table when a pretty girl in a black ankle-length apron appeared at his side. Light freckles were sprayed across a slightly bent nose under wild locks of blonde hair. She looked nineteen going on forty. Her name tag said "Jenny."

Ritter felt something wake up in his pants.

"Right this way, sir," Jenny said, leading him down the two steps to the redwood dock. Her purple eyes were dancing as he sat down on a woven chair. She didn't hand him the leather-bound menu she was holding against her breasts. "You look like a man who knows what he wants."

Ritter laughed at that. The whole evening had become glossy above the shimmering water.

A rowing team streamed by soundlessly, their coxswain at ease.

"Fish would be good," Ritter said.

The waitress bit her lip playfully. "Would you care to be more specific? Or should I guess?"

Ritter held her look. "I think we both know the answer to that, Jenny."

She blushed slightly but recovered quickly. "May I bring you something to drink with that?"

"Water," he said.

She gave him that look again. "Shaken or stirred?"

This was too easy, he thought. "What do *you* think?"

"Shaken it is." She hesitated.

"Is there a problem?" he said. It was possible she had bitten off more than she could chew, but he doubted it.

Jenny was frowning now. "You're not from around here, are you?"

"I'm not?" Ritter had taken great trouble to lose his Frankfurt accent two decades before. Most people thought he was from Hannover, home to High German. Jenny, on the other hand, had a tinny harbor accent that was one hundred percent Hamburg.

He wouldn't be surprised if she spoke Low German at home.

"No." Jenny sounded sure of herself. "You look like you've seen everything."

Ritter suppressed a laugh. "Why do you say that?"

"The crinkles around your eyes," she said, like she had just figured it out. "And you're, you're so well put together."

Well, now. That was specific enough to indicate serious physical interest. "Thank you."

"There's something mysterious about you, like a secret agent man."

Ritter felt his face go blank.

"Oops," Jenny said.

"Just don't tell anyone. Or I'll have to kill you."

Jenny gave him a look that could have raised the dead. "Is that a promise?"

"Yes," Ritter said. "When do you get off?"

She showed him sharp teeth. "Anytime you say, sir."

Sir.

"This is just my day job," she confided. "My night job is Down Under."

Ritter stared at her name tag again. This had better not cost him money.

A heavy shadow crossed overhead. He felt what could have been a raindrop.

"Gotcha!" she said triumphantly. "Down Under is an Aussie bar."

And you just showed your hand, he thought. "You working tonight?"

"Not anymore," she said.

Ritter felt a real raindrop. Then another. "We'd better find some cover," he said.

Jenny didn't disagree.

Their footsteps on the wooden deck were echoed by rapid-fire *pitter-patter* on the big umbrellas.

TWO

Fool for Love

Laura threw the navy-blue duty cap onto the matching canvas shirt in the sports bag. Both had knife-edge creases. The red seal of Hamburg rested on a twelve-pointed gold star riveted to the crown of the cap. The patch pocket underneath said "POLIZEI." The blinking blue lights embedded in the belt were against regulations. As were the missing sleeves and knee-high boots with twenty-centimeter spikes.

Ever since getting paroled from Hahnöfersand, Laura had worked in The Cage. Businessmen from as far as Munich drove up to St. Pauli to see a "policewoman" and female "suspect" locked in deadly—and intimate—combat behind bars. The draw was live sex. Real penetration with real nightsticks.

Laura zipped up the bag and looked at the clock. Veronica was working late again. That was getting to be a habit. No wonder she was so stressed.

Laura went into the kitchen and turned down the heat on the ground beef. The scent of chili filled the air. She walked past the mute TV onto the balcony and fired up a Marlboro Red. Exhaling a healthy lungful into the silver moon, she slapped shut the Zippo and shivered in her thin T-shirt. The things we do for love.

Down below, a black Mini Cooper swept into an impossibly small parking spot at the base of the bridge. The lights went out and the door swung open, followed by two luscious legs.

Butterflies fluttered in Laura's stomach. She ground out the butt on the railing and dropped it into an old pickle jar.

Back inside, she mixed the Tanqueray and Schweppes.

Out the corner of her eye, she saw the title shot for *The King of St. Pauli*. She put a wedge of lime on each glass and made a face at the plasma TV. It measured 101 centimeters. The high definition made it easy to see the dozens of hairs in Willi Kaiser's nose.

■ ■ ■

Walking up the stone steps of the white Victorian, Veronica looked away from the muscle car below and shifted the position of her shoulder bag. The twine handles of the oversized Versace shopping bag dug into the fingers of her other hand. The long-necked vase kept shifting position, causing the ball inside to bang around. She could already feel her sciatic nerve acting up.

Laura greeted her at the door with a nicotine kiss and a G&T, strong like she liked it, with a twist of lime.

"Sorry I'm so late," Veronica said, sucking on the straw and sneaking a look at the hall clock. "That ship captain from Bangkok took forever."

The pint-sized commander of the massive *Asia Dawn* container ship was one regular she didn't mind talking about. Foreign nationals were out of Laura's shakedown range. Still, Veronica didn't dare mention his name. Captain Meephuk. She never would have heard the end of that.

Laura let out a nasty laugh. "The monkey cage guy?"

"That's the one." Veronica let the leather bag down softly onto the marble-topped side table and continued to the living room, where she set down her burden with a muffled thump on the white shag carpet. She shook her carrying hand.

"Long as he tipped heavily," Laura said.

"Oh, yeah." Veronica allowed herself a half-smile. "He paid and paid and paid."

They laughed at the old joke together.

Veronica used the armrest to lower herself onto the couch,

careful to keep her back straight. As she rubbed circulation back into her hand, she noticed that the flat-screen TV on the far wall was on, but the sound was all the way down. Maybe Laura took her recent speech about the homeowners' association complaints to heart after all.

"What's in the bag?" Laura was pointing to the neck of the vase.

"It's a gift," Veronica said, leaning to her left and discreetly massaging her upper buttock with a thumb knuckle.

"For me?" Laura said excitedly.

"No, silly, for me. From the ship captain."

"Oh," Laura said, sticking out her lower lip.

Veronica saw her disappointment. There was only one way to fix that. "I thought you'd like it."

Laura looked at her uncertainly. "You thought I'd like something from that little perv?"

"Look at it," Veronica said. Her knuckles finally found the *piriformis* muscle. *Aaahhh.*

Laura did as she was told. "It looks like a big-ass bong!"

"Take it out," Veronica said with half-closed eyes. The kneading was producing good pain.

Laura lifted the vase by the neck. "Damn, this thing is *hea-vy!*" The big end got caught on the twine handles, so she kicked the bag away with a loud *whack!* It almost took out Veronica's Murano glass collection.

Veronica's eyes popped open in alarm. Nothing on the windowsill was broken, but the unicorn from Venice was shaking on its hind legs.

The ball started rolling around again. It sounded like a small roulette wheel. Laura shook the vase. "What the hell is *that*?" she said, turning it upside down and peering into the hole. The big end of the vase made the chandeliers above the coffee table tinkle.

"Careful!" Veronica said.

"Sorry, Cap'n!" Laura flipped the vase back down. It made a not-so-muffled thump when it hit the carpet. "What is it?" she said.

"What is what?" Veronica said, irritated.

"This thing!" Laura slapped the open end of the vase with her palm loudly.

Veronica tried to control her temper. "Keep your hands off it and I'll tell you."

Laura took one monster step back from the vase. "Look, Ma, no hands!"

Veronica waited a few seconds for her pulse to settle down.

"So?" Laura said.

"It's a monkey trap," Veronica said finally.

Laura stepped forward, bent over at a ninety-degree angle, and peered into the narrow neck with one eye shut. "How the hell do monkeys fit into *that*?" Her voice seemed to be affected by her squinting.

Despite her anger, Veronica had to laugh. That was Laura to a T. "They don't," she said. "The hunters put a ball inside."

"So that's what's making all that racket!" Laura grabbed the neck again.

"Laura!" Veronica said.

"But the hole is too small!" Laura demonstrated by jabbing her bird finger in and out of the hole.

"They glue the bottom on after they put the ball inside," Veronica said. She knew because she had asked Captain Meephuk the same question.

Laura jumped onto her stomach, catching herself with both hands, and examined the base. "You're right!" she said, her voice muffled by the carpet. "I can see the seam!" Then she pushed herself up onto her knees. "How does it work?"

"Monkeys put their hands inside to get the ball," Veronica said. "But when they grab it, they can't get their hands out."

"They got skinny-ass hands," Laura said, flexing her own.

"Yes, they do," Veronica said. "But when they form a fist, they can't pull their hands back out."

Laura scrambled to her feet, grabbed air a couple of times, and looked at her fist. Then she held it over the hole. "Oh, I get it!"

"They can't let go of the ball," Veronica said. "Their own greed captures them." Like you, she thought.

Laura flexed her fist some more. "Cool!" Then she stopped, a funny look on her face. "Whadda they do with the monkeys?"

Veronica smiled into her empty eyes. "Eat their brains."

Laura let that sink in and then pumped her fist. "Yeah, baby! That is *so* cool! Monkey brain tacos!" She laughed and threw herself onto the couch next to Veronica.

Veronica sat up quickly. To cover herself, she took a long draw on her G&T. "This really hits the spot."

"*You* really hit the spot," Laura said with *that* look in her eye.

Veronica ignored the pass. If it were up to Laura, they would do their live show every night, like they used to.

Black-and-white clips of Willi Kaiser showed on HHTV. Veronica wanted to turn up the volume, but Laura needed quality time when she first came home.

"It's thirty in the shade," Laura said.

Oh, boy, here we go, Veronica thought. Ibiza again. She tried not to let her impatience show. "You ought to be the weatherman on HHTV!"

"Tell me you don't wish we were there right now," Laura said.

Veronica bit her tongue.

Laura walked over to the mantle and touched the framed photo. The two of them were glowing under twin palm trees. A perfect sunset enveloped them in orange light.

On the other side of the room, HHTV showed Willi and his fifth wife entering a courtroom under a blitz of lights.

■ ■ ■

Veronica pushed back her plate. "That was great! There's nothing like a home-cooked meal." The tacos were perfect for this time of year. Her tongue was still burning from the chili sauce. Laura was a regular pyromaniac, even if she couldn't spell it.

"Bet you say that to all the girls," Laura said.

Veronica didn't hear her at first. She had thirty-seven emails on her phone, but nothing from the university hospital.

"Don't forget your yellow card tomorrow." Laura sounded snippy.

Veronica looked up mid-scroll. "How many times do I have to tell you? I don't have sex with clients!"

The last thing she wanted to think about was her monthly VD check at the gynecologist. Tomorrow of all days.

"Losing your license is a big—"

Veronica gave her a hard look.

Laura swallowed the rest of the sentence.

"Sorry," Veronica said. "I just had a long day."

"How about an after-dinner massage?"

■ ■ ■

"You've still got the magic fingers," Veronica said. Laura always managed to trigger her *supraspinatus tendinitis*. Only a bubble bath would relieve the sharp pain.

"They can do a lot more than that," Laura said.

Veronica felt a callused hand stray from her shoulder blade to her right breast. She shifted her weight just enough to make it go away. "My breasts are fine."

"You can say that again."

Veronica picked up the remote. HHTV was replaying the debate between Innensenator Mertens and Senator Althaus. "This is interesting," she said. "I heard part of it in the car on the way home."

Mertens looked a lot different in a tailored suit. Nobody would have guessed the top cop in Hamburg had monthly sessions with Mistress Veronica in the Black Room of Herbertstrasse. Not even Laura.

Veronica didn't let her mind go there. If she ever breathed a word, Laura and her old cellmate would blackmail the Innensenator into the poorhouse.

Laura stuck out her lower lip at the TV. "That's just politics."

"I wouldn't say that," Veronica said. "It affects us directly."

Laura was busy rubbing the excess oil on her own hard nipples.

"The Christian Democrats want to turn the Herbert into Silicon Alley," Veronica said. She hated to admit it, but it *was* a brilliant idea.

The rubbing stopped. "They want to turn it into a tit farm?"

Veronica didn't laugh. Laura wasn't the sharpest pencil in the box, but she drew straight lines. "No, silly, a high-tech business district, like in America. Althaus wants to gentrify the neighborhood."

Laura pulled her T-shirt back down. "Good luck with that. The only gents in St. Pauli are the johns."

Veronica's trigger point throbbed menacingly. Straight lines were overrated. "Times are changing. AIDS was bad enough, but the Internet is killing us. You remember those schoolgirls in Eppendorf?"

"Yeah," Laura said. "Their pimp is doing a dime in Santa Fu. What of it?"

"That's not my point." Veronica worked her shoulder, but that just made it worse. "Private houses are popping up like weeds. Deutsche Telekom will set up an e-commerce site for ten euros a month. You should hear Anita go on about profit margins. She makes the girls check their phones at the door."

"Thought you had some super-duper contract," Laura said. "Special conditions. Or you still a working girl like the rest of us?"

"I may be a specialist, but I still work hard! Who do you think pays for all this?" Veronica motioned around the restored apartment. Alone the heating lost in the high ceiling and out the high windows cost an arm and a leg. "How many dancers you know can afford a condo in Eppendorf?"

"I do my part," Laura said. "Besides, I don't care *where* I live. I just care *who* I live with."

Veronica almost felt sorry for her. The poor girl really had it bad. "Let me put it this way," she said, "if the Christian Democrats win, I'm out of the Herbert for good."

"Oh!" Laura said. "Can we go to Ibiza?"

Laura's childishness was misleading. You had to weigh your words carefully. She took them so literally—and held you to them. "One step at a time."

"Yes!" Laura said, pumping her fist again.

■ ■ ■

The debate was almost over when Veronica's lips were assaulted by another ashtray kiss.

Laura grabbed her bag and headed for the door. The creaky stairs in the hall didn't make a peep.

Veronica could never figure out how she did it. Maybe all those B&Es were good for something.

Veronica put the crusty dishes under water. Below the kitchen window, the muscle car *vroomed!* to a start. With a slow gurgle, the headlights strafed the neighboring villas and burned rubber.

Veronica walked into the bathroom, leaned over the clawfoot tub, and twisted the ceramic knobs counterclockwise. When the water was hot to the touch, she dropped the plug and added scented bubble bath. The tiles steamed up around her. She began setting out the candles.

The soothing sound followed her to the kitchen, where she uncorked a bottle of Cabernet and poured her first glass.

Excitedly, she walked back to the side table in the hall and plucked the envelope from her shoulder bag. Her heart skipped every time she saw the cobalt blue UKE logo. Universitäts-klinikum Hamburg-Eppendorf, the university hospital on the other side of Eppendorfer Park.

She set down her glass on the miniature neo-Roman column she'd picked up at that charming boutique on Rothenbaum-chaussee. Her hands were shaking as she lit the candles. She laughed when the logo attracted some fluffy bubbles. She shook them off, slipped the envelope under the glass, and stripped quickly. She put one foot, then the other, into the steaming suds. She twisted the faucets shut and settled down into her spot. Then she reached for the envelope.

Taking her second sip of wine, she began reading.

Dear Veronica Lühmeyer,

We are pleased to inform you....

Veronica let out a squeal of delight. Sometimes dreams did come true.

THREE

Fight Club

Innensenator Carsten Mertens watched the angry demonstrators on the wide plaza down below. Most were young women, girls really. They were chanting loudly with raised fists about animal fur, of all things.

He knew they couldn't see him behind the mirrored windows of his fourth-floor office in City Hall. But they should be able to see the city-state's patron goddess, Hammonia, and her Latin motto above the entrance. *Libertatem quam peperere maiores digne studeat servare posteritas.* Based on the black Xs taped across the nubile nipples below, he doubted very much that "posterity" would "strive to preserve the freedom won by our elders in dignity."

If the protesters were a bit brighter, they would direct their wrath at the Ladage & Oelke shop that stood directly behind them for two centuries. The family-run store still tailored frock coats for members of the Hanseatic Club. Mertens reminded himself to pick up his resoled wingtips the next day.

A hideous electronic scratching sound crashed into his reverie. He turned away from the window and went over to the oak-paneled wall, where the fax machine was ejaculating paper in uneven jerks that ended up on the floor. The protesters probably wouldn't like that either.

He stopped smiling. The letterhead said Kaiser Enterprises. "Not again," he said. Willi Kaiser was sending more "corrections" to his senate bill. The gangster took peer review literally.

Mertens sighed. To get anything done in this town, you had

to get your hands dirty. Kaiser, the so-called "King of St. Pauli," owned most of the "establishments" in the district. His support was essential to turning the historical Herbertstrasse into a national monument. Never mind that men window-shopped for girls in the houses that lined the street. Or that Kaiser had him on tape in the Black Room of Haus 7b.

Mertens looked at the first sheet of fax paper. Kaiser had written in the margins that historical monuments were free from property taxes, and he wanted the city-state to pay "care-holder fees" to property owners. Mertens laughed. If Kaiser had his way, the blue-collar workers who made up the Social Democratic voter base would have to kick money back up to the owner of Herbertstrasse, namely Kaiser. "Willi, Willi, Willi," Mertens said, crossing out the "suggestion."

■ ■ ■

An hour later, Mertens' armored Mercedes S-Guard pulled up outside the Rowing Club on the Alster River. He put down his *Financial Times* and got out, telling his driver to pick him up in an hour. Wafts of steamed lobster greeted him as he crossed the wide planks to the floating restaurant. It had been years since he was on a rowing crew. He kept his membership because of the contacts—and the food. Who said Social Democrats had to eat Bratwurst?

Mertens spotted the blonde goddess with oversized black shades at the far end of the pier-like dining area. She was wearing a red-and-white polka dot dress and matching party shoes. The angle of her neck told him she knew she was being watched.

He made his way across the deck over to her. "Hello there, beautiful," he said.

"Hello," she said seductively, removing her dark glasses. Her eyes were crystal blue and sparkling.

Mertens looked at the empty chair opposite her with more

than affected shock. "Don't tell me you're here all alone."

"Not anymore," the goddess said, flashing perfect white teeth. She motioned to the chair.

"What beautiful polka dots," Mertens said, sitting down gratefully. He was awestruck by the way they highlighted her stunning figure.

She giggled and bit a big red lip. "I wore them just for you."

"Will you marry me?" he said. It wasn't a joke. He felt like he was seventeen again.

"Only if you ask me." She could have been blushing under her deep tan.

It was an old game of theirs. Charlotte looked just like she had that spring afternoon as she pedaled around the Alster on her ancient Dutch bicycle in her trademark polka dots. After twenty-five years of marriage, Mertens still couldn't believe she was his. So fresh, so willing.

"And only if you run for mayor," she continued.

Goodbye, bicycle girl, Mertens thought. "One step at a time," he said. "First the historical monument."

If only he could forget about politics, just for a few hours. It never ended. In the corridors of power, you had no friends, only people who wanted something from you.

"You are a national monument," Charlotte said with a giggle.

"Those tennis lessons are worth every penny," Mertens said, admiring his wife's curves. He didn't know whether she looked better with or without the dress. It was an old question that didn't have an answer. *The path is the goal.*

"*Buongiorno!*" she said, reminding him that her new tennis instructor had an Italian accent and dark good looks.

Mertens nodded to the waitress, who was waiting patiently with the menu. She obviously knew who he was. "I'll start with a Tanqueray and Schweppes with a twist of lime," he said, taking the menu.

"Yes, sir," the waitress said. Her ass was smiling at him as she walked away.

Charlotte balled her fist at him playfully. "Why I oughta—"

"Another fifteen-rounder, huh?" Mertens said, opening the menu. He didn't mention the dark rings under her eyes. The night before, he was woken by the late-night boxing match in the living room downstairs.

"Hardly," she said. "But Klitschko knocked that big Samoan down three times in the fifth."

"Leapai?" He looked up. "I thought he was Austrian—"

The waitress was back with his G&T.

"That was quick," Mertens said, taking the tall glass eagerly.

"We aim to please," the waitress said.

Charlotte stared at her rival. "If it walks like a duck and quacks like a duck."

The waitress made a quick retreat to the kitchen.

Mertens took a deep drink. He knew better than to stop Charlotte on a roll.

"Klitschko bounced that aborigine all around the ring like a basketball," she said. "If the ref hadn't stopped him, he would have killed him." Her face was flushed.

"Speaking of aborigines," Mertens said. "How's your Italian Stallion?"

Charlotte was outraged. "What?" she said. "I want you to know that Tony is highly cultivated. He holds a degree in comparative literature."

"I'll bet," Mertens said, with a laugh. "That explains why he teaches pretty married women double-handed backhand."

"It beats obsessive vacuuming."

"Ouch," Mertens said. Charlotte must have heard him with his new steam cleaner. He loved the way it cleaned out those hard-to-get spots between the white tiles on the bathroom wall.

"I'm sure your therapist has a name for that," she continued.

"Not that I've ever met her."

"What makes you think my therapist is a *her*?"

"Because I've never met her."

Mertens marveled at his wife's circular logic. It was a beauty to behold. "That comes under doctor–patient confidentiality," he said.

"You can ask her tomorrow."

"Is it that time again? I forgot to check my calendar."

Charlotte laughed. "While you're at it, you might ask her about Alzheimer's. Oh wait, you asked last month."

Mertens pretended to slap his wife with his *Financial Times*. But he was already thinking about his "therapy session" with Mistress Veronica the next day.

FOUR

Breakfast of Champions

Ritter woke with a jolt. The mattress was soft, the sheets sticky. Early morning sun was peeking through rattan blinds. Where the hell was he? A safe house in Kandahar? A hospital in Istanbul?

He was pretty sure he wasn't dreaming anymore. Last he remembered, he was running for his life up a rocky hillside. Base camp was just over the ridge, but he had to double back to sidetrack a white Toyota Hilux with a mounted PKS machine gun. He ducked into the central train station in time to see gray men in gray suits following him. Somehow, he got cornered by towelheads in a latrine on Rhein-Main Air Base. Which was strange. The Taliban didn't exactly have a big footprint in Frankfurt.

Ritter blinked hard and tried again. The walls morphed from red to yellow to green to blue to purple and back to red. The lava lamp on the makeshift nightstand sure was moody. The rhythmic light show was punctuated by loud snoring.

Ritter looked over. Jenny. Waterbed. Hamburg. Thunder. Lightning. Rain. The loud memories came flooding back.

He never would have thought such a little girl could make so much noise—or bring him in so hard. He checked his wrists for marks. He hadn't been cuffed that tight since Level 3 SERE training at Bagram.

A cone-shaped breast rose and fell under a wild mass of red–yellow–green–blue–purple hair, each snort sending a gentle ripple his way. Even in the ever-morphing psychedelic dawn, he could make out a mouthful of dark nipple.

He peeled back a sheet that stuck in all the wrong places and reached for his black jeans on the Navajo rug. A loose plank under a wool arrowhead squeaked.

The rising cone looked about ready to peak. He waited for it to crash, sending another wave of patchouli his way.

He scanned the floor under the desk. He vaguely recalled his shorts hitting the engineering lamp after she tossed them away. He gave up and pulled on his jeans. His T-shirt and leather jacket went on by themselves while the search for his boots began. He located his Iron Rangers under the bed, next to some industrial-grade dust balls. One sock was AWOL.

He frog-marched across the rug, keeping an eye on the reddest–yellowest–greenest bush he had ever seen. No hint of hair removal, despite her age.

The erect nipple jiggled to a stop mid-snore. He looked above the smooth peak into the dreamy face on the pillow. He was rewarded with a languid sigh that rolled with the waves, revealing modest curves. He felt a last surge of lust mingled with regret but knew what he had to do. He grabbed the *MOPO* off the ground. The door opened silently. Then he was on the other side.

▪ ▪ ▪

Back at Best Western, Ritter slipped a faded green folder into the *MOPO* and hit the carpeted stairs next to the elevator. At the first landing, he stuck the newspaper under his arm and zipped the sweater jacket up to his Adam's apple. Frying bacon drifting up the stairs competed with the erotic blend of cigarettes and patchouli clinging to his nasal membranes. It wasn't cold enough for a turtleneck. April rarely was, even up here. The worn carpet muffled his descent.

He felt himself smirk. Less than twenty-four hours in town and he couldn't keep it in his pants—the night before his new job. He hoped the collar covered the monkey bite. He spotted the teeth marks in the mirror over the sink when he came in. Another reason not to shave. Served him right for bedding down a waitress half his age.

He had popped two paracetamols, but his lower back was still killing him. It wasn't just the spongy mattress. He tried not to think about the Snoopy doll bouncing in the fluid colors of the lamp.

At the base of the stairs, Ritter walked past the front desk and into the dining room. The frying bacon smell won. The tables against the wall were covered with every conceivable breakfast food. He took the rectangular lid off a stainless-steel tray and scooped out bacon strips, scrambled eggs, and fried potatoes.

Back at his table, he set down the plate and made space for the *MOPO*. He opened it to the folder stamped "Polizei Frankfurt – Confidential."

As he chowed down, he took a final look at the documents Polizeipräsident Rosenfeld had handed him the morning before. Hard to believe his former boss was under indictment—for torture. But easy to believe Rosenfeld took the fall himself to protect his protégé. Ritter hadn't seen loyalty like that outside of what the *Amis* called "Injun Country." *Leave no man behind.*

The single-spaced A4 pages contained no letterhead or watermark, just blunt biographies of five detectives and the chief inspector of LKA 411, the Homicide Division in Hamburg, with official portraits stapled in place. Rosenfeld had typed them himself on his old mechanical Olympia. As he put it, "Print is the future." They both laughed bitterly. No electronic trail.

One bio in particular had caught Ritter's attention on the train.

> *Dietmar ("Motz") Beck born and raised in harbor bar. Altercation with Hells Angels at age 16, deep scar in scalp from motorcycle chain. "Protected" by local underworld boss Willi Kaiser, reputed "King of St. Pauli."*

Numerous disciplinary hearings and reprimands for insubordination and excessive force. High clearance rate, excellent courtroom witness.

Ritter studied the academy photo. Nothing remarkable or even intelligent about Beck's blunt features. He wouldn't stand out in a crowd. Aside from the usual cop stare, he could be a truck driver or a dock worker.

The nickname was telling, though. Motz, as in *motzen*. So Beck was a complainer. That meant his bark was worse than his bite. Except for the scar. Blowhards didn't stand up to one percenters.

And then there was Beck's ex-partner.

KHK Lars Hanson, DOA 27 March result of motorcycle accident under questionable circumstances. No evidence of foul play. Beck blames local casino owner with ties to Albanian mob. Hanson rumored to have gambling problem.

Anybody who'd spent time in the trenches knew loyalty among comrades was thicker than blood. That made Beck dangerously unpredictable. Ritter's kind of people—under normal circumstances. Problem was, these weren't normal circumstances.

The snitch legend created by Rosenfeld established an unshakable alibi. It was the only thing standing between Ritter and his own indictment. But it had a serious downside. He had to play a role that would make an instant enemy of a violent detective with a score to settle. Rosenfeld said it gave his alibi "legs." Nice theory. But the man on the ground knew better. *No plan survives contact with the enemy.*

FIVE

Pay Dirt

Motz didn't hear the door open behind him. The broken man in the steamy mirror had his undivided attention. He was trying to say something, but blood just bubbled out of his mouth. His body was sprawled on the dirty cement like everything was broken inside. *Lars! Don't you die on me!* The bubbles turned into a wet laugh. A black pool grew rhythmically under his wet hair. *Lars! Stay with me!*

"Hmmmph!"

Motz blinked back tears.

Little Sophie was standing on spindly legs at his height. As always, she had jumped onto the toilet lid next to the sink, towel at the ready. Her eyes were closed, like she was savoring the last moments of sleep.

Motz stifled a sob.

After a loud intake of breath, a hoarse voice began singing. "The itsy bitsy spiii-der"—there was a dramatic pause—"climbed up the water SPOUT!"

The sob caught in Motz's throat.

"Daddy, you're not doing it right!" Sophie objected. She was staring at him with one open eye.

Motz nodded and dipped the safety razor into the hot water.

The eye closed. Another loud breath. "Down came the raaa-ain..."

Motz dutifully shaved away a strip of soap.

"...and washed the spider OUT!" Sophie emphasized the last word by wiping the strip clean with the towel.

"Out came the suuu-un..."

Motz shaved another strip.

"...and dried up all the RAIN!"

There was a loud knock on the door. "Hey, hurry up in there! I gotta go." Sophie's big sister didn't like their morning ritual.

"And the itsy bitsy spiii-der..."

Motz switched sides.

"...climbed up the spout AGAIN!"

"I mean it!" the voice yelled.

Sophie did a fake spider shiver at the door.

Motz's eyes welled up again.

■ ■ ■

Back in the bedroom, Motz watched Sabine struggle into her white nursing uniform. With her figure, it was a striptease in reverse.

"Zip me up?" she said.

"With pleasure." Motz had trouble getting the zipper to go the right way.

Sabine bumped him with her ample bosom and kissed him firmly on the mouth. Her tongue seemed to have a mind of its own.

When Motz came up for air, he said, "Remind me to bring home smoked eel every night."

Sabine giggled and grabbed her car keys. "Hanna!" she yelled. "Time to go!"

Motz holstered the P6 and threw on his black leather jacket.

Sophie's big sister emerged from the kitchen with both backpacks. She threw the smaller one hard enough to knock over the little spider.

After Sophie recovered her balance, she stuck out her tongue at her big sister.

Motz grinned at Sabine. "That's my girl!"

"Love you," Sabine said.

"Love you more," Motz said.

"Love you most," Sabine said, already halfway to the car.

Motz watched his wife and daughters pile into the Volvo station wagon just beyond the picket fence. He had come a long way from the mean streets of St. Pauli.

The car pulled away with a small toot of its horn. Motz waved back and reached for his shades. Behind the blue lenses, he followed the rear signal light around the corner of the quiet street. Then he eased on his Wehrmacht helmet and jump-started the Harley.

■ ■ ■

The chopper bounced through the gated entrance to Diebsteich Cemetery and followed the gravel path back to the Hanson family plot. Motz parked it behind the hedge, where frequent visitors hid their tools. He opened his battered saddlebag and pulled out the gloves and tulips. Then he yanked a spade out of the dirt and headed for the big mossy headstone Lars had always talked about. He tried to ignore the fresh grave with the temporary wooden cross. He crouched down, pulled the plastic vase out of the ground, and began digging.

Ten minutes later, he was sweating profusely. He should have brought a real shovel. This short-hoe shit was getting him nowhere. After throwing his jacket over the headstone, he dropped to his knees and came up with another handful of damp dirt. Or what he hoped was dirt. *Ashes to ashes, dust to dust.*

The thunder showers the night before hadn't done much to clear the air. If anything, they made the new day even more oppressive and cloying. Motz felt a migraine gathering ominously in the distance, waiting to strike. He sure wasn't going to miss April. But at least the rain had loosened the ground around the grave.

With each handful of dirt, the holster dug deeper into his side. He wiped his brow with his forearm. Too late he remembered it was peppered with dirt. The mark of Cain. "Goddamn it, Lars!" he said. "What the hell've you got me into now?"

Before the spade went back into the ground, his eyes swept the grassy knoll. No commandos in Darth Vader outfits jumped out of the junipers. No hoarse voices screamed for him to chew crabgrass. No red lights danced on the crossbones of his black T-shirt.

The sickly sweet smell of dead flowers made him want to gag. Swallowing fresh panic, he forced himself to double down. He reached in and scooped another handful. And another. The motion was becoming mechanical. Then his gloves hit something hard and flat. Pay dirt.

He traced a groove around the brick with his fingers. Then he began widening the wall of the hole until it became more square than round. *Be there or be square.* He heard fear in his own laugh.

Carefully, he lifted out the first brick. Underneath the dirt clods, the plastic glistened meanly. The size and shape were unmistakable, like stacks in the property room. He wiped off enough dirt to see the holographic "50" on the right side. "God help me," he said.

A dozen scoops later, he got his fingers under the bottom brick. Five, just like Lars had said two days before he was killed. *Just in case.* Motz should have known. He could barely hear the words over the pounding in his chest.

Sunlight flashed on dirty plastic. Knowing he was crossing an invisible line, he stuffed the first brick into his saddlebag. His stomach tightened a notch. He reached for the next. No way to be discreet about a thing like this. It looked like what it was. A crime in progress. He heard a telephoto lens whizzing and purring and clicking from an "unmarked" van with one-way glass. He saw a black-and-white close-up of his ugly mug stuck to an Internal Affairs bulletin board, a thick line connecting it to a photo of Lars. His jaw was clenching spastically by the time the last brick was in place.

"The early bird gets the worm."

Motz froze. At first, he had trouble placing the voice. It was so weak, it could have been his imagination.

"Frau Hanson loved yellow tulips." The voice was paper thin and trembling. But it was real.

Oh shit, a civilian. "Yeah," Motz said, leaning back on his heels. "She sure did." Like he had a clue. He realized he was on his knees.

What he saw could have been Lars' grandmother. For all he knew, it *was* Lars' grandmother. Aside from Loni and her son, there weren't a lot of Hansons at the funeral. Just a sea of blue uniforms and a twenty-one-guard salute.

Motz made a show of replanting the new tulips. The stems disappeared in the oversized square, so he pulled them out and started shoveling more dirt into the hole. His left hand was a bulldozer, like when he was seven.

"You're a member of the family?" the shaky voice said. It wasn't exactly a question.

"Something like that." Just your friendly grave robber, getting his share from his dead partner. Motz grabbed the plastic container, jammed the tulips inside, and rammed the container into the shallower hole. They fit this time. He held them in place while he shoveled the rest of the dirt around the container.

"Dietmar!" The voice wasn't shaky anymore.

"What?" Motz said. Nobody had called him by his real name since grammar school. Then he saw the old worn cane in the arthritic hands. Oh shit! It was—

"Don't pretend you don't know me, young man!" The cane twitched angrily, sending small chunks of dirt his direction.

"Frau Spiess?" Motz stared at the thick red rubber tip in disbelief.

He knew it had circular grooves on the bottom to give the cane more traction—not to soften the blows meted out to wayward schoolboys.

"That's right," she said in triumph.

Motz just gaped. The old lady looked half dead, but her beady eyes hadn't changed a bit. It was his third-grade teacher. The one who gave him shit five days a week. How long had it been? Thirty years? His math wasn't that good, but—

"What's in the bag?" Frau Spiess demanded, poking the cane at his chest violently.

Motz sidestepped more flying dirt and instinctively held up his hands to ward off blows. Back in her classroom at Grundschule St. Pauli, Frau Spiess took such defensive moves as an affront to her authority. Once, she got so angry that she flailed the cane wildly at his face, leaving bruises on his hands. The other kids thought it was hilarious, but Motz knew she really wanted to hurt him.

"The bag?" Motz said lamely. He hoped the old bat was too nearsighted to have seen the plastic-coated bricks. That was all he needed. A rubberneck who knew his name and disliked him personally. Frau Spiess would make a perfect witness for the prosecution. If they let her, she would fit the noose herself.

"Yes, Dietmar, the bag," she said, slightly out of breath from all the exertion. "What's in it?"

"Oh, just some personal things." Motz's mind raced. After all these years, Frau Spiess still didn't wear glasses. That meant she had twenty–twenty vision. Or was just stubborn. He checked her eyes for cataracts. They didn't make glasses for—

"You keep personal things in a grave?" she said.

Motz didn't have an answer for that.

"Show me the bag, young man!" Frau Spiess said, jabbing the cane at him again. It was shaking. She was breathing heavily, like she was about to keel over.

The thought gave Motz hope. "We're not in third grade anymore," he said.

Frau Spiess glared at him for a moment. Then she made an angry movement in his direction with the cane. "You haven't changed one bit, Dietmar!"

"Yeah, yeah," Motz said. "I've got work to do."

Frau Spiess gave him a final glare. "I've got my eye on you, Dietmar!" Then she turned on her heel and took jerky steps back to the next plot. Her white hair was braided and pinned in a wide circle in back.

When her thin figure disappeared behind the hedge, Motz exhaled. He hoped to God she didn't have a mobile phone. Knowing her, she'd fax in an "anonymous" complaint to the Polizeipräsidium.

SIX

Human Qualities

As the Charger blasted up Rothenbaumchaussee, Mick Jones belted "Should I Stay or Should I Go" from the kick panels. Laura hammered the steering wheel, staring down the looks of pencil-dick commuters. Fuck 'em if they couldn't take a joke.

Laura accelerated into the Klosterstern turnabout, snarling at a metallic gold Porsche Cayenne and sending a little rat-dog yipping for cover. She banged on until Nonnenstieg, where she cranked down the volume. "Mommy wouldn't approve," she said to the dash.

The Charger bumped onto the curb with a final blast of its tubes. Home sweet home. Laura slammed the CD into the cracked *Combat Rock* case, threw it into her sports bag, and shouldered open the door.

Locking up, she scanned the bridge for the impossible spot Veronica had found the night before. No Mini Cooper. Her heart sank. Then she reminded herself of the street sweeper. Veronica knew how to stay ahead of that meter maid twat.

Laura landed a healthy loogie in the junipers outside No. 13 and bounded up the stairs and through the open door, landing with both All-Stars and making the tiles squeak. Then she sprinted up the stairs. At the second landing, she coughed loose a chunk of nicotine to acknowledge the effort. With excited fingers, she jiggled the key into the lock. "I'm home!" she said to the open doorway.

Nothing.

Maybe Veronica was still in bed.

Laura slammed the door, threw down her bag, and raced to

the bedroom. "Rise and shine with twenty-five!" she yelled.

No Veronica there either. The bed was made. What the fuck?

Laura ran to the kitchen. Veronica's handwriting was under a refrigerator magnet. Laura's heart stopped.

> L,
>
> *Had to go in early. Special request.*
> *Have a good day! See you later alligator.*
>
> V.

Laura's heart started back up. That was close. For a second there, she thought it was a Dear John letter. Nope. She got to live another day. Miss Veronica just had a "special request." Like that twisted monkey fuck the night before. Veronica sure knew how to pick 'em.

Laura skipped back to the front room, waved hi to the monkey vase, and grabbed her bag. After dumping it in the laundry room, she stuck *Combat Rock* between her teeth and grabbed a couple of squat brown bottles from the top case of Astra. She used to carry the heavy beer cases up the steps herself, but Miss Veronica put an end to that, insisting on a "discreet" ooh-ooh-ooh delivery service. Laura flipped one bottle upside down and used it to pop the other. She kicked the cap into a nearby trash can on the way down. Rim shot. She guzzled beer.

By the time she made it to the stereo, she felt the first healthy burp vibrate against the picture over the mantle. *Their* picture. "Sorry," she said. Then she kissed the CD. "It's just you and me, babe." She jammed it into the player. "Know Your Rights" boomed from oversized AudioQuest speakers. She marched to the beat, downing the Astra to keep from spilling it all over Miss Veronica's nice white carpet.

When Laura's first frenzy was over, she grabbed a small baggie from the watch pocket of her 501s and dry-swallowed her first two pills. By the time "Car Jamming" came on, her scalp was tingling in time. She fired up a Red with her Zippo—fuck Miss

Priss, she'd air out later—and reused it to open the next bottle, which she downed with one go. She did the same with the Red and headed to the laundry room for reinforcements.

Joe Strummer followed her with "Rock the Casbah."

She grabbed two more Astras and sang along.

The Sheik he drove his Cadillac
He went a' cruisin' down the ville
The muezzin was a' standing
On the radiator grille

■ ■ ■

"Frau Lühmeyer?" The voice sounded authoritative and reassuring. An experienced but energetic fifty-something.

Veronica put down the Ebola article, grabbed her briefcase, and extended her hand in one fluid motion. "*Guten Tag, Frau Doktor.*"

The admissions officer shut the door soundlessly, motioned Veronica to one of two Bauhaus armchairs, and went to the mesh-backed swivel chair behind the desk.

Veronica squinted against the sharp rays of sunlight ricocheting off the miniblinds. They were only partially blocked by a tree branch.

"Oh, sorry," the admissions officer said. She swung around, stood up, and changed the angle. "The sun is especially bright after the rain."

"No complaints here," Veronica said. She was just glad to be there.

"So." The older woman settled back into her chair and scooted up to the desk smoothly. "I'm sure you're eager to see your results."

"Actually, I'm a little nervous," Veronica said. She figured honesty was the way to go. *Win friends and influence people.*

"That I can understand." The admissions officer pulled a pair of tortoise-shell glasses from her silver-streaked hair, opened a blue folder to the second Post-it, and put her finger on something. Her green eyes met Veronica's. "The bad news is that you didn't make the first hundred."

"I see," Veronica said. She felt white noise gathering behind her eyes.

The admissions officer placed a chart on the desk so it faced Veronica. "Your grade point average of 1.5 gets you 750 of 900 points. Your HAM-Nat score of 75 percent gets you 300 points. Taken together"—she pointed with her silver Cross pen—"you have 1050 points, just over the 1000-point threshold."

Veronica braced herself for the crash. She had done well on the 90 multiple-choice questions about natural science, but not enough to overcome her mediocre school record.

"The good news is that you will be invited to take HAM-Int."

Veronica could barely hear above the roaring in her ears. "Excuse me?" she said. Why would they invite her to take the second exam?

"That's right," the admissions officer said. "UKE is interested in more than grades."

Veronica exhaled. "I was scared there for a moment." The roaring receded with each thumping heartbeat.

"No need to be." The admissions officer handed Veronica the applicant copy of the chart. "Experience has taught us that human qualities are as important as intellectual qualities."

All Veronica could do was blink.

"As you know, UKE is the only medical school in the country with such a two-tier system. Out of three hundred students selected each year, one hundred are the best students—on paper. The other two hundred are chosen for a mixture of intellectual and human qualities. You, of course, fall into the latter category." Her tone made it sound like the better group.

Veronica looked at the chart. "Lühmeyer, Veronica" was

scheduled to take the psychological test, HAM-Int, the following Friday.

"Given your nursing degree and internship, I think we can be cautiously optimistic. University of Lübeck has a very good reputation, as does the University Clinic of Schleswig-Holstein. I don't want you to be overconfident," the admissions officer said in a hushed voice, "but, just between the two of us, I would say you stand a good chance of being admitted."

Veronica stood up abruptly and extended her hand. "Thank you!"

"Don't thank me yet." After a brisk handshake, the admissions officer motioned Veronica back to her chair. "Now let's sit back down and talk strategy." The glasses were back in place. "As you know, our testers include professional actors from Studio Hamburg, so you need to be on your toes and stay in character." Her tone had a wink in it. "Here are some sample questions from last year's HAM-Int." She handed Veronica another piece of paper.

Stay in character. Veronica wanted to laugh. The psychology exam was starting to sound like her day job. Her eyes jumped to the first question.

> *Explain to a patient the difference between an analog and a digital clock.*

She shook her head in happy disbelief. The psych test was going to be a cake walk.

When she looked up, the admissions officer was beaming. "What did I tell you?"

Something flashed through the blinds. A tree branch was moving. The bird on top had something glittery in its beak. The black head and white body were unmistakable. A thieving magpie. Probably snagged a gold watch from one of the doctors. Veronica had read somewhere the birds were monogamous. Talk about hell. She laughed out loud.

"That's the spirit!" the admissions officer said.

SEVEN

Thin File

Inspektionsleiter Klaus Ebeling hummed Mozart's *Requiem* cheerfully. A china cup was steaming next to the right patch of his green herringbone jacket. Black tea mingled with rich leather and understated pine aftershave. A well-manicured nail with matt finish kept time on the green leather desk pad.

Ebeling knew today was going to be a good day. It wasn't just the concert at the Elbphilharmonie the night before. At long last, LKA 411 was moving in the right direction, his direction. As head of the Homicide Division, he now had the coveted corner office on the top floor of the Polizeipräsidium.

From the bank of windows on the right, Ebeling could follow old-fashioned steamboats plodding up and down the outer canals of the Alster River. They carried higher-end tourists to and from the wide sidewalks of Jungfernstieg, the address for concentrated wealth in his beloved city center. As his father, the late and much-bereaved tea magnate, Karl-Heinz Ebeling, had never tired of telling the young Klaus, the old family dynasties that owned and operated Hamburg did not and could not distinguish between trade and politics. Money was power. It was the lifeblood of the city-state.

To get a glimpse of the ivory towers of commerce, all Ebeling had to do was turn around. His antique oak desk was positioned strategically in the corner so he could see anyone entering his domain.

He took another sip of the bitter brew. The delicate curve of the lip was precise and correct. The cup belonged to an elaborate set his grandfather had brought back from Shanghai in 1929, along with an iron Buddha and a few tons of carved cherrywood furniture. The teacup clattered in the saucer with a happy sound.

Ebeling opened the green folder titled "Ritter, Thomas." It arrived from Frankfurt by special courier the night before. There was no return address, just a "Confidential" stamp. Polizeipräsident Rosenfeld was taking no chances.

Slowly, Ebeling paged through the thin biography. Born in 1975, Thomas Ritter had earned his *Abitur* in 1993. Like him, Ritter was a man of education. In 1997, Ritter graduated from the Bundeswehr University in Munich. His father was a brigadier general who headed air traffic control for the German Army in Frankfurt, where he worked closely with the Luftwaffe and NATO.

Like father, like son, Ebeling thought. His own father used to call him a loser. He snorted. Not everybody could be a "tea baron." The royal pretensions of the Hamburg trading families always struck Ebeling as ridiculous. The city-state was founded by merchants, not royalty. Like the other members of the Hanseatic League, it had no duke or castle, just mountains of money made by businessmen not known for scruples.

Ebeling turned the page and stopped. Ritter had a degree in psychology. Good Lord, Ritter wasn't like his father at all! The workaholic tea baron despised the "idle talk" of psychotherapy. He always said it was just an elaborate excuse for failure. *Idle hands are the devil's workshop.*

Reading further, Ebeling saw that Ritter did six years of mandatory service in Frankfurt. He wiped his frown with a linen napkin. Obviously, Ritter had to work off school debt to the Bundeswehr. Unlike Ebeling, he was no prep school kid. No boarding school in St. Gallen. No special privileges for the son of a general.

Ebeling turned the page. It was 2010. Ritter was with the

Homicide Division in Frankfurt. Ebeling turned back a page. Bundeswehr. Then forward again. Homicide squad. Nothing between 2001 and 2009. His frown deepened. Ritter was off the grid for almost a decade. That could mean only one thing. Black ops. Why did the head of the Polizei Frankfurt arrange the quiet transfer of a top homicide detective just before his own forced retirement?

Ritter obviously had trouble in Frankfurt. Ebeling had owed Rosenfeld for that customs tip the previous month. God knew how many kids would have died on the streets of Hamburg had the container ship from Turkey made it all the way into the duty-free port. They found only one bag strapped to the bottom of the ship, but it was pure Afghan Gold. Rosenfeld didn't wait long to call in his marker.

Ebeling liked that. Ritter wasn't the only one who needed help. His former boss did too. That meant Rosenfeld now owed Ebeling. And Ritter was now Ebeling's secret weapon. Ebeling beamed at the file. This could really work out.

■　■　■

Meike Voss snuck another look at the lean guy sitting outside Ebeling's office. His long black hair, olive skin, and two-day beard were offset by penetrating blue eyes. The tight black jeans and worn work boots somehow matched the high forehead, long nose, and strong jawline. The hands belonged to a surgeon. The turtleneck didn't hide the red mark on his neck—the size of a hungry female mouth. The shrink was right. A guy with another girl was more attractive.

When Ritter changed position, Meike's eyes retreated to the monitor. She frowned. It wasn't just that ComVor wouldn't let her look at the file. The personnel system didn't even recognize her "stark thomas" query, like he had never worked for the Polizei Frankfurt. That only piqued her curiosity. She wouldn't put it past

Ebeling to have put a block on the file. He seemed to take pleasure in frustrating his detectives.

■ ■ ■

Ritter felt the redhead's hazel eyes. He pulled the turtleneck higher and adjusted his position in the uncomfortable chair. He must have pulled a lumbar muscle again. The damp air didn't help. Against his will, he saw the pert breasts bouncing gently against his chest in the multicolored light. He hoped the waitress was street legal. She could have tied a pretzel with that tongue.

The hot redhead across the hall was now "busy." The photo stapled to Rosenfeld's sheet didn't do justice to the curves she was trying to hide under the oversized sweater and cargo pants.

> *KOK Meike Voss born in Hamburg-Barmbek to crane operator and hairdresser. Graduated Hochschule der Hamburger Polizei with "satisfactory." Special interests: computers, flea markets, male coworkers.*

The pigtails and rubber rain boots didn't fool Ritter. In his experience, girls with that kind of figure were always hot-blooded. Their minds might tell them one thing, but their bodies always got the upper hand. As if to prove his point, the hazel eyes were sneaking a peek at him again. Ritter didn't blink. He was amazed at his own post-coital bravado. The more you do, the more you can do.

EIGHT

Day Shift

In the front office of Herbertstrasse 7b, the four day-shift girls gathered in a semicircle for their morning "stand up" meeting. In a night course at the local community college, their *Puffmutter*, Anita Krenz, had been taught the value of short meetings. The best way to keep them that way was to force everybody to stand.

Half-glasses in place and clipboard in hand, Anita reviewed the schedule for the day. "Tanja is in Cage 1, Magda in Cage 2. Chantal is breaking in Angelique in Cage 3. Cage 4 is closed until we get the window repaired."

"What's wrong with the window?" Magda wanted to know.

"It doesn't lock properly. You know what the wind can do." Anita liked the question. Magda's alertness showed promise. Her counterfeit residence permit said she came from Gdansk. It had cost Anita plenty but paid off in the first week.

"My uncle could take a look," Magda said. "He would give us a special discount."

"No, we need receipts for the tax man," Anita said. She'd seen the work those Polacks did. Not exactly made in Germany.

"When's the window man coming?" Tanja asked.

Anita was glad to change the subject. "End of the week. He doesn't want to bring his cough into the house."

"God forbid," Tanja said, all but crossing herself.

Anita sighed. Tanja was obsessed with germs ever since she saw that TV show with all those squiggly things under the microscope.

Tanja frowned. "But won't that affect our profit margins?"

"Two girls are a profit multiplier," Anita said. Her rectangular glasses had a soft landing on her salon-tanned cleavage. The gold chain held them in place. "You know that." *Our profit margins.* Tanja didn't have a clue what a margin was. She still hadn't figured out that she was paying rent for her window. Profit margins were a house problem, not a girl problem. Now wire-frame bikinis, that was a girl problem.

"Oh, sorry, I forgot Chantal and Angelique were doing mother–daughter." Tanja flexed her lithe calf to show off the dragon tattoo.

"That's okay." Anita put her glasses back in place. "There's one more thing. Mistress Veronica has a special client at noon. So be on your best behavior."

The four girls nodded their heads reverently.

"And now," Anita looked at Tanja, "it's time to do your duty."

Tanja squealed over to the sink with baby steps that made her tits jiggle for joy. She returned with a tray of five full schnapps glasses.

Everybody grabbed one.

Anita made the usual toast.

Bock, Bock, Bock!
Pille, palle, punz!
Alles Geld für uns!

Everybody clinked glasses.

One by one, Anita slapped each girl on the ass loudly for good luck. The girls giggled and wiggled to their window seats. Day shift had begun.

■ ■ ■

Upstairs in the Black Room, Veronica made her final preparations. She had changed out of her blue pantsuit and into red latex tights, spikey red boots that reached well above her knees, and a shiny black wig. Her face was powdered white. A bullwhip was attached to her right hip.

Today was not just any client. Mertens might be flesh and blood, but he was still the Innensenator. With his pending senate bill, he was more important than Willi Kaiser.

Veronica walked around the room like a caged tiger. She stopped in front of the tool rack and applied antiviral disinfectant to the mouth guard with a fresh pack of cotton swabs. Then she examined the manual resuscitator. The bag mask valve was in order. After that, she checked the leather straps and chrome-plated chains on the St. Andreas cross, climbing the wall with her spikes. The thing didn't budge. It was almost too solid, like the chalkboard. When Anita's carpenter built something, it stayed built.

Veronica took a closer look at the chalk holder. "Shit!" she said. Nothing but small fragments. Mertens wouldn't make it past a dozen sentences on those nubs. She ran into the storeroom and yanked open the cabinets. She found all different sizes, shapes, and colors of dildos, enemas, masks, restraining devices, even the "sewing kit" a urologist had given Anita.

Then she spotted the blue box of Pelikan Blackboard Chalk. It was supposed to hold twelve pieces, but it was empty. How could she have been so foolish? The whole morning, she had the nagging feeling that she had forgotten something.

She threw open the door of the Black Room and ran down the stairs as fast as her spikes would let her.

She ran into the office, and Anita looked up in alarm from her Day-At-A-Glance. "What's wrong?" she said.

"I'm out of chalk!" Veronica held out the empty box for Anita to see.

Anita put down her florescent pink marker and checked the box. No chalk. "Don't worry, we'll fix this," she said. She opened one desk drawer after another. That done, she turned to the metal cabinet and began scouring the shelves.

"I knew it," Veronica said.

"Hold on." Anita walked around her desk and into the narrow

hallway behind the sink.

Veronica heard a lot of muffled scraping and scuffing. Once, it sounded like Anita hit her head on something. The closet door latched again.

Anita walked back into the room. "Nothing back there. I'll call Frederic, let him know it's an emergency." She was already punching the number on her landline.

"Thanks, Anita. I don't know why I'm so jumpy today."

First UKE, now Mertens. Two worlds that could never ever meet. And Laura, the human wrecking ball, with that yellow card. Veronica's workday had barely begun, and already she was a nervous wreck.

"Take a deep breath." Anita cradled the phone on her shoulder as she examined the box. "He puts on his pants one leg at a time like everybody else."

"You're right," Veronica said, not believing a word. "I'm just being silly."

Anita spoke into the phone. "*Moin*, Frederic. We need you to make a delivery ASAP." She winked at Veronica. "You got a pencil? Good. One box of Pelikan Blackboard Chalk. The blue box of twelve."

"White," Veronica said. All she needed was for that creep to bring blue chalk.

Anita nodded and waved Veronica away. "White chalk, not colored chalked. That is very important, Frederic. White chalk."

Veronica headed for the stairs.

"That's right," Anita said. "Blue box, white chalk."

Veronica slipped on the first step.

Anita was still talking on the phone. "What? We don't have time for prepayment! This is an emergency! And bring the receipt. We need it for the tax man."

The front door buzzed.

Veronica prayed it wasn't Mertens.

NINE

Loose Cannon

"Hauptkommissar Ritter!" Inspektionsleiter Ebeling sounded like he was pleasantly surprised by an old university buddy. "Welcome to LKA 411! I trust you are settling into the *Hansestadt*."

"Thank you, sir, yes." Ritter didn't like the two-handed shake, but at least it was firm and dry. Was there a hint of irony in Ebeling's voice? Ritter forced himself not to check his collar.

"Please," Ebeling said, motioning him into the office. Then he turned to the redhead. "KOK Voss, would you be so kind and bring in the file on the forklift driver?" Without waiting for an answer, he shut the door. "She's really quite good, you know. Please, take a seat." He nodded to three comfortable leather chairs facing the desk and an impressive view.

Ritter didn't get it. Why would a homicide detective run errands for the boss? Hamburg wasn't exactly the boondocks.

"I think she's eager to meet you," Ebeling said.

Ritter touched his collar.

"You do drink tea, don't you, Herr Kriminalhauptkommissar?"

"Of course," Ritter said, clearing the first hurdle effortlessly. The off-center knot in the thin green-and-black school tie hadn't escaped his notice. It matched the herringbone, Oxford cloth, cuffed flannel, and unkempt wingtips. He crossed his legs at the knee to mirror Ebeling. He'd always heard old Hanseatic League types were Anglophiles, but this fish-head was straight out of *Buddenbrooks*.

"Don't look so surprised," Ebeling said. "Polizeipräsident

Rosenfeld speaks very highly of you."

"Excuse me? Oh, righ—"

"Right over here, Voss," Ebeling said over Ritter's left shoulder.

A thick red folder slapped the desk. The redhead turned and gave Ritter a frank once-over. A healthy farm girl trying desperately to look cold, distant, and urban.

"Thank you, Voss," Ebeling said. He winked at Ritter.

Voss stomped out of the room. Her freckles were glowing almost as brightly as her red rain boots. The door closed firmly behind her.

"Excitable girl," Ebeling confided. "Comes from a long line of dock workers. Now, where were we?"

"You were speaking of Polizeipräsident Rosenfeld," Ritter said.

"That we were." Ebeling picked up the green folder, resumed reading, grunted to himself, licked a forefinger, and turned to the next page, which seemed to engross him completely. He nodded a few times and once noted something in the margin with an engraved Montblanc fountain pen.

Two minutes of silence were supposed to put Ritter on edge. He was very aware of sitting below Ebeling's eye level. An old *Stasi* trick.

Rosenfeld's summary fit the picture in front of him. *Tea baron.* Check. *Boarding school.* Check. *PR.* Check. *Political animal.* Check.

Ritter's new boss stared at him coldly.

Ebeling took off his blond horn rims and massaged the bridge of his nose. "Interesting reading," he said. "A trifle thin, but that's to be expected." He fit the glasses back in place. "Given your background." He seemed disappointed at the lack of reaction. "As you well know, teamwork is everything, especially in the Homicide Division. LKA 411 is made up of six homicide squads of five investigators. Each squad is led by one man."

Ritter could imagine how the redhead would react to the word "man."

"Given your rank as Kriminalhauptkommissar in Frankfurt, your solid clearance rate with the Homicide Division, and, of course, your sterling recommendation from Polizeipräsident Rosenfeld, I think you would make an ideal lead investigator in LKA 411."

Ritter didn't try to hide his surprise. "But I'm new here."

"Exactly."

"What about the rest of the squad?" The last thing he needed was envious coworkers.

"Let that be my concern," Ebeling said.

Another red flag. "Who am I replacing?"

"The late Kriminalhauptkommissar Hanson." Ebeling seemed to take a special interest in his ink blotter. "He died four weeks ago. Tragic motorcycle accident." He straightened the blotter.

Ritter nodded respectfully. "I hear he was a good man." Rosenfeld called Hanson "an army of one." He also said there was some holdup on the star in the entrance hall of the Polizeipräsidium. Something to do with the rat squad.

"As I said, a real tragedy," Ebeling said. "He left behind a lovely wife and a son."

"KHK Hanson died in the line of duty?"

"No, he was on his own time." There was a slight pause. "Unfortunately, not everyone feels that way."

"Sir?"

"His long-time partner, Kriminaloberkommissar Beck, is convinced that local gangsters were somehow involved," Ebeling said. "We have absolutely no evidence to support Beck's claims. Still, he persists in his private vendetta."

"Vendetta?" That was all Ritter needed. If anybody could figure out his real role in Frankfurt, it would be a detective hell-bent on revenge.

Ebeling nodded impatiently. "Beck doesn't know when to give up. Our staff psychologist says he's still in the denial phase.

I think he's letting his emotions get in the way of his work."

"They were close?"

"Too close." Ebeling paused for a moment and then grinned. "Beck is on your squad. He now works for you."

"Great." Ritter got a close look at Ebeling's green teeth. What was it about old money and bad dental work?

"You'll have your hands full," Ebeling said cheerfully. "Beck is a real loose cannon. Completely unpredictable."

■ ■ ■

While Ebeling opened the red file, Ritter readjusted his position in the leather chair.

"The victim was a forklift driver," Ebeling said, flipping through the glossy photos with evident distaste. "His wife reported him missing seven weeks ago. The day after a crane pulled his forklift out of the Elbe River." Ebeling looked over his glasses. "Apparently, he miscalculated a loading ramp on Steinwerder."

"He was loading a cruise ship?" Ritter said. Based on the photos of the *Queen Mary 2* in *MOPO*, it would take a dozen forklifts just to load the luggage.

"No, he was on the east side, at an old container depot."

That made more sense. A death next to a luxury ship would have made international news.

"A body washed up at the water bus stop on Finkenwerder a few days later," Ebeling said.

"The one that scared all those Airbus employees?" Kind of hard to forget that one. It was all over the wire. The corpse got caught in the rotors of a ferry on the Elbe.

"Exactly," Ebeling said. "I'm impressed, Herr Kriminalhaupt-kommissar. You have done your homework. I would have expected nothing less."

Ritter was beginning to wonder if Ebeling was the source of

Rosenfeld's intel. "Were you able to confirm his identity?"

"Yes," Ebeling said. "The rotors didn't leave enough for fingerprints or dental records, but the DNA was a perfect match."

Ritter's squad in Frankfurt had a similar problem with a woodchipper a few years earlier.

Ebeling cleared his throat. "There's something else." He paused. "The forklift driver was a confidential informant."

"Oh." That wasn't in Rosenfeld's file.

"So confidential we didn't know about it." Ebeling fingered one of the glossies. "After his disappearance, we discovered he had been working for KHK Hanson. Unofficially."

"I see." Ritter could imagine how the death had affected Hanson. Stockholm Syndrome worked in both directions.

"You do?" Ebeling said.

Ritter told the voice in his head to shut the fuck up. *Active listening*, they called it in interrogation training.

"Hanson said he was investigating a local casino. Casino Esplanade, to be exact." Ebeling gave him a hard look. "The owner is one Sulejman Hasani. He's a person of interest in half a dozen homicides in the past few years."

Maybe Beck was on to something, Ritter thought.

"That's not all," Ebeling said. "Hasani owns a lot of real estate in St. Pauli."

"Around the Reeperbahn?"

"Yes." Ebeling looked at Ritter strangely. "And a container terminal on Steinwerder."

"Where the forklift driver had his ... accident."

"Yes," Ebeling said. "Of course, KHK Hanson didn't believe it was an accident. It being his informant and all."

Ritter bit his tongue. He would have thought the same thing.

"One more thing," Ebeling said. "Internal Affairs thinks KHK Hanson might have had a gambling problem."

"At Casino Esplanade?"

"Don't make that mistake," Ebeling said, visibly agitated.

"Sir?"

"KOK Beck blames Hasani."

Ritter nodded curtly.

Ebeling seemed to take that as agreement. "I will let you do the honors." He scooped up the folder as he stood.

Ritter took it with both hands. It was heavier than it looked.

TEN

Old Friends

Motz down-shifted the chopper over jaw-bobbing cobblestone. The back entrance to Mr. Wu's bounced into view. The red brick looked purple through his blue lenses.

Kaiser's enforcer was sharing the morning air with a sawed-off sidekick. His new partner had psychotic spikes of blue hair and mirror shades. The enforcer was straining the seams of his sharkskin suit with each stroke of the fingernail file.

Motz brought the Harley to a smooth gurgling stop near the black wrought-iron bars covering the windows. He rolled the hog back onto its kickstand, whipped a leather-clad leg over the seat, and removed his helmet. Then he unstrapped the saddlebag.

The nail file stopped.

Motz looked at everything and nothing as he crunched gravel toward them. "*Moin moin,*" he said too cheerfully.

"*Moin,*" the enforcer said through what sounded like a steel slit.

Motz held open the saddlebag. Five plastic-coated bricks of fifty-euro notes stared back at him. The wet dirt had begun to smear the raw leather inside.

The enforcer clucked approval.

Motz threw the bag over his shoulder and raised his hands to half-mast.

The enforcer's practiced paws patted him down—and stopped. He yanked the P6 out of Motz's holster.

"I look that dumb?" Motz said. Slowly, he reached into his hip pocket with his thumb and forefinger, producing the magazine.

Next to the enforcer, the little psycho was trembling like a rabid poodle. His right hand was clenching something in his coat pocket.

Motz figured a stiletto or switchblade. "Better cut Snapper's caffeine intake," he said. "Wouldn't want him to blow a gasket."

The enforcer checked the breach of the P6. Clean. He handed back the gun but pocketed the magazine.

Motz returned the P6 to his holster.

The enforcer pulled open the grated steel door. "Let's not keep him waiting," he said. The sound of rusty springs was lost in a chaos of kitchen clatter.

Lots of heavy chopping going on, Motz thought, falling in line. His nose was immediately overwhelmed by a hot spectrum of spices. His back muscles twitched nervously. The psycho's bite was undoubtedly worse than his bark.

After leading Motz past the bar, the enforcer stopped and pulled back red beads hanging from a black lacquer doorframe to reveal a large dining area. Only one table was occupied. It was tucked away in the far corner on a kind of platform with red satin sashes tied to the posts on either side of the single step. "After you," the enforcer said.

Ducking under the beads, Motz saw Willi Kaiser holding court on the platform, his favorite bodyguard standing with crossed hands at his back. Behind them was an elaborate gold-on-black tapestry that depicted an ancient orgy.

Willi's eyes behind his big black frames were larger than Motz remembered. Maybe he had a new prescription. He wasn't getting any younger. Even his bushy eyebrows looked different. Probably dye.

Kaiser glanced at the doorway in fake surprise. "Motz!" he said, flashing teeth that had gotten magically whiter and straighter with age. "How good of you to join us!"

Motz figured implants. He knew for a fact the mob boss had

lost two front teeth to a Hells Angel back in ninety-five. After that, he'd pull out his flipper *before* bar fights.

The carpet shook under Motz's boots. A sash brushed his shoulder as he stepped onto the platform. He stopped just shy of the table. Slowly, he took off his shades, folded them, and hooked them into his holster. The entire time, he kept his eyes on Kaiser's.

Neither man blinked.

Motz felt the enforcer shift his weight at the base of the stair behind him.

"You have something for me," Kaiser said.

Motz removed the saddlebag from his shoulder and held it out.

Half a second later, the enforcer relieved him of his burden.

Kaiser showed more teeth when the first brick hit the table, but his look never wavered from Motz's. His smile grew with each *plunk!* One, two, three, four, five. Count 'em.

A scraping sound broke Motz's eye lock just before the flying saddlebag hit him. His forearm took the brunt of the blow.

"It's all there," Motz said, returning the bag to his shoulder. His forearm stung.

"I know it is," Kaiser said. He had yet to glance at the bricks, let alone touch them.

"Fifty thousand," Motz said. "Three for the principle, one for back interest, one for delivery."

Kaiser dipped his fingertips in his teacup and made a show of wiping the nails with a napkin.

"No one bothers his family," Motz said. He still hadn't figured out how he was going to pay. Willi didn't do protection for free.

The wiping stopped. "We are not animals," Kaiser said. "We were just discussing our non-pork-eating friends." He paused half a beat. "The ones with the," he cleared his throat delicately, "blowtorch."

Motz winced. The bloated, faceless corpse would haunt him

for years. They lost it when the state prosecutor decided not to file. Insufficient evidence, she said. Now the old bastard was letting him know he knew details they had withheld from the press. He must have had an informant very close to their team. Motz hoped it wasn't Lars.

"Blowtorch," the bodyguard said, leering at Motz obscenely.

Kaiser held up a glistening fingernail.

Silence filled the room.

The bodyguard stared at mahogany.

"We are old school," Kaiser said.

Here comes the price tag, Motz thought.

"We take care of our own," Kaiser said.

Just name your price, Willi.

"Now run along," Kaiser said, waving Motz away. "I have work to do."

So that was it. Willi was taking a rain check. Sometime soon, Motz would get an anonymous call. Something small, like a license plate check. Thanks, Lars. That graveyard dirt would stick to his hands forever.

Motz whipped out his glasses fast enough to feel the bodyguard twitch. The tablecloth turned light blue again.

Kaiser poured himself more tea with a steady hand.

As Motz clomped out of the room, he felt a dozen eyes tracking his back like heat sensors. The psycho was nowhere to be seen.

Kaiser's enforcer pulled back the red beads again and slammed the P6 magazine against Motz's chest. Motz pocketed the eight rounds and "accidentally" bumped the enforcer with his shoulder.

Passing through the steamy kitchen, he half expected the sting of a stiletto between his shoulder blades. The back door opened with a loud squeak. A wave of fresh air cooled his sweat.

When he reached the Harley, his fingers were acting up.

He would have to reload the P6 later. He grabbed his helmet but didn't put it on.

Across the street was a black van with darkened windows. Something was covering the front plate.

■ ■ ■

Motz's chopper flew past Casino Esplanade and bounced across Kennedybrücke. On the other side, it made a curving right down Ferdinandstor, glided under a low, wide bridge, and gently bumped up onto the sidewalk. The four-week-old blood stains were now part of the gritty cement, which shook with the steady *ka-chunk!* of a freight train crossing overhead.

Motz grabbed the cartridge from his hip pocket and slammed it into the base of the P6. The ninth round went into the chamber. He grabbed his phone and hit "Honeybee."

Gentle rays of sunlight peeked through the rail lines and warmed his scar.

"Motz," Sabine said on the other end. "Is something wrong?"

"Everything's fine," he said. "I just wanted to hear your voice."

"Oh you!" There was a slight pause. "You sure everything is okay?"

Something screeched above Motz's head and took the sun with it. Another train slowing for the main station. When it finally passed, he could hear Sabine again.

"Where are you?" she said.

"Ferdinandstor." The scene of Lars' non-accident. It was something they avoided talking about directly.

"Oh."

"I'm fine, really."

"Maybe you should talk to that counselor after all," Sabine said.

"I just needed to talk to Lars." Motz felt her nodding.

"I'm bringing Loni something later on," Sabine said.

"Say hi for me." Sabine was never that close with Lars' widow, but she always came through when it counted.

"Are you really sure you're okay?"

Motz felt the worry in her voice. "Love you."

"Love you more."

"Love you most."

Motz pocketed the phone and grabbed his helmet. In the distance, a loudspeaker announced the arrival of an InterCity Express from Frankfurt.

ELEVEN

Pasha Import/Export

Mustafa checked his hair in the brass plate with his free hand. The other clutched the stainless-steel briefcase tightly. You didn't let go of seven million euros in cash—unless ordered to by Uncle Sulejman.

Mustafa's view was impeded by the chiseled "HANSABANK." Behind his reflection, an old-fashioned white river boat chugged away from the steps of the Alster Pavilion with a fresh load of tourists.

An armed guard opened the door to the bank.

Mustafa walked in. He was greeted by cool marble and more brass. At the information counter, he handed the girl his card and said the manager was expecting him. The card said: "Pasha Import/Export GmbH." No address, no phone number.

The girl looked at him uncertainly, walked back to the corner office, and knocked on the doorframe. The bank manager came out with fake friendliness on his pink face. "Good morning," he said. "Grube is my name."

Mustafa shook the soft hand firmly but did not offer his own name.

"My office is in back," Grube said and led the way.

Mustafa followed him into an office that smelled of old leather, brandy, and cigars.

Grube motioned him to a comfortable armchair and took a seat behind the wide desk. "So, how may I help you, Herr...?"

"Hasani."

Grube coughed like something had gone down the wrong way.

When he recovered, he said, "How may I help you, Herr Hasani?"

The fear in his voice told Mustafa the banker was intelligent and well informed. That simplified things. "My uncle would like to propose a real estate deal."

"A real estate deal?" Grube didn't ask who his uncle was.

"Yes" Mustafa said. "He is prepared to give you seven million euros." He patted the briefcase.

"That is very generous of your uncle," Grube said. "What would he like in exchange?"

"The deed to Herbertstrasse 7b," Mustafa said. "You know, the whorehouse owned by your mother."

The banker's face got pinker. "Excuse me?"

"The price is more than fair."

"Haus 7b is not for sale," Grube said.

Mustafa pulled a photo out of his jacket and placed it on the desk. It was a villa on Behler See. The house Grube grew up in. The house his mother still lived in.

Grube leaned forward and gasped.

Mustafa stood up. "The briefcase is yours to keep. A little token of our agreement."

TWELVE

Candid Camera

Andreas Scherf eased the Mercedes S-Guard down into the dip and back up, mindful of the scrape marks on the asphalt, and then over to their spot in back.

The tan 1953 Chevy next door had a brown metallic top and tons of chrome. The rear wheel guard spelled "Powerglide" in that funky fifties script. All the letters were connected to a baseline, like a marquee. They belonged to Helen Patch, the president of Sex Workers United.

Andreas first saw Helen on HHTV wheezing on about "my girls." She looked like what she was. A former domina with diabetes and a back ticker. But her eyes were young and intelligent, someone you would pick out of a crowd. If Andreas liked girls, she would be his type. Big and bouncy, with a firm handshake and a heart of gold.

"Another long meeting," Innensenator Mertens said over the back seat. "Pick me up at three."

Andreas saluted the mirror, but the door had already shut with a *hummpf!* Instead of putting the Mercedes in reverse, he reached into his overcoat on the seat and pulled out his new Leica V-Lux. Propping the telephoto lens on the headrest, he zoomed into Mertens' silver mane, which was too big and jerked around the frame. Andreas zoomed out to the entire parking lot, then back into the brick building.

By the time Mertens made it to the back door, Andreas had managed to get a close-up of him in profile. The camera clicked a dozen times in rapid succession. One of the things Andreas had learned at his weekend photography course at the Speicherstadt was to squeeze off as many shots as possible. You could separate the wheat from the chaff afterwards.

Andreas thought he heard the back door to the union building buzz. Then Mertens was gone.

Andreas hunkered down in his seat and flipped through the results. The first two were blurry, but the third was perfect. Even on the small screen, anyone could see it was Innensenator Mertens. And it had the SWU logo under Mertens' nose. Andreas knew it was just beginner's luck, but he took it as a good omen.

So much for the *before* shot. Now for the *after*. When Mertens left the building, Andreas would have just a second or two to catch his face.

He would never forget the first time he saw that goofy costume. After dropping off Mertens at his monthly SWU meeting, Andreas had headed to his favorite café, Mother's Fine Coffee. The Sardinian owner made killer espresso, but the real draw was the window seat facing Davidstrasse. It was hilarious to watch pin-striped johns trying to fit in with blue-haired NyQuil addicts and slobbering Rottweilers before they disappeared behind the high red gate to Herbertstrasse.

Andreas had just taken his first sip of bittersweet espresso, followed by a delicious drag on an unfiltered Gauloises, when a new St. Pauli freak walked by. Some loser with long blond locks, monster dark glasses, clinking gold chains, and a slinky red jogging outfit. Andreas figured him for a wannabe pimp when it hit him. He knew that walk! It couldn't be. But it was! Why the hell would Mertens be dressed up like that?

Andreas almost swallowed his Gauloises when the golden locks disappeared behind the red gate. Mertens visiting a whorehouse? That didn't make any sense. His wife was a knockout. More than once, she'd given Andreas a look that almost made him wish he were straight.

Andreas had every reason to be thankful to Mertens. The Innensenator had hired him as his personal chauffer on the strength of Helen's word, despite his police record for his aborted career as an underage "film star." Yes, a judge had sealed the file when Andreas turned twenty-five, but Mertens doubtless had access. Helen said the chauffeur job normally went to cops on the way up the career ladder, so Andreas should be doubly thankful. She also said Mertens was "sympathetic" with Andreas' "difficult childhood."

Andreas really was thankful. But old habits were hard to break. He didn't give things away. He sold them. And now he had something very big to sell. Like always, he went to the highest bidder. It didn't take him long to figure out who would have the biggest interest in his photomontage of the Innensenator. The old queer worked one floor below Mertens in City Hall.

Their first meeting had been a big disappointment. Andreas was told in no uncertain terms that his photos of "somebody with long hair and a jogging outfit" entering Herbertstrasse wasn't enough. How could anybody tell it was really Mertens? They needed a positive ID, as well as the monthly schedule. That was when Andreas got the idea of shooting Mertens entering SWU in a suit and exiting in his costume.

Now, from the cushy leather seat of the Mercedes, Andreas made sure his Leica was still set to timestamp all frames. The he reached up and adjusted the side mirror to face the back door to SWU. He knew from experience that Mertens didn't waste time changing clothes. A close-up of his exit in full costume was the money shot.

THIRTEEN

Bad Teacher

Mertens rounded the corner to Herbertstrasse with a spring in his step. Under his costume, he was wearing the latex underwear Mistress Veronica had picked out for him at Boutique Bizarre on the Reeperbahn.

He stepped through the red gate and walked between two rows of small houses sandwiched together. There were no lights behind the floor-length windows this time of day, just beautiful shadows. He was always impressed by the quality of the human mannequins. Most looked like remarkably attractive housewives in bikinis. Not unlike Charlotte a decade earlier. Somehow, the thought of a secret rendezvous with his own wife excited him even more.

At the middle of the block, he turned left, passed through a narrow corridor, turned right, and walked up to 7b. The door opened before his thumb hit the buzzer.

"Welcome, stranger!" The *Puffmutter* was beaming from ear to ear. Her cleavage glistened.

"Thank you, Anita," Mertens said, wiping his sneakers on the mat and stepping through the doorway. He smelled something cool and fresh.

"It's been too long." Anita nudged Mertens up the staircase with her battleship breasts.

"Yes, it has," he said. "I'm afraid I've been very busy."

"Well, now you can relax. You are in very good hands."

Mertens nodded. He didn't trust himself to speak anymore. His throat was pounding.

At the top of the stairs, Anita stopped and knocked on the shiny black door.

■ ■ ■

Footsteps approached, a creaky lock turned over twice, and the door squeaked open. Mistress Veronica took up most of the doorframe.

Anita disappeared from view.

The woven leather whip snapped this way and that, like a cat on the prowl. "You sure took your time," Mistress Veronica said. The black wig set off her unnatural pallor. Her waxy breasts were held in place by thick black laces.

Mertens heard Anita make her way down the stairs behind him.

The whip cracked near his left ear.

"Cat got your tongue?" Mistress Veronica said.

"Y-yes, mistress," Mertens stammered.

The whip snapped near his feet. "Enter, slave!"

"Y-yes, mistress." He stepped into a room that was entirely black. Floors, walls, ceiling, everything. The sight always took his breath away.

Mistress Veronica slammed the heavy door. The big key twisted and the iron latch fell into placed. She turned and scrutinized the blond wig, gold chains, and running outfit with evident distaste. "What's this, *The Seventies Show*?"

Mertens looked at the ground in shame. "I'm sorry, mistress."

"You can say that again. You're a sorry excuse for a slave," she said. "You're not even good enough to lick my boots."

The whip ripped the blond wig off his head. A spikey boot kicked it across the room. "Disgusting!"

"I'm sorry, mistress," Mertens said, letting go. He really was in good hands.

"Strip, slave!"

"Yes, mistress."

The whip cracked next to his ear. "I don't have all day, slave."

■ ■ ■

Veronica tightened the last strap until Mertens winced. She stepped back and surveyed her work. The leather bonds held him firmly in place. He was covered from head to foot in black latex. The rubber ball between his teeth was secured with a wide rubber band that stretched behind his head. The jogging outfit was laid out neatly on an old stool nearby, the wig on top. The sneakers were lined up underneath.

Veronica grabbed Mertens roughly by his latex-clad face and forced him to look at the old-fashioned blackboard bolted to the wall. The same sentence was written over and over in angular cursive. "I will not talk in class." Three times, there were slash marks where the tiny piece of chalk had slipped out of Mertens' hand. "How many times did I tell you to write it?"

"Mmmfff mmmfff mmmfff!" he said behind the ball.

"That's right, slave. One hundred times. So how come I only see thirteen sentences?"

"Mmmfff mmmfff mmmfff!"

"The chalk broke? That's no excuse. Failure is not an option in my classroom."

"Mmmfff mmmfff!"

"Are you trying to make me angry?"

"Mmm mmm!"

"You calling me a liar, slave?" The whip snapped viciously.

"Mmm mmm!"

"Thirteen sentences?"

"Hmmm."

"What's the penalty for thirteen sentences?"

Mertens stopped squirming.

Veronica grabbed his jaw again. "Thirteen lashes."

Mertens whimpered.

"You wimp. I'll make a man out of you yet." She touched her leather whip lovingly.

The whimpering went up an octave.

"You like that, do you? Good. Because today's lesson is the meaning of pain."

"Mmmmmm! Mmmmmm! Mmmmmm!"

"What did you say?" Veronica tilted her head. "You'll have to speak clearer than that."

More unintelligible complaints came from behind the ball.

"I still can't hear you," she said in a singsong voice.

The red ball moved up and down on each syllable for emphasis. The pupils staring at her were huge, like a mouse cornered by a cobra.

"Don't be a crybaby or I'll give you something to cry about!" The cobra in her hand cracked for emphasis.

The whimpering got louder.

"Okay. Some slaves have to learn the hard way." Veronica turned on a spiked heel, took three measured steps to the middle of the room, and turned again. The whip followed her with an electric sound.

It whistled past Mertens' left ear. He jerked his head to the right. The ball muffled his scream.

Veronica admired her own precision. Practice makes perfect. "What did you say?" She did it again.

This time, the whip got caught on the crossbars. Mertens jerked forward. The cross didn't budge.

Veronica made her mistake work for her. She grabbed the belt around Mertens' neck and tightened it.

He shook his head violently.

She stuck the butt of the whip against the ball. At the same time, she gently massaged his crotch with a lithe knee.

Behind the ball, Mertens began to moan in rhythm with the knee.

The knee eased higher.

Mertens' head began to shake again.

Veronica slapped him. "Now you think about what we talked about!"

She pulled a sleeping mask over his eyes and stretched the elastic behind his head, making sure not to loosen the red ball.

Mertens began to whimper again.

Veronica marched out of the Black Room, through the hall, and into the break room. She kicked the door shut, sat down on a white leather swivel chair, and set the kitchen timer to fifteen minutes. Thirty seconds later, she was absorbed in HAM-Int Sample Question 7.

FOURTEEN

Yellow Card

The foaming tide tingled Laura's scalp. Coconut oil mixed with the earthier scent coming from the fine blonde hairs curled up in the damp warmth of the black thong. She could taste the salt on Veronica's tan line.

Crashing waves shook Laura awake. She was still staring at the photo. On that white beach, Veronica had compared Laura to a young boy. In that moment, Veronica finally crossed the line. It wasn't a compliment, it was a promise! Laura had never thought she would be loved. She loved back so hard it hurt.

She looked down at the word "*VERTRAUEN*" tattooed in green gothic script across her hard pecs. Trust was everything. She called it her necklace of pain. Good pain, pure pain, the bittersweet kind that lasted through thick and thin. Every anniversary, she added a new tattoo. First came the chain around her ankle. Then the barbed wire around her biceps. She laughed. If she kept this up, she would run out of skin by forty.

Something rolled across the hardwood floor in the hallway. The empty Astra bottle was heading for its partners in the kitchen. She jumped up and followed.

■ ■ ■

An hour later, the candles were burned down to their silver platters. Drops of red wax had dribbled over the raised edges and onto the coffee table.

Laura ran the back of her hand against her face. It came back slick with sweat. She tripped over another Astra bottle. "Whoa, sailor!"

she said and stumbled toward the bedroom. She shielded her eyes from the sunlight. The radio clock said ten thirty.

"Shit, past my bedtime." Laura cackled at her own joke and fell onto the waterbed face first. After the waves died down, she snuggled in. Two minutes later, she jerked awake, cold slime on her cheek. She wiped away the drool. Something sharp brushed against her ear. What the fuck? She sat up abruptly, felt around with her hand, and came up with a yellow card with a city stamp on it.

"*Scheisse!*" she said, wide awake now. It was Veronica's get-out-of-jail card. She pushed off the bed and began hunting for her All-Stars. She was glad she hadn't taken her goodnight pill yet. She found the first high-top in the living room. "Your friend can't be far off," she told the shoe as she tied the laces just below the tattooed chain. On hands and knees, she found the shoe's partner next to the couch.

When she finally made it down to the street, she saw city workers trimming trees and a meter maid getting closer. "Fuck you, bitch!" she said and keyed the Charger. It *vroomed!* to a start and burned rubber.

∎ ∎ ∎

Laura's baby gurgled up and over the curb opposite Herbert-strasse, in front of "*Der blaue Engel.*" She stumbled out of the white leather bucket seat. Bracing herself against a West cigarette poster, she panted like a dog until the nausea went away. Then she walked through the open gate.

A bobtail truck was backed up outside 7b. Veronica's boss and some guy were arguing loudly on the other side.

"Don't shake your head at me!" Anita yelled.

Laura stepped past the driver with a raised right hand, like the Indians did in *Old Shatterhand*. "How," they always said. She cracked herself up.

"Veronica's busy," Anita said, her eyes still trained on the driver.

"Brought her something," Laura said.

Anita waved her past impatiently. "Go on in."

Laura walked into the courtyard. *Su casa, mi casa.*

"And don't forget to close the front door!" Anita yelled after her.

Laura raised her right hand again. *How, white woman.* She was laughing so hard she stumbled over the first step. "Shhhh!" she said. "Veronica's busy."

Outside, the argument continued.

"Don't you walk away from me!" Anita yelled.

"I've got work to do!" the truck driver yelled back.

"We're not done here!"

Laura bolted the door from the inside. It felt good, like she was a member of the family. She decided to wait in Anita's office. Veronica didn't like surprises.

Laura pulled up short at the door to the office. Some creep was standing at the bulletin board—right in front of *their* Ibiza picture. Laura was instantly sober, alert, ready. "Help you," she said, stepping into his space.

The creep jumped back. "I'm the gofer, Frederic." He extended his hand. "I was just delivering chalk to Mistress Veronica." His accent was oily.

Laura ignored the limp hand. "I know who you are." *Mistress.* What a weasel. "What're you doing?"

"I was just delivering—"

"At the bulletin board." Laura stepped even closer. "Special interest in that photo?"

"It doesn't do you justice," Frederic said.

"Fuck you say, asshole?"

Frederic looked down.

Goddamn right. "You made your delivery. Fuck you still doing here?"

"Anita—Frau Krenz—told me to pick up the envelope," Frederic told the ground.

"The envelope," Laura said. The little shit was begging for an ass whooping.

"For the chalk." Frederic pointed to the brown envelope on Anita's desk. It had his name written in all caps.

"Fucking chalk," Laura said. She snatched up the envelope and ripped it open. A ten-euro bill fluttered to the ground. "What're you waiting for?" Laura said. "Pick it up."

■ ■ ■

After the creep left, Laura tried to settle down. She breathed in coffee, cigarettes, and schnapps. Just like home. She fired up a Red and walked to the bulletin board. She exhaled happy smoke at their picture. Then she remembered the yellow card. She took a final drag and smashed the butt into the big-ass Jägermeister ashtray on Anita's desk.

Something familiar caught her eye. *Moderne Schulbänke*. She didn't touch the old book, just tilted her head to get a better look. Veronica was "particular" about her "source material." Judging by the number of Post-its, she had spent half the night going through the old volume. No wonder she had been so ragged out lately. She was too committed to her work.

Silently, Laura flipped the combination to Veronica's birthday. The lock opened with a satisfying *klatch!* The door swung open to Veronica's shoulder bag. Laura reached down—and froze.

Her heart was pumping big time as she yanked out the clear plastic folder. The printout said "UKE." She squinted. It had a bunch of numbers in columns and some totals at the bottom. "Fuck is this?" she said. Then she saw "*Studienbewerber*." University applicant.

Everything went ear-shattering black, then deafening white. Laura screamed but nothing came out. Decimals swam in front of her eyes. She rocked back and forth on her knees.

U-fucking-K-E. Veronica hadn't said word one about medical school, let alone a test. Of course, she used to be a nurse of some kind, but that was years ago, long before they met. Laura sniffed. Veronica had already taken the entrance exam. That meant she didn't want Laura to know.

The room went white again, Ibiza a distant memory, their big plans blown to shit. Just like that. The bitch had boarded the UKE express. Laura grabbed the locker and banged her head against it. Over and over. *Bang, bang, bang, bang, bang.*

She opened her eyes, and the blinding whiteness was gone. The train had left the station. She looked up bitterly at Ibiza. It had only existed in her mind. Veronica had played her for a fool. All these years.

Veronica thought she was something better. She wanted respectability. She wanted out of the life. Out of Laura's life. And everybody in the world knew except the one person who mattered. Laura's eyes burned. Her stomach dropped. The love of her life was leaving.

Then it hit her, like that time in Hahnöfersand. She knew what she had to do. The bitch would pay, big fucking time.

Laura laughed in the faces of the happy couple on the bulletin board. She jumped up and rammed a thumbtack into Veronica's eyes. Over and over and over. When she was done, the photo hung a bit crooked and her lover's face was tattered cork.

Somebody was going to learn the meaning of commitment. Love is as love does. No pain, no gain. Goodbye respectability, hello respect. Laura grabbed the UKE form, slammed the locker, and ran out of the office.

FIFTEEN

The Bunker

Andreas steered the Mercedes S-Guard into the parking garage under the Reeperbahn. The former air raid shelter was as good a place as any for the handoff. Few tourists knew it existed. And most of the local business owners were still in bed sleeping off their night shifts.

Andreas pushed the red knob and pulled the ticket. It took two tries with his gloved fingers. When the white bar went up, he eased the car down the polished cement ramp. The steel-belted radials squeaked on each slow turn.

It took Andreas a full minute to make it down to the third level. He drove to the last cement post, the one with the stenciled "301," and did a U-turn. He kept the lights on and the engine running.

After the longest ten minutes of his life, he heard a faint squeal of tires. It went away and then came back stronger, this time with headlights. He shielded his eyes until the passenger window was even with his own. The darkened glass slid down silently. Deep in the shadows, something flashed. Rimless glasses. Senator Althaus.

"You have something for me," Althaus said in that Hanseatic lisp of his.

Andreas grabbed the envelope and handed it through the window. He was glad he had sealed it. He thought he heard the memory card slip around under the prints.

Althaus slit open the envelope with something shiny, turned it upside down with his hand underneath, and held up the tiny memory card. "This the only copy?"

"Of course," Andreas said. Other than the duplicates on the encrypted flash drive he had just placed in his safe deposit box.

"Hmmph," Althaus said. He pulled out the glossies and paged through them.

"I think you'll find the last one particularly interesting," Andreas said. He was proud of that shot. His high-resolution Canon photo printer made it possible to see Mertens' eyes behind the ridiculous dark glasses.

Althaus flipped to the back and gave out a phlegmy laugh. "Oh dear, Carsten," he said to the photo. "Where do you find such tasteful outfits?"

"I thought you'd like it," Andreas said. He wondered idly how many of those stinky cigarillos Althaus was up to now. The old pervert liked to hold them between his second and third fingers while getting blown by pageboys at his desk in City Hall.

"That ought to do it," Althaus said, slipping the glossies back into the envelope.

"The money," Andreas said.

"Always the impatient young man," Althaus said with another tubercular laugh.

"I don't have all day," Andreas said, pushing away the unpleasant memory of his short tenure in Althaus' office. He thought he heard a car coming.

A large fat envelope slapped onto Andreas' window frame. He ripped it open. The gloves made it hard to count.

The sound got louder. It was accompanied by a flashing yellow light.

Althaus' window slid up as his car slithered around a post like an eel, gliding to the exit ramp on the other side.

Andreas tried to open the briefcase, but it kept slipping out of his grip. In desperation, he tore off the gloves with his teeth, popped the lock, and dumped the envelope and its tumbling contents inside.

The flashing light belonged to a truck. A door slammed.

A security guard crossed in front of the light and knocked on his window.

"Car trouble?" the uniform said.

"Just the navigation system," Andreas said. "Stupid thing thinks this is the IKEA lot."

The uniform laughed. "Computers."

"Have a good day," Andreas said.

The flashing light backed up, bounced off the posts, and sped toward the exit.

Andreas put the Mercedes in gear and squealed around the "301" post, sending the briefcase into the passenger door and down onto the floorboard. The wind cooled his sweat as he hit the first ramp. Too late, he heard cement scrape the belly of the car.

SIXTEEN

We Have a Problem

The timer buzzed. Break time was over. Veronica put down the sample test. That was the future, this was now. Time to get back in character. She straightened her spine, took a deep breath, and opened the door.

As she entered the Black Room, she snapped her whip menacingly. "Did you behave yourself while I was gone?" she said.

Mertens didn't move a muscle. He didn't even wince when she cracked the whip next to his head.

"Cat got your tongue?" Veronica said.

Nothing.

Veronica stepped closer. That was when she saw his blue lips. "Oh my God!" she said. She checked his eyes. Nothing but whites. Asphyxiation.

Panic grabbed her by the throat. She fought it back and went into crisis mode. *When you're in a hurry, slow down.* At least his skin was warm. She unstrapped the ball. His entire face was blue. She forced open his mouth and cleared it. The tongue was where it belonged. But there was something whitish at the back, blocking his windpipe.

She unstrapped him, unshackling his ankles first, then his wrists, holding him up with her body. He weighed a lot more than she expected. She somehow worked her way around to his broad back without dropping him and then grabbed her left fist above his navel and pulled violently against his abdomen. Something flew out of his mouth.

She turned him around with effort, lowered him to the

ground with even more effort, and checked his throat. Clear. Then his pulse. Nothing. Then his heart. Nothing. Her own heart was keeping time with the black walls closing in around her.

She turned him on his side, like they taught in nursing school. Then she raced over to the wall, popped the door of the steel wall case, and pulled out the resuscitator. Running back, she put the mask over his nose and mouth and started pumping the red ball. God knew how long he had been out. She prayed there was no brain damage.

■ ■ ■

After ten minutes of pumping, Veronica removed the mask and looked horrible reality in the face. Mertens was dead. She stood up on wobbly spikes. The black walls were closing in again. This time, she panicked for real.

She stumbled over to the door and tried to open it. It didn't budge. Her heart was going through the roof. Somehow, her fingers remembered the big key between her breasts. On her third try, she got it into the lock and turned it hard. Once. Twice. Freedom.

She felt cold air. The heavy door banged against the wall behind her. Her spikes gouged carpet going down. She hit the landing so hard the right spike got stuck, slamming her against the wall. Pulling the spike loose, she limped down the next flight of stairs, barely registering the muffled complaints from behind the red walls.

By the time she hit the office, Anita was waiting with an open mouth. "What's wrong, honey?" she said.

"Our worst nightmare," Veronica said. And then under her breath: "Our special client is dead."

The tan drained from Anita's face.

Veronica tried to push past her. "We've got to make some calls," she said.

Anita grabbed her by the arm. "Show me."

Veronica peered over Anita's thick shoulder. The corpse was even harder to look at from the doorway.

Anita's shoulders dropped.

Veronica caught her as she slid down the doorframe. Together, they ended up on the floor.

Veronica helped Anita to her feet. Slowly, she guided her down the steps. The girls in the doorways looked scared. Veronica shooed them away.

Back in the office, Anita pulled herself together. "Willi," she said, walking around the desk. She speed-dialed Kaiser Enterprises.

SEVENTEEN

Team Building

Ebeling led Ritter down the hall without any small talk. He stopped at an open door and knocked.

Ritter saw three detectives look up from their desks. An old guy, a young guy, and the redhead. Kaminsky, Müller, Voss.

"There's someone I'd like to introduce," Ebeling said. "Kriminalhauptkommissar Thomas Ritter from Frankfurt."

Ritter stepped into the room.

"KHK Ritter comes highly recommended," Ebeling said. "He will be taking over for KHK Hanson. He is your new squad leader."

The redhead stood up and strode over to Ritter, her hand extended. "Meike Voss," she said.

Ritter shook her hand once and broke cleanly. "Ritter."

The older detective took Meike's place. "Olaf Kaminsky," he said. "And this is Dirk Müller." He grabbed his partner by the arm. "He's a bit shy."

Müller gripped Ritter's hand too firmly.

"Where's Beck?" Ebeling demanded, walking to the middle of the room.

"I'm sure he'll be here any minute now," Meike said.

"What did I tell you?" Ebeling said to Ritter. "KOK Beck is the first one out and the last one in."

Meike said nothing.

"That's going to change, starting now," Ebeling said. "Isn't that right, KHK Ritter?"

Ritter nodded noncommittally. He saw a biker in full colors at the other end of the hall. The animal sported a shaved head, black leather, and shades. He was approaching rapidly. Make that a blond buzzcut, with tattoos on thick hairy forearms. The one percenter looked like he should be cuffed, hooded, and shuffling in leg irons, accompanied by half a dozen special ops with face masks.

"KHK Ritter?" Ebeling said.

"Yes, sir," Ritter said, forcing himself to look at Ebeling. His muscles tensed.

"As we discussed in my office, there are going to be some changes around here."

"Yes, sir." Ritter watched the hall with his ears. The heavy footsteps were getting closer. Each was accompanied by a dull clink. Motorcycle boots.

"Loyalty is a two-way street," Ebeling said. "As you well know."

Ritter felt his face go blank. Just how much had Rosenfeld told Ebeling?

The clinking stopped abruptly, one meter away.

Ritter saw a beefy red face, boxer's nose, thick neck, wide shoulders, and barrel chest stretching a black leather vest and black T-shirt. The vest had a brown leather bulge.

"I don't need to remind you—"

For such a big man, the biker moved fast. He whipped off his blue shades, his angry brown eyes measuring Ebeling for a coffin.

"—that one bad apple can spoi-"

The biker reached for his holster.

Time stopped.

In silent slow-motion, Ritter pushed Ebeling sideways. The wall shook. He felt the impact but stayed with the biker, whose eyes were bulging. His red face was turning purple. A deep scar pulsed under the blond buzzcut.

Ritter's forearm pressed tightly against the biker's windpipe. Each hand clenched the other elbow tightly.

Time started again.

Followed by a roar of voices.

Ritter looked up at half a dozen navy-blue uniforms with weapons drawn. All were aimed at his head. Apparently, the bad guys wore vests here too.

Ritter felt a hand on his shoulder. "Let him up, son," an authoritative voice said. Ebeling.

It took a moment for that to sink in. Ritter let go of his elbows, slowly. He was rewarded with a horrible retching sound. Something big and heavy rolled to the side. Something else began to slam the ground. It sounded fleshy.

Ritter stood up and did a slow one-eighty of the hallway. He counted three SIG Sauer P6s, one Walther P99, and two Heckler & Koch P2000s returning to holsters. All eyes were still on him. They were not friendly.

"Kriminalhauptkommissar Ritter," Ebeling said. "Allow me to introduce your new partner." He gestured toward the ground. "Kriminaloberkommissar Beck."

The biker was now leaning on an elbow. His breathing was still labored, but his face was a more natural red. His black eyes had lightened to a halfway human brown. They almost looked intelligent. A long string of pink spittle hung from his lips. Sticking out of his inside pocket was the broken arm of aviator glasses with shattered blue lenses.

Ritter's face got hot. The biker on the ground looked nothing like the official photo in Rosenfeld's file. No dress blues or hat, just a white skull and crossbones on a black T-shirt with the words "FC St. Pauli."

"KOK Beck, please welcome KHK Ritter to LKA 411," Ebeling said. "KHK Ritter will be running day-to-day operations around here." Ebeling beamed at Ritter like he'd invented him. "For the interim." He winked at his new protégé.

Nervous laughter from the assembled uniforms seconded

their obvious disbelief.

Ebeling's eyes strafed the officers lining his hallway. "Don't you all have work to do?" he said.

The uniforms dispersed noisily. A few gave Ritter a parting look that told him his ordeal was just beginning. His snitch cover must have made the rounds. Attacking his new partner just confirmed what everybody already thought.

"Now would be the time to shake hands," Ebeling said.

Ritter forced himself to reach down to the biker, who was sitting up now. Touching him again didn't seem like a good idea.

Motz batted away his hand and pushed himself up onto one knee. A long scar made an uneven path through the stubs of blond hair, which were shot through with white.

With a low grunt, Motz stood up the rest of the way. His coarse features darkened with the effort. The bulk was deceiving. His eyes were almost at Ritter's level and sharp as a Bowie knife. The scar was pulsing again.

A lazy smile meandered across Motz's face. It didn't reach his eyes. "Heard about you," he said. His hand was extended toward Ritter's midsection.

Reflexively, Ritter grabbed it. "Heard about you too."

"Nothing good, I hope," Motz said.

The hand closed around Ritter's thumb. He knew he'd been had. All Motz had to do was lean forward slightly. Excruciating pain would force Ritter's knees to buckle.

Motz nodded his head imperceptibly. The pain shooting through Ritter's thumb went up a degree. The smile never left Motz's lips.

Ebeling stepped between them. "Nice that you could join us, Beck," he said to Motz. "KHK Ritter will be replacing KHK Hanson."

The pressure on Ritter's thumb went away. His hand began to tingle.

"No one can replace Lars," Motz said.

"Yes, well, we have to move on," Ebeling said.

"We?"

Across the room, a phone rang. Meike ran over and snatched it up. "Voss," she said.

Ebeling looked at her with annoyance. "Actually, Beck, you're late for your appointment with the counselor."

"What appointment?"

Meike was writing frantically.

"The one we made last week," Ebeling said. "As you will recall, the other option is suspension without pay."

Motz snorted.

"Well? I'm waiting, Beck."

Motz turned to Ritter. "Late for my electroshock. See you around."

"Herr Inspektionsleiter!" Meike said, walking up quickly.

"Yes?" Ebeling said, his eyes still on Motz. "What is it, Voss?"

"We got a bad one, sir."

Ebeling finally looked at her. "I'm listening."

"Innensenator Mertens is dead," Meike said.

"What?!" Ebeling seemed more outraged than shocked.

"They found him in Herbertstrasse," Meike said.

"Is this some kind of joke? Carsten would never—"

"It gets worse, sir." Meike looked scared. "They found him in some kind of S&M room."

Ebeling was at her desk a second later. "Inspektionsleiter Ebeling," he said into the phone. "You're sure?" There was a pause. "Who called it in?" Another pause. "Good God! Who else knows?" Ebeling's voice was shaking. "Keep it that way! We'll be there in twenty."

Ritter felt footsteps behind him.

Ebeling had trouble putting the phone back in its cradle. "That was Davidwache," he said. "Innensenator Mertens is dead.

He was found in a house on," he cleared his throat, "Herbert-strasse."

The room rumbled.

"Quiet!" Ebeling held up his hand. "I don't need to tell you how sensitive this is. The Polizeipräsident reports directly to the Innensenator."

"Reported," Motz said from the doorway.

Ebeling whirled around. "What are you still doing here, Beck?"

"My job," Motz said.

"You really do want a suspension, don't you?" Ebeling's eyes were flashing as he turned to his other detectives. "KHK Ritter will be leading the investigation. No information leaves this room! None! Or you can all forget your pensions! Have I made myself clear?"

"Very," Meike said.

"What about Forensics?" Motz said.

"Need to know," Ebeling said.

"And the coroner?"

"Need to know, Beck."

Ritter felt the snitch in him make his move. "Has the state prosecutor been informed?"

Ebeling gave him a cold look. "Why?"

"Isn't that the normal procedure?" Like it mattered. Ritter was disgusted by how well he was playing his role.

"This isn't Frankfurt, Herr Ritter," Ebeling said.

Ritter stiffened.

"The state prosecutor takes long lunches," Meike explained.

"Keep me posted," Ebeling said and walked away.

Ritter turned to his new partner. "Kriminaloberkommissar Beck? We're driving together. On the way, you can give me background on Mertens—"

"Sorry, I don't know much about S&M," Motz said.

"—and Ebeling."

"Ebeling is into pain?"

"I have the impression they know each other."

■ ■ ■

Ritter studied the chrome "Eldorado" on the dashboard. "Not exactly standard unmarked," he said.

"Got it out of impound." Motz made a smooth gliding right onto the street. "The former owner won't be needing it anymore."

At the north entrance to Stadtpark, Motz whipped the skinny wheel with the heel of one hand, pulling them onto Ohlsdorfer Strasse. His other hand was holding what appeared to be an eight-track.

Ritter stared at the worn label of the fat Led Zeppelin cartridge in disbelief. "Black Dog" had to be as old as he was.

Motz slammed the tape into the ancient player and cranked the dial. After a few vinyl pops and cracks, Robert Plant's high-pitched wail filled the Caddy.

> HEY, HEY, MAMA
> SAID THE WAY YOU MOVE
> GONNA MAKE YOU SWEAT
> GONNA MAKE YOU GROOVE

Guitar and bass exploded in unison from the door panels. Motz was keeping pace on the wheel.

> HEY, HEY, BABY
> WHEN YOU WALK THAT WAY
> WATCH YOUR HONEY DRIP
> CAN'T KEEP AWAY

Robert Plant's wail was followed by another explosion of electric guitars. A blissful look in his eye, Motz turned onto Barmbeker Strasse with two wide loops. The big boat glided over the cobblestone smoothly. Painfully loud feedback followed in its wake. The glittery "T" bounced back and forth happily.

Ten blocks later, a deafening silence filled the Eldorado. Motz had cranked down the volume.

Ritter popped his ears with his palms. "You got spare gloves?"

Motz headbutted toward the dashboard.

Leaning forward, Ritter spotted the tiny chrome lock. He pushed it tentatively. Nothing.

Motz's hand came out of nowhere. The glove compartment popped open. Inside was Ted Nugent, Jefferson Airplane, Boston, Jethro Tull, Lynyrd Skynyrd, Stevie Ray Vaughan—and an ankle holster. Uh oh. A Smith & Wesson .38.

"What's that, your throw-down gun?" Ritter said. He wondered how far over the line this squad had gone.

"Yeah, belonged to the previous owner. Pimp named Karate Tommy," Motz said. "Went missing."

The gun had print-resistant black tape wrapped around the butt. "What's with the grip?" Ritter said.

"Makes it harder for Forensics."

EIGHTEEN

Pre-Med

The Eldorado turned into Herbertstrasse, past a small crowd held back by uniforms, and through two-meter-high iron gates. Relics of the 1930s, they were covered with red paint and oversized cigarette ads. The steel signs were legendary.

ENTRY FOR MEN UNDER 18
AND WOMEN PROHIBITED

The day before, Ritter had read in *MOPO* how the girls working here used to dump a bucket of urine on neighbor kids who ran through on a dare. Housewives in search of wayward hubbies got two. Now, here was the legend, up close and personal.

Motz lowered the volume and killed the engine with a final blast.

A uniform walked up. Mid-fifties, with a paunch and a silver bar on his shoulder. Probably the head guy from Davidwache.

Ritter stepped out onto the cobblestone. "KHK Ritter. I'm leading the investigation."

The uniform had a firm handshake and nicotine breath. "Polizeioberkommissar Pohl," he said. "I was the first on the scene."

"What have you got?" Ritter said.

Pohl looked at the crowd warily. "The Innensenator," he said behind his hand. "Found him dead in the S&M room of Haus 7b. *Puffmutter* called it in."

So the madam knew Pohl well enough to call him directly, Ritter thought. "She identify herself on the phone?"

"Yes, sir. She was very precise." Pohl looked at Motz, like that meant something. The two seemed to know each other too.

"How did he die?" Ritter said.

"He choked on something," Pohl said. "Rudi—I mean the coroner—can tell you more."

"He with the body?" Motz asked.

"You know Rudi," Pohl said.

"Show me," Ritter said.

Pohl led them through the hallway and into the courtyard. "This is 7b," he said, giving a heads-up to another uniform at the door.

Ritter felt eyes from the banks of windows along the courtyard. The girls were prettier than the street hookers in Frankfurt. Herbertstrasse gave new meaning to the words "window shopping." It looked like an upscale boutique for mistresses or even second wives.

Pohl led them up the three steps to the office. "The body is upstairs," he said, pointing to a steep wooden handrail glistening with black acrylic paint.

"Tell your men to keep the witnesses inside," Ritter said.

"Yes, sir," Pohl said.

Ritter started up the stairs. Motz and Pohl straggled behind, like they didn't want to be overheard.

At the second landing, Ritter was greeted by an open doorway to a pitch-black room that seemed to absorb several high-intensity crime scene lights. Inside, a fat man in white paper coveralls was examining a body wearing a skin-tight black costume. The owner had silver-gray hair plastered to his skull. Somebody had outlined the body with white tape on the black floor.

Ritter introduced himself in a loud voice. "Ritter, LKA 411. I'm leading the investigation."

It took the coroner a moment to get to his feet. He looked like a cross between a butcher and a grandfather. White stubble was sprinkled around his wide skull. Ritter knew the type. The kind of guy who got more human the more bodies he disemboweled.

"Deichmann," the coroner said finally. "You can call me Rudi." He didn't extend his gloved hand.

"What have we got, Herr Doktor?" Ritter said.

Rudi pointed to the corpse. "Death by asphyxiation."

"Oh, Jesus," Motz said behind Ritter.

"You can say that again," Rudi said with a deep laugh. "The chief of chiefs."

"Above my pay grade," Motz said.

Ritter cut through the banter. "Time of death?"

"About twelve thirty," Rudi said. "No rigor mortis. Body is still warm."

Ritter looked at his watch. It had been a little more than an hour. "Tell me about the victim."

"Innensenator Carsten Mertens." The coroner wasn't laughing anymore.

"Positive ID?"

"Yes!" a voice from the next room yelled. The owner was a young guy in white coveralls and hood. He stepped into the main room, holding something in a small transparent bag. It contained a national ID card. Mertens looked almost as bad in the photo as he did now, except his silver-gray hair was more wavy than flat.

"Social Democrat bigwig," Rudi said. "Mayor's right hand."

"He's a Social Democrat?" Ritter said. "Is that important?" He thought of the taxi driver the day before. *The Sozis will show those fascist bankers!*

"In this town, yeah," Motz said.

"Explain."

"The Social Democrats run everything, always have," Motz said. It sounded like he didn't think that was good or bad, just an empirical fact.

"Almost always," Rudi said.

So there really was a power struggle in town, Ritter thought. And the victim was the mayor's right hand. That could make this a political killing. "Who knows about the death?"

"Just us," Rudi said.

"Keep it that way," Ritter said. Of course, there was no way to keep something like this secret. Still, they had to pretend, if only to cover their asses.

"And half of St. Pauli," Motz said. "Especially the competition."

Ritter's new partner wasn't as dumb as he looked. That could be an advantage in their line of work. "Bad for business?"

"Fatal," Motz said.

Ritter agreed but forced himself back into his by-the-book role. "So we have a motive but no suspects," he said. Ebeling would have approved.

"Oh, yes, we do," Motz said.

"We do?" Ritter said.

"All the real estate agents in town."

"Explain," Ritter said again, even though he had a pretty good idea where this was going. *That'll stop all those real estate sharks.*

"Herbertstrasse is the most expensive property in Hamburg."

"This place?" Ritter said. A St. Andreas cross was bolted to the black wall. It had shackles at each extremity. Next door was some kind of cage with greasy bars big enough to hold a lion. Or a man.

"Law of supply and demand," Rudi said to his kit. He seemed to be having trouble with the latch.

"Great," Ritter said. "So we have a strong motive, too many suspects, and a city-wide scandal."

"Good thing you're in charge," Motz said.

Ritter knew he deserved that one. Motz kept surprising him with his speed. His banter was blunt but effective. "Who's next of kin?"

"Charlotte Mertens," Rudi said. "Former beauty queen from Hannover. Likes big horses and gala balls."

"Former is good," Motz said.

Rudi agreed. "She's all over the society pages in tight party dresses with plunging necklines."

"Unbelievable," Motz said, shaking his head at the latex-clad corpse. "The bastard has prime rib at home and he goes out for dog food."

■　■　■

"I've got one thing to brighten your day," Rudi said. "Looks like somebody stuffed something halfway down his throat." He handed Ritter another plastic bag. The contents looked sticky. "He must have inhaled it. Probably formed an airtight seal."

Ritter didn't like his imprecision. "Probably? Where did you find it?"

"On the ground," Rudi said.

"On the ground?" That made no sense—unless somebody tampered with the body. "How did it end up on the ground?"

"Heimlich maneuver," Rudi said. "I found the typical bruise pattern around the *xiphoid process*. Just above the abdomen," he added.

Oh. That changed everything. "So somebody tried to save him."

"My guess would be a domina," Rudi said.

Ritter's spine tingled as the first puzzle piece fell into place. "Who was working in here?"

"That's where it gets interesting," the Forensics guy said. "Found this in the break room." He handed Ritter a much bigger plastic bag. It contained an A4 sheet of paper with a blue logo up top.

"Universitätsklinikum Hamburg-Eppendorf," Rudi said. "UKE to its friends."

"University hospital," Motz explained.

"Home to my little laboratory," Rudi continued. "Ten minutes from the Präsidium."

Ritter didn't like the happy talk. Excitement clouded judgement.

Early assumptions could distort an investigation. Time to step back. He took a closer look at the form in his hand. "What's HAM-Int?"

"Psychological test for medical students," Rudi said.

"Look at the cover letter." The Forensics guy handed Ritter another bagged A4.

Ritter put it on top of the first.

"It's addressed to one Veronica Lühmeyer."

"Look her up on POLAS," Ritter said.

"Already did," the Forensics guy said, whipping out his phone. "Lühmeyer, Veronica. Born: 1988, Lübeck. Occupation: Domina. Employer: Anita Krenz, Herbertstrasse 7b."

"What?" Ritter said. "The medical student is a domina? Here, in this whorehouse?"

"Yes."

"That's not as strange as it sounds," Rudi said. "Dominas know a lot about medicine. Some, like this one, are former nurses."

Ritter felt the ground shift. "And you say she works here?"

"In this very room," the Forensics guy said.

Ritter braced himself against the wall. "You call it in?" he said, taking small breaths.

Rudi was studying him strangely, like he knew.

"Didn't have to," the Forensics guy said. "She's downstairs with the *Puffmutter*."

To cover his dizzy spell, Ritter crouched next to the body. "Any defensive wounds?"

"Just the marks from the straps." Rudi paused. "Suffocation can enhance orgasm."

"Like that kung fu actor?" Motz said.

A wave of nausea hit Ritter. It had a hot, bitter aftertaste. He spotted an evidence bag near his boot. Worst case, it could double as a vomit bag. "Could it be the domina just made a mistake?"

"You'll have to ask her," Rudi said. "But, in my experience, no. They're real pros."

"And she's a med student," Motz said.

"Not yet," Rudi said. "But she might make it. Her scores are above average."

"What about drugs?" Ritter said, swallowing bile.

"I'll let you know after I do the blood work," Rudi said.

"How long will that take?"

"Give me a couple of hours. My men will be up here shortly to pick up the corpse."

Ritter wanted to nod, but his throat was on fire.

■ ■ ■

After Rudi left, the Forensics guy walked back in with the check-out list for Ritter. "Sign here." He pointed to the spot on the clipboard with a ballpoint.

Ritter took the pen and added his initials. His hand was surprisingly steady, like nothing had happened. "Where's Mertens' driver's license?"

"He didn't have one." The Forensics guy tapped the clipboard for emphasis.

"So he's got a driver," Ritter said. That was normal for such a powerful politician.

"That would be my guess," the Forensic guy said.

"Not one of ours," Motz said.

"Why not?" Ritter said. "Doesn't the Innensenator get a police driver?" In Frankfurt, Polizeipräsident Rosenfeld had offered Ritter the post. He declined because he knew it was just a stepping-stone for somebody with political ambition.

"He rejected it," Motz said. "Now we know why."

Anybody who declined a police driver valued privacy more than safety. Now Mertens had neither. "What about fingerprints?" Ritter said. "I mean, other than the UKE paperwork."

"It's kind of weird," the Forensics guy said. "We haven't found any fingerprints in here yet."

Ritter looked around again. The room was too orderly. "Somebody cleaned up." He would have to ask the domina about that.

"Actually, these people are obsessive about cleanliness. They've got antiviral cleanser by the liter. And jumbo packs of cotton swabs." The Forensics guy motioned to the break room with a gloved thumb. "It looks like a doctor's office back there."

"They got a thing about latex," Motz said.

The Forensics guy laughed.

Ritter didn't like the lazy banter. These *milieu* types were pros at wiping down crime scenes. They knew physical evidence was the problem—not witnesses, who could be silenced. If he didn't come up with something tangible very quickly, his high-profile investigation would never get off the ground. That was probably why Ebeling picked him to walk point. He looked at the corpse under the St. Andreas cross. "This is no laughing matter," he said.

The Forensics guy sobered up. "There's something else." He pointed to the blond wig, dark glasses, gold chains, and jogging outfit. "We think the victim was wearing a disguise."

"That explains how he was able to walk right in here without attracting attention," Motz said. "That shit looks like it belongs on a small-time pimp. The gold chains are a nice touch."

Ritter had to agree. Mertens certainly hid his secret well. Like they said, the best way to rob a bank was in broad daylight.

"Of course, we'll have to compare the hair in the mask and the hair inside the wig," the Forensics guy said.

"We don't have that much time," Ritter said. Proving that Mertens wore a disguise didn't get them any closer to finding his killer.

"We've got witnesses," Motz said. For once he didn't seem sarcastic.

Ritter looked at the skull and crossbones on his T-shirt. He hoped that meant his new partner had experience squeezing information out of lowlifes. They'd have to take the gloves off on this one. Especially down here. From what Ritter could see, everybody in St. Pauli was iffy. Even Pohl didn't look entirely kosher.

"Oh, I forgot," the Forensics guy said. "Every room has a panic button." He pointed to a red knob under the light switch. "Nice, huh?"

Just what Ritter needed earlier. He tried not to think about the dizziness and nausea. That sometimes brought it back. "Where does it go?" If the domina had hit the button earlier, it might indicate there was a third party in here.

"The front office would be logical," Motz said, walking over to the red knob. "Want me to try it?" He held up the heel of his hand to demonstrate his willingness.

"No, hold off," Ritter said quickly. "Let's see if they tell us on their own."

■ ■ ■

At the landing, Ritter dialed a number and watched two burly guys from the coroner's office struggle down the narrow stairway with the temporary gray casket. He knew from experience that corpses were heavier than they looked.

"Talk to me," Ebeling said on the other end of the line.

"We've got a positive ID on the victim, sir," Ritter said. "It is the Innensenator. He suffocated on an X-shaped cross."

"A St. Andreas cross."

"Yes, sir." Apparently, Ebeling already knew.

"Keep a lid on this. No statements to the press. You know what's at stake."

Yeah, your career, Ritter thought. Ebeling had to know a leak wouldn't come from him. He just needed a scapegoat when the shit hit the front pages. "People are already talking," Ritter said.

"Only in St. Pauli, not Hamburg proper." The old boy tone was unmistakable. Us versus them. "I will inform the next of kin personally."

"We need to interview them first, sir," Ritter said.

"No, she needs to be shielded from the press," Ebeling corrected him.

She. So Ebeling knew the victim personally. "But sir—"

"Herr Kriminalhauptkommissar, you, of all people, know how much damage bad press can do."

Ritter was stunned. Ebeling knew he would do time if his real role in what the Frankfurt press was calling the "Lemke Affair" ever came out. And Ebeling knew he knew. That was why he was being so obvious with his "next of kin" word games. He was covering for somebody, and his new lead detective would help him.

"I think we understand each other," Ebeling said.

"You forgot to say *or else*," Ritter said. He felt Motz's eyes on him.

"I never forget," Ebeling said and hung up.

"Me neither," Ritter said to dead air.

"Ebeling?" Motz said.

Ritter nodded. "He's informing the widow himself."

"Son of a bitch!" Motz said. "He's tampering with a witness. He's telling her what to say."

Ritter couldn't have put it better. "In the car, you said he knew Mertens personally."

"Those rich fucks all know each other," Motz said. "They play by their own rules."

"Ebeling is rich?" Rosenfeld's description didn't leave a lot of doubt.

"Filthy," Motz said. "The bastard comes from an old trading family."

"Ebeling said he was protecting her from the press."

"He's protecting a trophy wife from proles like us!" Motz said.

Motz sounded like the taxi driver. "Whatever happened to Social Democratic solidarity with the workers?"

"In Hamburg, the Social Democrats *are* the ruling class," Motz said.

"Nice town you fish-heads got here," Ritter said.

"Guess you didn't get the memo in Frankfurt," Motz said. "Fish stinks from the head."

Ritter tasted something bitter again. "We don't have fish in Frankfurt, just rats."

NINETEEN

Next of Kin

Ebeling called the mayor on his private line. "Carsten is dead."

"What?" the major said.

Ebeling didn't pull his punch. "We found him in an S&M room in Herbertstrasse."

There was a gasp at the other end. "My God! There must be some kind of mistake."

"There is no mistake," Ebeling said. "We have a positive ID."

"Who knows?" The mayor's voice was cold as ice.

Well, that was quick, Ebeling thought. Mertens was instant collateral damage. "We're trying to keep a lid on it, but you know how it is down there."

"Don't try, succeed," the mayor said. Translation: You're on the hook. Keep me out of it.

"We will," Ebeling said.

"Does Charlotte know?"

Like you care, Ebeling thought. "Not yet. I'm on my way over there now."

"Good man," the mayor said. "Keep me posted."

Click.

"Yes, sir," Ebeling said. Cold bastard, he thought. The mayor wouldn't be caught dead with the widow of a sex fiend. He was probably calling an emergency meeting of his spin doctors. The Herbertstrasse bill was now as dead as its sponsor.

■ ■ ■

Tucked deep behind the Anglo-German Club on Harvestehude Weg, Ebeling pushed the brass chime and discreetly stepped back from the big black door for the camera. It was cool between the white stone pillars. The double-paned windows were twice as tall as he was.

Behind him was a huge expanse of green lawn and well-trimmed oak trees and junipers. The gravel driveway curved around in both directions. His green Jaguar glistened at the base of the wide curved steps. There were twenty-five in all. He had been to many cocktail parties here, but counting steps was a habit.

"Klaus! What a nice surprise!" The voice was flirtatious, like it might have a gin and tonic under its belt.

Ebeling turned around. "Charlotte." He touched her bronze shoulders and kissed her on both cheeks. Only when she released him did he notice her hair and skin were damp. The silk bathrobe clung to her perfect body like a second skin. He was pretty sure she had just stepped out of the shower.

"What brings you to our humble abode, darling?" she said. "Did Carsten show you our gorgeous pictures from Vai beach? It was like swimming in emeralds." Charlotte Mertens' electric blue eyes sparkled, like the visit was an inside joke.

Ebeling hesitated. "I have some bad news, dear," he said finally. "It's about Carsten. He had an ... accident."

Charlotte's hand went to her mouth. "An accident? What do you mean accident? Where is he?" She looked around Ebeling's shoulder to his Jaguar, like her husband might be inside.

"UKE," Ebeling said. Technically, that was correct. The Institute for Forensic Medicine was on a far corner of the UKE campus. Of course, Carsten was now on a cold slab, his vital organs on scales.

"Oh, my God!" Charlotte said. Then, after a moment, she pulled herself together with a resolve that surprised Ebeling.

"I have to see him!" She looked down at her bathrobe. "Just give me a moment to—"

Ebeling grasped her hands gently. "I'm afraid he's dead." He hated himself for saying it.

"What?!" Charlotte shook him loose.

"I'm sorry."

"Dead?" Charlotte made a guttural noise that could have been a laugh. It was not pleasant to hear. "That's impossible! He was in perfect health this morning! He swam his usual thousand yards while I made break—"

"I'm afraid it's true. The coroner just confirmed it." Ebeling wanted to take hold of her arms.

"The coroner?" Charlotte's eyes crossed.

Ebeling caught her on the way down. He carried her into the darkness of the villa and laid her down on a Victorian couch held up by carved feet.

He rushed to the bar, squirted carbonated water into a cut-glass tumbler, and brought it back to the couch.

After a mini sip, Charlotte sat up, gasping. "What happened?"

"We found him in St. Pauli," Ebeling said as gently as he could. "It looks like murder."

Charlotte pushed him away. "St. Pauli?"

Ebeling played for time. "I wish there was a good way to say this."

"Say what?"

"We found him in a ... bordello." He really hated himself for that one.

"A what?"

"Herbertstrasse." Helplessly, he watched Charlotte's eyes go wide. There was nothing he could do.

"What? Never! Not my Carsten! It can't be true!" Charlotte looked around the room wildly.

"He suffocated." With a rubber ball strapped to his mouth,

Ebeling thought. Good God, Carsten.

"Suffocated?" Charlotte's body started shaking. "This can't be happening!" She jumped up and ran to a guest bathroom.

Ebeling expected to hear retching noises. Too late, he realized she was ransacking the medicine cabinet.

When he threw open the door, pills flew across the room. He picked up the bottle. Tranquilizers. He forced Charlotte to the toilet, kicked open the lid, and put his forefinger down her throat.

She vomited up yellow capsules that stank of gin. Then she started coughing uncontrollably, hugging the toilet for dear life. In time, she managed to take in big gulps of air.

* * *

Half an hour later, Ebeling was sitting in a deep leather armchair in the drawing room, perpendicular to the massive stone fireplace. Charlotte was sitting in a matching chair across from him, sipping more water.

"Do you feel well enough to talk?" Ebeling asked. He opened his leather-bound notebook and unscrewed his Montblanc, the picture of calmness. He was just an old friend taking an alibi statement from a new widow. This was purely routine.

Charlotte nodded inside the tumbler.

"I'm sorry, Charlotte, but I have to ask you where you were at noon." Ebeling felt nothing as he said the words. They were spoken by a stranger in a strange place.

"At noon? I was at my tennis lesson." Charlotte could have been talking about the weather.

"Where was that?" Ebeling said as pleasantly as he could.

"Rotherbaum Tennis Club, where else?" Charlotte made it sound like a silly question. Maybe it was.

That was when Ebeling dropped the bomb. "How were you and Carsten getting along?"

Charlotte's eyes went wide again. "What?"

Ebeling couldn't believe it either. He was even more surprised that it didn't bother him. After years behind a desk, he hadn't lost his killer instinct. This was a murder investigation that would make or break his career. He repeated the question.

"You don't think—" Charlotte stopped.

Ebeling studied her face for any sign that she might be acting. An unnatural grimace. An eye tick. Any facial movement that didn't fit.

Charlotte slammed down her glass. Water splashed onto the stone island between them. "You bastard!" she screamed. "We were never happier!" Her eyes flashed. "We kidded each other all the time. We played all kind of games. Just last night, we played *Strangers on a Train*. He picked me up like a one-night stand! How many people married twenty-five years do that?"

Charlotte wasn't beautiful anymore. Her face was a twisted mask of snarling wrath. If she was acting, she was damned good.

"Certainly not you and your dried-up prune of a wife!" she said. "You probably gave her a blender for Christmas." She laughed bitterly. "You're not half the man he is!"

Ebeling almost welcomed the body blows. That made what came next easier. "Did the two of you kid each other about Herbertstrasse?"

Charlotte gasped in disbelief. "You, you—"

Ebeling bore ahead. "What can you tell me about the Black Room?"

Charlotte got her voice back. "The black what?"

Ebeling wasn't impressed by her outrage this time. Wives always knew. "How much did you know?"

"About what?" Charlotte said. "I don't know what you're talking about!" She reached for her tumbler and stopped, staring at the splattered water like she didn't know what it was doing on the stone.

"Yes, you do," Ebeling said with conviction. "You knew he had an appointment today."

"An appointment?" Charlotte looked up quickly. "Yes, of course. He had his monthly therapy session today. So what?"

"Therapy." Ebeling wrote that down.

"Yes," Charlotte said, getting up onto unsteady feat and stumbling over to the bar. "Maybe *you* should visit one." She poured clear liquid into a fresh glass and threw it back. Then she poured herself another.

Ebeling figured gin neat. He had to pick up the pace before she got too sloshed. "Who was his therapist?" he said.

"How would I know?" Charlotte said, sipping this time. "Some woman." She laughed too loudly. "We joked about it. Don't you joke about things?"

"Some woman." Ebeling wrote as he spoke. "Where did he have his, um, therapy sessions with this woman?"

Charlotte looked at him with hatred. "What is this, Klaus? An interrogation? Should I call my lawyer?"

"I don't know, should you?" Ebeling said. He was beginning to wonder himself.

Charlotte made a spitting noise and downed her drink. "Some friend your turned out to be!"

"Did you know his appointments were in St. Pauli?" Ebeling said. Some friend indeed, he thought. But he was in a cold business. His career was on the line. *Don't try, succeed.*

"No, Klaus, I didn't know his appointments were in St. Pauli," Charlotte said. A sob caught in her throat. "Oh, God!" she wailed. "This can't be happening!"

Ebeling wanted to believe her, but he had to be sure. "When was *your* appointment?" he said.

"*My* appointment?" she said. "What the hell are you talking about? I don't see a shrink. I got all the therapy I need right here." She laughed loudly at her own joke and splashed more gin into her tumbler.

"At the Rotherbaum Tennis Club," Ebeling said, paging back in his notebook. "You said you were there at noon."

"Oh, that," Charlotte said behind cut glass. "Ten o'clock."

"How long was your lesson?"

"It lasted until eleven thirty. I had lunch with Brigitte." Charlotte was slurring her speech now.

"Brigitte who?" Despite the circumstances, the question reminded Ebeling of a bad knock-knock joke.

The empty glass had a hard landing on the bar. "Brigitte von Daggenhausen."

Ebeling dutifully scratched the name on the pad. "How long did you have lunch?" He would check her alibi later.

"We left about one." Charlotte reached for the gin but then changed her mind. "Brigitte had a hair appointment in Harvestehude."

Ebeling nodded but wrote nothing down. "What is the name of your tennis instructor?"

"To-ny," Charlotte said in a singsong voice.

"What is Tony's last name?" Ebeling asked, his pen poised.

"Lorenzo. He's very nice. He comes from Calabria." She sounded like a teenager now. The spent emotions and alcohol had taken their toll.

Ebeling stared at the word on his pad. The Calabria region of Southern Italy was a known mafia hotbed. Organized Crime said the Italian national police had recently rounded up over a hundred wise guys in the capital city alone. "Has this Tony been here very long?"

"I think he's got a temporary visa," Charlotte said, yawning expansively.

I'll bet, Ebeling thought. Good Lord, the wife of the Innensenator.

Charlotte was drifting again.

Ebeling put the cap back on his Montblanc and tucked it into the leather pad, which disappeared into his jacket. "Would you like to see Carsten?"

Charlotte seemed to think the question was funny. Then her laughter went south. A horrifying wail came out of her chest.

"I'm so sorry." Ebeling watched Charlotte's nails claw her bathrobe. He was pretty sure she couldn't hear him anymore.

TWENTY

Good Cop, Bad Cop

Motz shook his head. It didn't make sense. Ritter wanted to be the BKA heavy, the bad federal cop. Motz was supposed to play the good local cop.

When he objected, Ritter said something about "psychological inversion." When that didn't work, he said, "I'm everything she hates."

That Motz understood.

Then: "Just do it, Herr Kriminaloberkommissar."

That Motz understood even better. Familiar territory, Ebeling territory.

Ritter had a slightly different take on the old Polizeischule drill. Hand on heart meant get close. Hand on belt meant go dirty. Clenched fist meant hit hard. Hand around fist meant back off. Finger to throat meant stop now. Finger up meant my turn. Finger to nose meant switch roles.

Motz had to remember that go dirty thing. Hand on belt. That was a keeper.

There were footsteps on the landing. First Pohl appeared in the doorway, then Veronica Lühmeyer. She seemed afraid to enter her own workroom. Her eyes were trained on the crude outline of a corpse taped to the ground.

Ritter dismissed Pohl and introduced himself to Veronica. Motz did the same. She shook their hands mechanically.

"Frau Lühmeyer," Ritter said. "What happened in here today?"

"I've been asking myself the same thing," she said. Her eyes were haunted.

"What happened, Frau Lühmeyer?" Ritter said again.

"I wish I knew. I was just—" Veronica appeared lost in thought.

"You were just what?"

"I was returning from my break. He was just hanging there. It was all wrong." She sounded despondent.

"He was hanging where?" Ritter said.

Veronica pointed to the X-shaped cross bolted to the wall.

The shackles were lined with black velvet. At that moment, Motz lost all sympathy for the domina. This was a torture chamber for rich sickos.

"Innensenator Mertens was hanging on the St. Andreas cross?" Ritter said.

The way he spelled it out made Motz wonder if he was recording the interview.

"Yes." Veronica looked down.

"How did he get on the cross?" Ritter said.

"I put him there," she said to the ground.

"How did you do that?"

Motz enjoyed the repetition. Lull her to sleep, then hit her hard.

Veronica looked up briefly. "It's kind of complicated."

"We have time," Ritter said.

Veronica exhaled. "Well, you stand him on a stool in front of it. Then you attach his wrists and ankles, in that order."

Motz spotted a medieval-type stool near the cross. It had three squat legs.

"Then what do you do?" Ritter said.

"Normally, I strap a rubber ball to his mouth." She was nodding to herself.

Motz didn't like the picture in his mind. The fucking Innensenator, of all people.

"Did you strap a rubber ball to his mouth today?" Ritter said.

"Yes," Veronica said. "It's not as uncomfortable as you might think." She seemed to be gaining confidence.

"Did you kill him?" Ritter said. He was clenching his fist.

Motz didn't need the signal. That was a direct hit.

"God, no. I just told you—"

"Were you alone with him?" Ritter said.

"Yes, but—"

"Was the door locked?" Ritter said.

Damn, Motz thought. The fucker was relentless.

"Of course. I always—"

"You were alone in a locked room with a man you bound and gagged—"

"Wait a minute!" Veronica yelled. "You're putting words in my mouth." She looked to Motz for help.

He stared back. Ritter already had her on the ropes. Just a few more blows, and they could all go home.

"The man you bound and gagged suffocated—"

"But I was on my break!" she screamed.

Ritter stepped into her face. "Carsten Mertens died an agonizing death, Frau Lühmeyer, and all you have to say is, you were on your break?"

Veronica stood to her full height. No fear in her eyes now, just contempt. "That's not what I said."

Ritter didn't back off. "Oh yes, it is. That's exactly what you said."

"You're not listening!" Veronica screamed.

"Yes, I am," Ritter said, like a patient boxer. "You confessed to killing the top cop in Hamburg."

So much for a technical KO, Motz thought. Ritter was going for the real thing.

"The hell I did," Veronica said. "I just found him that way."

"Which way?" Ritter said.

Veronica pointed to the white tape on the ground. "That way, damn it."

"You mean dead," Ritter said.

"Yes, dead," Veronica said. "Blue in the face. Dead, dead, dead. Was that what you wanted to hear, Herr Kriminalhauptkommissar? Or is it too tough for you to understand?"

"Why did you kill him?" Ritter made it sound like she had confessed and he was curious about her motive.

Motz snorted. Who needed hand signals? Ritter was good cop, bad cop wrapped into one.

"What?" Veronica screamed. "Are you hard of hearing? I was on break."

Ritter's fist was clenching and unclenching spastically.

Here we go, Motz thought. KO time.

"Frau Lühmeyer, take a good look at the outline of the man you killed," Ritter said. When she didn't respond immediately, he grabbed her roughly by the arm. "Look at it."

Veronica spun into him. "Let go of me," she said, pushing against his chest.

Ritter's fingers clamped down on latex.

"You bastard," she said, gasping for breath. Her other hand flailed. Tears crisscrossed the white powder on her face. Then her body went limp.

"You catch on quick," Ritter said, his other hand on his heart.

Motz saw the signal. Get close. Time for fake outrage. "Herr Kriminalhauptkommissar," he said.

Ritter ignored him.

Veronica gasped wetly. A string of saliva hung from her lips.

In one quick motion, Ritter pulled her to the center of the room.

Motz stepped back.

Ritter grabbed her behind the neck. "Take a good look," he said, forcing her head closer to the white tape.

Veronica stumbled. She jumped up and hissed at Ritter. "You son of a bitch. You can't treat me like this."

"Wrong," Ritter said. "I can do whatever I want. You killed the Innensenator. That's a game changer."

"I didn't—"

"Yes, you did." Ritter threw her up against the St. Andreas cross. Her head hit the crossbar with a thud.

"That's enough, Herr Kriminalhauptkommissar!" Motz yelled. "This is Hamburg, not Frankfurt."

"She's guilty as hell!" Ritter yelled back.

"I said enough!" Motz really meant it this time.

Veronica was trembling against the crossbars.

"Are you okay, Frau Lühmeyer?" Motz said.

"I'll–live." Veronica touched the back of her head. She was panting shallowly.

"I apologize for my colleague," Motz said. "He's new in town."

"Ought to—put him—on leash," she said.

"I thought that was your department," Ritter said, casually hooking a leg over a strange wooden cage about the size of a big doghouse.

Motz didn't let the thought distract him. "Are you okay?" He tried to put his arm around the domina's shoulder, but she shrunk back. "I'm not going to hurt you. *Nobody* is going to hurt you." He really meant it.

Veronica nodded weakly.

"We're under a lot of pressure," Motz said. "A lot of unwanted publicity. A lot of unanswered questions. A lot of pressure from City Hall."

"I can well imagine," Veronica said.

The domina was regaining her composure a bit too quickly for Motz's taste. "Let's just sit down and have a little talk," he said. He pulled over the medieval stool. "Sorry, that's the best I can do on short notice."

Ritter took out a pocketknife and began cleaning his nails.

TWENTY-ONE

Strong Horse

Sulejman Hasani looked at the first monitor next to his immaculate desk. A shadowy figure in a pakol cap, white beard, cape, and shepherd's cane was standing at the front desk of the casino—and staring directly into the black-and-white monitor.

"He's here," Hasani told his bodyguard. He figured it would take the old Afghani five minutes to make it up to the fourth floor with that stiff leg of his. They said he was the only member of the wedding party to survive the drone attack.

Two minutes later, the squirrely Sunni was standing outside the office door, staring into another monitor. Hasani cursed softly and pressed a button.

The door opened. The bodyguard stood at attention. A distinguished gentleman in a colorful outfit entered.

Hasani stood up, smoothed his white dinner jacket, and came out to greet his visitor. "*Assalam Alaykum*," he said, extending his hand. Peace be upon you.

The Afghani removed his hand from his robe. "*Assalam.*"

Hasani ignored the missing "*Alaykum.*" For Sunnis, Bektashis like Hasani were heretics. But that didn't stop them from doing business.

Hasani motioned his guest to a small armchair and returned to his desk, glancing briefly at the blackjack tables below. "I trust you had an uneventful journey." He pressed a white handkerchief to the left side of his nose.

The bodyguard placed a small glass of green tea next to the bowl of almonds and plate of *girda* bread.

"Security is especially rigorous at Karzai International this time of year," the Afghani said.

Hasani motioned to the bread. "Please."

"You are very thorough." His guest broke off a piece.

"My form of *taqiyya*," Hasani said.

The Afghani stopped chewing. The camel jockey obviously didn't like jokes about religious dissimulation. "Your Arabic has improved since we last met," he said at last.

"You are too kind." Hasani turned over the handkerchief and pressed it to his nose again.

"No one can harm us if Allah is with us," the Afghani said.

"*Allah akbar.*" The Afghani had evidently heard about Hasani's mistreatment by the Serbian infidels. Good. Hasani liked business partners who did background checks. Paranoia kept you sharp.

"We have a common enemy, no?" the Afghani said.

"NATO is a weak horse," Hasani agreed.

After talking around the subject, the two men got down to business.

"Why did you ship under a Turkish flag again?" Hasani said. "We agreed on Yemen."

"That attracts too much attention."

"Exactly."

The Afghani looked at Hasani strangely. "I hear you are having trouble with customs."

"Nothing we cannot handle," Hasani said. They called the customs officials the "black gang" because they got so dirty climbing containers with flashlights in their mouths. The poor, underpaid fools.

"What about the divers? They keep finding our packages."

"Let that be my worry," Hasani said.

"It is your money."

"That it is." Hasani dabbed his nose again.

"So you want the big shipment under a Yemeni flag?"

"No, I want it under a German flag." Hasani was enjoying himself now.

"What?"

"A Bundeswehr flag, to be exact," Hasani said. "You're delivering to Mazar-i-Sharif."

"Are you out of your mind? Camp Marmal is crawling with German soldiers!"

"*Our* German soldiers," Hasani said. "Let me explain."

■ ■ ■

Hasani watched the Afghani's hat and cape descend the carpeted steps. When he turned around, his bodyguard was frowning. Hasani folded his handkerchief. "This is not the final shipment," he said.

The bodyguard's frown deepened.

Hasani walked back into the office and over to an antique cabinet. "It is the *only* shipment." He opened one of the ornate doors and pulled out a stone bottle and two matching goblets. "Our friend thinks this is about politics. He thinks the Taliban is the future." Hasani paused. "Our friend is wrong. Real estate is the future." He poured the wine into the goblets. "Soon we will own this town."

The bodyguard looked awestruck.

Hasani handed him a goblet and took the other. "We outlasted the Axelmans, Tito, Milošević. Now, it is NATO's turn." He raised his goblet over his head with both hands.

The bodyguard did the same.

"*Tâ ezel bezminden ikrâr eyliyen, şi'îleriz.*" Since the gathering of Eternity, we are Shia.

The bodyguard responded with the familiar chant. "*Bunda ol ikrârı tekrâr eyliyen, şi'îleriz.*" Here, making this confession yet again, we are Shia.

The two men drank in silence.

TWENTY-TWO

Hippocratic Oath

"Frau Lühmeyer, I need you to tell me exactly what happened today," Motz said. "Take your time. Details are important."

The two of them were sitting on expensive chrome and leather office chairs he had rolled in from the break room.

"I understand." Veronica's eyes strayed to the white tape on the ground. They got that haunted look again.

Motz jumped up and grabbed the plastic tarp Forensics left behind. It crackled when he shook it, then floated down to cover the tape, like a comforter. "There," he said. "That's better."

"Thank you," Veronica said.

Motz sat down on his comfortable chair again, careful not to roll away. He took a spiral notebook from his jacket and flipped it open, cheap ballpoint at the ready. "Okay," he said. "Whenever you're ready."

Ritter's knife paused.

Veronica took a deep breath. "Well, we had an appointment at noon, like always. He arrived right on time."

"At noon," Motz said. Nice and easy.

"Yes, he was always punctual. After Anita handed him off to me, we got right down to business. Herr Mertens doesn't—didn't—care much for small talk. It's a time issue."

I'll bet, Motz thought. The clock is always ticking. He wondered if she charged by the hour or by the job. "Did you lock the door?"

"Yes," she said. "That is one of the first things I learned here. Everything we do is based on trust."

"Tell me about the ball," Motz said.

"The ball?" Veronica seemed mildly annoyed. "It's just a rubber ball that fits in the mouth. There are different sizes for different mouths"

"What's it for?" Motz said.

"It takes away his speech." Veronica's eyes brightened. "He no longer has any say. It's a control thing. He can't issue orders."

Motz had the impression she liked that part. "Is it, um, sexual?" he said.

"No, definitely not. What we did was simply domination and submission. Nothing really sexual, more about letting go."

"Uh huh." Motz looked at his notes. "This ball, does it have a strap?" He remembered the white Vs on Mertens' cheeks. Rudi said they matched the straps on the ball.

"Yes, it's—" Veronica looked around the room.

"At the Polizeipräsidium," Ritter said, standing up from the monkey cage. "Hope you don't mind." His knife closed with an audible click.

"Our lab guys are examining it," Motz said, giving Ritter a warning look. "Just routine. What happened after you fit the ball into Mertens' mouth?"

"I went to my office," Veronica said. "That's the room where you found these chairs." She patted the arm of her own.

"You left him alone?" It was Ritter again.

What the fuck, Motz thought. Ritter had better not blow this.

"Yes," Veronica said to Motz. "I always teach him a lesson. He never knows how long it will last. It teaches him he's not in control."

Motz's pen started moving again. He underlined "control" and "lesson." And willed Ritter to put a sock in it.

"It's an important lesson." Veronica sounded like she was talking about Sunday school.

"No, it's murder," Ritter said. "Or at least involuntary manslaughter."

Motz threw down the notepad.

Veronica looked at the ground like she was trying to read his writing upside down.

Motz scooped up the pad and slapped it shut.

"He was fine when I left him," Veronica said.

"He's not fine now," Ritter said.

Motz held up the notepad. "That's enough, Herr Kriminalhauptkommissar."

Veronica thanked Motz with her eyes.

Motz blinked *you're welcome*. He and Veronica had their own signals. "Frau Lühmeyer, you said something about a lesson."

"Yes," she said.

He leaned toward her. "If I understood you correctly, you left the room to teach Mertens a lesson."

"It's not the leaving that's important," she said. "It's the staying away that counts. He never knows how long."

Boy howdy, Motz thought. That's the difference between involuntary manslaughter and first-degree murder. "How long did you, um, stay away?"

"Fifteen minutes."

"Are you fucking kidding me?" Ritter said.

Motz rolled his chair between them, shielding Veronica with his body. "Frau Lühmeyer, did you just say fifteen minutes?"

"Yes. When you're bound and gagged, fifteen minutes can feel like fifteen hours."

Motz couldn't argue with that.

"What the hell!" Ritter said. "That some kind of union-mandated break?"

Motz was close enough to smell Veronica's breath. Peppermint. "Is that part of the kick?" he said.

"No, it's part of the therapy," she said. "The client is made to feel helpless. He has no control over his environment. He is entirely dependent on others."

"What happened next?" Motz said.

"When I came back—" Veronica's hand went to her mouth.

"When you came back? What happened then?" Motz was squeezing his fist so tight the knuckles were white.

"I—, I knew—"

"You knew—" Motz cut off the thought just as she had.

"I knew he was in trouble." Horror filled her eyes again.

"How did you know?"

"His head was hanging at a strange angle. And his eyes"—a sob slipped between her fingers—"were wrong."

Motz was all ears, her best friend. "His eyes were wrong," he said.

"Nothing but whites." She looked like she was watching it on film.

He nodded like he saw it too. "What happened then?"

"I removed the ball and got him down fast. His lips were already blue."

"What did the blue lips tell you?"

"That there was no blood to his brain," she said.

Motz nodded, the picture of concern. "He was in danger?"

"Mortal danger," she said.

"What happened then?"

"What do you think? I grabbed the BVM and tried to resuscitate him." Veronica had moved as far away from him as she could in her chair.

"A bag valve mask?" Ritter said. He was standing next to her now, his finger on his nose. Switch roles.

Veronica nodded and blinked at the same time.

Motz wanted to ask what a bag valve mask was, but Ritter cut him off. His finger was raised. My turn.

"We found the BVM." Ritter was crouched next to Veronica. "Did you bag him?"

She nodded again quickly.

"Did he respond to BVM?"

"No." Veronica was staring at something they couldn't see. "No vitals. His heart had stopped. I kept pumping, but I knew it was hopeless."

Motz looked back and forth between them. Pumping?

"How long did you pump?" Ritter said.

"Ten minutes."

"That's a long time," Ritter said. "Most people would have given up after five."

"*Primum non nocere.*"

"What?" Motz said.

"Do no harm," Ritter said, finger on throat. Stop now. "Part of the Hippocratic Oath."

Motz looked away in disgust. The Hypocritical Oath was more like it.

"You really tried to save him, didn't you?" Ritter said.

Veronica nodded vigorously.

"I believe you," Ritter said.

Veronica looked like she wanted to kiss him.

Ritter touched his belt. Go dirty.

Oh, hell, Motz thought. Everybody always gave him the shit jobs, even the new guy. "Didn't work out too well, did it?" he said. You want dirty, I'll give you dirty.

"Wh-what?" Veronica said.

"Wh-what?" Motz said, mocking her. Then he jumped up and threw back the tarp. "Take a good look, *Mistress* Veronica. See what you did."

"But I just told you—"

"Do no harm. Yeah, I got that part." Motz realized he was angry at both of them. Overeducated snobs talking Greek instead of plain German.

Ritter rotated Veronica's chair away from Motz and put both hands on the arms. "Do you just have the one BVM bag? The one in your office?"

Motz wanted to hit him. And slap the uppity domina for good measure.

Veronica shook her head. "We have another one in the White Room."

"What's the White Room, Veronica?" Ritter said.

Good question, Motz thought. Is that for good little boys and girls? Or is it the really sick shit?

"It's our clinical area," she said. "It's set up to look like a medical clinic."

Motz snorted. The really sick shit.

"Interesting," Ritter said. "Do you work in the White Room too?"

"Oh, no! Never!" Veronica said. "That's in my contract." There was a hint of hysteria in her voice.

Now I've heard everything, Motz thought. Wouldn't want to violate your contract now, would we? Whips yes, enemas no.

"Why is that?" Ritter said.

"You have to separate fantasy from reality, especially in this business," Veronica said.

"Tell me about it." Too late, Motz realized he had said it out loud.

TWENTY-THREE

Be Obvious

There was a knock at the door.

Hasani finished securing the cabinet door and walked over to his desk. His nephew, Mustafa, was nervously checking his hair in the monitor. Hasani pressed a button and the door opened.

Mustafa walked in.

Hasani looked at the briefcase in his hand. It was nearly identical to the one he normally used. Kaiser and his games. The only thing missing was the small scratch Hasani himself had made next to the handle. "Did everything go okay?" he said.

"Like clockwork." Mustafa walked up and placed the briefcase next to the desk.

His nephew sounded too sure. Overconfidence made people careless.

"You were not followed?" Hasani said. It would not surprise him if the German police were watching their locker at the central train station. It was time to switch drop boxes again.

"No, Uncle Sulejman," Mustafa said. "I was very careful."

"I certainly hope so." Hasani looked at his nephew's hands until they began to tremble. "That will be all."

Mustafa half bowed and left without a word.

The bodyguard closed the door behind him.

■ ■ ■

Back at his desk, Hasani opened the briefcase. It contained a brown envelope with a blue Polizei Hamburg stamp. Subtle, he thought.

He clicked open his switchblade and slit the duct tape with a practiced motion. Inside were five plastic-wrapped stacks of fifties, damp dirt clinging to them. More games. He would put the bills through the counting machine later, but he knew all fifty thousand euros were there.

By paying off his archenemy, Kaiser showed weakness. In his younger days, the "King of St. Pauli" would have delivered Mustafa's finger. Now he was paying *jizyah* tax like a good *dhimma*. Hasani wanted to laugh. Instead, he went on the offensive.

"Send two of your men to Norbert Grube's house in Blankenese," he told his bodyguard. "And send two more to watch his mother's villa." He pulled out the tax form his nephew had retrieved from Kaiser's accountant. "It's on Behler See, about an hour northeast of here."

The bodyguard read the address out loud twice, as a memory aid, the way Hasani had taught him.

When he was done, Hasani turned the form facedown.

"We will be discreet," the bodyguard said.

"No, be obvious," Hasani said. "That is the second part of the message. I expect the HansaBank manager will need some encouragement to do the right thing."

TWENTY-FOUR

Involuntary Manslaughter

"This yours?" Ritter said to Veronica. "It's got your name on it." He was holding an A4 evidence bag.

Veronica glanced at the piece of paper inside. "Oh that."

"UKE," Ritter said, like she had answered his question. "That's the university hospital, right?"

Veronica barely nodded.

"*We are pleased to inform you*," he read. "It sounds like they really want you."

Veronica shrugged.

"Are you applying to medical school?" Ritter said, like he was mildly curious about her career plans.

"Yes," Veronica said carefully.

"It says here that you passed the natural science test." Ritter pointed to the bagged letter. "When did you get the results?" He was annoyingly cheerful.

Motz could see Ritter's banter was getting to the domina. Maybe he knew what he was doing after all.

"This morning," she said. "I—"

Motz cut her off. "This morning? Do you mean to say—" Then he saw Ritter's hand around his fist. Back off.

"This morning you did what, Frau Lühmeyer?" Ritter said. He wasn't cheerful anymore.

"I—" She cleared her throat. "I picked up my test results."

"At UKE?"

"Yes, of course," Veronica said in a stronger voice. "Where else?"

Ritter ignored the question. "Did you talk to someone there?"

Veronica hesitated. "An admissions officer."

"What was the admissions officer's name?"

Motz liked that. Ritter was breaking her down her defenses, forcing her to cooperate.

"She can't find out about this!" Veronica said in desperation. "It would kill my chances!" There were tears in her eyes.

Motz took out his pad again. *She.*

"What is her name?" Ritter said. "We will be discreet," he added in a softer tone.

The hell we will, Motz thought. He flipped to a new page and handed Veronica his pen.

She stifled a sob as she wrote down the name. She held the back of Motz's hand to support the pad.

"Thank you," Motz said, back in good cop mode. "I know that wasn't easy." He could feel her trembling.

She let go of his hand and waved away a tear.

"Frau Lühmeyer, one thing bothers me," Ritter said. The softness was gone. "I just can't get that ball out of my mind."

Me neither, Motz thought. That and the slimy piece of paper in Mertens' throat.

"What?" Veronica said, wiping her eyes.

"The coroner says Mertens suffocated to death," Ritter continued.

Veronica grabbed her upper arms, like she was cold. "That's what you told me."

"And *you* told me he had a ball in his mouth when you realized something was wrong," Ritter countered.

Veronica shivered in silence.

"Here's the problem," Ritter said. "We found a slimy piece of paper on the ground. The coroner is pretty sure Mertens choked on it."

Now we're getting somewhere, Motz thought. Again. He had been building up to the same question fifteen minutes earlier.

Veronica froze.

"But you already knew that, didn't you?" Ritter said.

"I don't know what you're talking about," Veronica said, rubbing her thighs like the latex was cold against her skin.

She knows, Motz thought.

"How did the paper get in his mouth?" Ritter said.

Veronica knotted her brow.

Motz didn't buy her act. She was too smart not to have seen that question coming.

Ritter looked at her coldly. "You said you put the ball in his mouth," he said.

No response.

"You would have seen a large, balled-up piece of paper in his mouth, right?" Ritter looked at Motz. "I know I would have."

Still no response.

"What, you didn't see anything?" Ritter said, like he was confused.

Veronica was shivering violently now.

"Where are your test scores?" Ritter said.

Under a microscope back at the Präsidium, Motz thought.

Veronica looked at Ritter helplessly.

"Forensics tells us your scores were on that piece of paper," Ritter said.

"What?!" Veronica yelled. She jumped up. Her chair shot across the room behind her and crashed into the monkey cage. "Are you crazy?"

"No, just thorough," Ritter said.

Time for the kill shot, Motz thought.

Veronica stalked around the room like a trapped tiger. She didn't look cold anymore. "Are you saying I choked Mertens with my own test scores?" She cackled. "That's ridiculous! Why would I do that?"

"Well, *did* you choke him with your own test scores?"

Ritter said, walking up to her.

Veronica whirled on him. "No!" she screamed. "Why would I?"

Because you're a freak show, Motz thought.

"So how did they end up in his mouth?" Ritter persisted.

"I–have–no–idea!" Veronica yelled. She was shaking with rage now.

Yes, you do, Motz thought. You know exactly what happened.

Ritter turned to Motz. "She has no idea."

Motz snorted.

Ritter turned back to Veronica. "The coroner says the bruise patterns on Mertens' chest are consistent with the Heimlich maneuver." Ritter's hand was on his heart.

Not again, Motz thought. She's on the ropes. Go for the knockout.

"You're a registered nurse," Ritter continued. "You know the Heimlich maneuver."

"We've already been through that," she said.

Ritter nodded agreement. "You knew something was caught in his throat." His tone was gentle, almost intimate.

That stopped her cold.

"You tried to save him," Ritter said, respect in his voice.

"Yes, of course," she said, grabbing her arms again.

"So how did your test scores end up in his throat?" Ritter said matter-of-factly.

Kill shot, Motz thought.

Veronica jumped back, like she'd been hit by a bolt of electricity. "I don't know! How many times do I have to say it?"

Ritter didn't seem fazed. "Okay, let's try something else."

Veronica took a deep breath and shook her head at the ground.

Motz exhaled loudly. What the fuck, he thought. Why didn't Ritter just finish her off?

"A moment ago, you said the door was locked," Ritter said. He made it sound like the domina was a witness instead of the prime suspect.

"Yes, of course—"

Ritter ignored the snippy tone. "Does anyone else have the key?"

"Anita," Veronica said. "But it's with all the other keys in the lockbox."

"Who is Anita?" Ritter said, glancing at Motz.

Motz's pen was waiting.

Veronica hesitated, like she suspected a trap. "Anita Krenz, my boss. She wears the key to the lockbox around her neck."

Motz wrote down the name and "*Puffmutter*."

"Is the box always locked?" Ritter said.

"Yes, definitely. Anita insists on it." Veronica seemed worried by her own words. Maybe they were pointing in the wrong direction.

"This morning too?" Ritter said.

"Yes, of course." Veronica frowned.

They could throw away the key now, Motz thought. The domina just cut off any reasonable line of defense.

"Frau Lühmeyer?" There was concern in Ritter's voice.

"Yes?" Veronica looked disoriented, like he had interrupted her thoughts.

"I thought we lost you there for a moment," Ritter said.

That's when it hit Motz. The domina was covering for somebody they didn't know about. She had talked too openly about her *Puffmutter*, so it had to be somebody else. He would have Forensics check the keys to make sure nobody had ever made duplicates. If they were lucky, the keys were registered, so duplicates had to be formally approved by the owners.

"I was just thinking about something," Veronica said. "Anita rules this house with an iron fist. She says exceptions are evil."

Nice try, Motz thought. All this easy talk about her *Puffmutter* was meant to throw them off track.

"I like that," Ritter said breezily. Then: "Were you alone with Mertens?"

Motz liked the lack of transition. Ritter knew she was lying too. "Yes, but—"

"The whole time?" Ritter persisted. He sounded almost as angry as Motz felt.

"Yes, but I would never—"

Ritter slapped his thighs and stood up. "Frau Lühmeyer, put yourself in our shoes. A domina is alone in a locked room with a man whom she binds, gags, and leaves alone for fifteen minutes. When she returns, he has suffocated."

Veronica looked at him in horror.

"Frau Lühmeyer, if you were us, what would you think?" Ritter said.

"I don't know." She had that faraway look again.

Ritter shook his head. "Frau Lühmeyer, I'm afraid we have to take you into custody."

Hallelujah, Motz thought. Finally.

"Why? I've told you everything you need to know!" She looked at Motz in desperation. "I'm cooperating."

Motz didn't respond.

"That's just it," Ritter said. "You aren't."

"But—" She looked around the room again, pulsing with dangerous energy.

Motz moved to block her path to the door, getting ready to shield his eyes from her claws. She looked capable of anything.

"Frau Lühmeyer, I don't think you murdered Mertens," Ritter continued, as though he hadn't noticed their movements. "I know you tried to save him."

"Then why—" Veronica stopped when she saw Motz at the door.

"You're withholding something," Ritter said.

No shit, Motz thought.

"But I told you I don't know how it happened!" Veronica was pleading with both of them now.

Ritter stepped into her field of vision. "The man choked to death in a locked room on your watch," he said. "Under the circumstances, *I don't know* doesn't cut it."

Veronica started shaking again. "Am I under arrest?"

"Yes," Ritter said. "You are."

Motz slapped his notepad shut. So much for that. Now all they had to do was find the real killer.

"What are the charges?" Veronica asked.

"Involuntary manslaughter."

Veronica collapsed in her chair.

TWENTY-FIVE

Behler See

Norbert Grube pushed the accelerator to the floor and felt his Mercedes coupe grip the road. The lush greenery of his favorite park flew by on the left, but the sinister black van in his mirror stayed right where it was. It had followed him all the way from HansaBank.

He knew that Clausewitz Barracks was only a couple of blocks away. The army base would have provided him with personal safety, but he was worried about his wife and kids. The coupe climbed the steep hill with no effort.

As Grube approached the high green hedge of No. 42, he clicked the remote to open his gate. That was when he saw the green Land Rover out front. He wanted to speed away, but it flashed its lights at him. Something about the signal was calming. As the gate rolled open, the black van appeared in his mirror again. He raced through the gate, up the driveway, and into the garage. The door was already closing behind him. He switched off the engine and got out, shutting the car door quietly.

Outside, he heard the van roar its gurgling engine three times, like a teenager pumping the gas of a hotrod, each time louder and longer. Except these weren't teenagers. They were Albanian killers. And he was their prey.

The Land Rover did the same. Its engine was deeper, and its muffler made a popping noise each time the driver blasted the pipes.

Before Grube knew it, both vehicles were roaring back and forth at each other. It was childish. The thought was not reassuring.

Grube snuck to the side window of the garage and peered over the iron-framed sill. Down below, the black van was inching toward the Land Rover, like a boxer. The Land Rover came out to meet its opponent in front of the gate. After a long moment, the black van changed its mind and sped away.

Grube exhaled. Kaiser was even better than his word.

■ ■ ■

After Grube drained a crystal tumbler of twelve-year-old single malt—and assured his wife, Annette, that everything was okay— he decided to check on his mother. Those Balkan types were big on family. Which meant, when push came to shove, they would go after yours. Grube tried not to think about a black van pulling up in front of the family estate.

After refilling his tumbler, he closed the door to his oak-paneled study and dialed the Behler See number by heart. Hopefully, his ninety-one-year-old mother hadn't "forgotten" to put her hearing aid in again. She thought it made her look old to her private physician, who did house calls once a day. It didn't help that her twenty-two-inch analog TV was blasting through the thick walls of the villa around the clock. A few years before, Grube had somebody wire the land line to the doorbell, which gonged like a church bell. He let it gong twenty times, hung up, redialed, and sipped some more single malt.

Finally, somebody picked up the phone and made fumbling noises that sounded like hand-to-hand combat. A rerun of *Bonanza* was blaring in the background. Apparently, Hoss was having another disagreement with Little Joe.

Both were interrupted by an overly loud voice. "Grube residence, Hildegard speaking."

Grube sighed. "*Mutti*, how many times do I have to tell you not to give out your name on the telephone." He knew his mother was holding the oversized phone on the cart next to her Barcalounger.

It was a prototype developed for his father in the 1970s. The shoulder clamp on the receiver was the size of the widow's shrunken white head.

"Who is this?" the loud voice said. "I'm going to hang up now!"

"*Mutti*, wait! It's me, Norbert, your son." Your only son, he added in his mind. Not for the first time, he wished he had siblings to share the burden.

"Norbert? Why didn't you say so?"

Grube held the receiver away from his ear. "I just did."

"Watch your mouth, young man," she yelled, her voice carrying across the room. "I'm still your mother."

"I know that, *Mutti*. I just have a lot on my mind." Grube realized he was yelling too. His wife would knock on the door soon if he didn't lower his voice.

"Why aren't you working?" his mother demanded.

"I'm at home," he said in an indoor voice.

"That's where you belong." It almost sounded like a threat. "Your father, God rest his soul, worked himself to death."

Grube sighed again. "Yes, I know. I was there."

"You were where?"

Grube decided to change tactics. "Annette and I would like to visit you this weekend."

"It's been ages since I saw the kids," his mother said. "I have something for them."

"They don't live with us anymore," Grube reminded her, his voice too loud again. "Björn is in New York, and Sven is in Brussels. It's been over ten years now. They both have families of their own. You remember those baby photos we showed you?"

"Never you mind," his mother said.

"We'll be sure to bring the pictures." Grube heard loud gunfire on the other end. He hoped it was on the Ponderosa.

TWENTY-SIX

Panic Button

"Willi Kaiser still own this place?" Motz asked. He was on the landing outside the Black Room with POK Pohl.

"Yeah," Pohl said. "He must be going to the mattresses by now."

They watched Ritter bring Veronica Lühmeyer to the landing.

"We need to talk some more," Motz said to Pohl. "Later."

Pohl grunted and nodded up at Veronica.

"You two know each other?" Motz said.

"Sure," Pohl said. "We go way back."

"Take Frau Lühmeyer into investigative custody," Ritter said to Pohl. "Involuntary manslaughter."

Veronica got that desperate look again.

Pohl took her by the arm. "It's just routine," he said and turned her toward the stairs.

Yeah, right, Motz thought.

Ritter finished sealing the room. "Let's brace this *Puffmutter*," he said.

Veronica stopped outside the office. "Can I get my things?"

Ritter and Motz slowed their descent.

"Of course," Pohl said.

Veronica walked into the office and hung up her key on top of its twin.

Motz and Ritter watched from the doorway. Both keys had black rubber handles. Those next to them had white rubber. The rest were similarly color coded. Red, blue, yellow, green.

"Both of those black keys for the S&M room?" Ritter said.

"For the Black Room, yes," Veronica said. She worked the combination on her locker. "That's why the key has a black label." The lock snapped open.

Motz was impressed. The domina hadn't completely lost her attitude.

"Why two keys?" Ritter said.

"One for Veronica, one for me," somebody said. It sounded like a heavy smoker.

Motz gave the speaker a quick up-and-down look. Sixty, handsome, built like a brick shithouse, with a studio tan, half-glasses, expensive hair, French nails, and some serious cleavage that looked well kept. Next to her was a bulletin board full of vacation photos of girls who could have been swimsuit contestants. In the middle, there was fragment of a photo under a thumbtack, like somebody had ripped it down.

"Who are you?" Ritter said.

"Anita Krenz, the concierge. Who are you?"

Motz liked that. These Herbert people really had spunk.

"Kriminalhauptkommissar Ritter. We ask the questions."

Motz stepped forward. "Beck," he said and nodded curtly at Anita. "Don't mind the Kommissar's manners. He's new in town."

The *Puffmutter* nodded back. They understood each other.

"Beck!" Ritter warned.

"Kind of the dominant type, isn't he?" Anita said to Motz.

Motz grinned. She was his kind of people.

Ritter stepped between them. "Why one key for you, Frau Krenz?"

"Just in case," Anita said.

"In case what?" Ritter said.

"In case Veronica needs help." Anita winked at Motz.

"How would you know if she needed help?" Ritter said.

"She has a panic button," Anita said. "Like all my girls."

"Where?"

"In the Black Room, where else?"

Motz began wondering who was interviewing who.

"What happens when she pushes the panic button?" Ritter said.

Anita finally looked at him. "A warning light flashes."

"Show me."

Anita took three heavy steps to her desk and pointed to an inclined panel next to the phone.

The buttons were marked G1, G2, G3, G4, Black, and White, in matching colors. Standard services were printed on a card taped to the wall. Inquisition, Mommy Dearest, Doc Proc, and Yellow Rain. The *Puffmutter* ran a tight ship.

"Where is the panic button located in the Black Room?" Ritter said.

"Next to the light switch when you enter," Anita said.

Ritter grabbed one of the black keys from the rack and threw it to Pohl, who had just reappeared in the doorway.

Pohl fumbled the key but held onto it.

"Go upstairs and push the button," Ritter ordered.

After glaring at Ritter for a couple of beats, Pohl headed for the stairwell.

Motz could guess what he was thinking.

"And reseal the room before you come back down," Ritter yelled after him.

Pohl just raised the key with his bird finger as he ascended the stairs.

Motz grinned again.

Thirty seconds later, a red light flashed on Anita's desk.

"What did I tell you?" she said.

"Why no sound?" Ritter said.

"To give us a jump on the scumbags. We don't want to warn them."

Motz had a pretty good idea what happened to johns after the button was pushed.

A tortured laugh made him turn around. Veronica was staring at her locker. A yellow card was sticking out of her purse.

"Something wrong, honey?" Anita asked.

"Yes, no, everything," Veronica said.

Motz could see her point. She was fucked, no matter what. But that wasn't it. Something had just spooked her. "What's that yellow card?" he said.

Veronica's laugh became a sob.

"It's just a doctor's appointment," Anita said at his shoulder.

Motz kept his eyes on the card. "May I see it, Frau Lühmeyer?"

Veronica held open her bag for him.

"Thank you," Motz said. He pulled out the card. It had a city stamp. One of those monthly checkups for sexually transmitted diseases. That would spook him too. A VD test was quite a fall from a med school acceptance letter. He decided to hold off on bagging it until Veronica was gone.

"Satisfied?" Anita said. The friendliness was gone.

"Who knows the combinations to these lockers?" Ritter said.

"The girls provide their own locks," Anita said. "House rules."

Ritter turned to the door. "Polizeioberkommissar," he said.

Motz followed his look. Pohl was back.

"Frau Lühmeyer is ready," Ritter said.

Pohl walked into the office and touched Veronica on the shoulder. She flinched.

"Everything is going to be okay, honey," Anita said.

Ritter stepped in front of her.

"It's time to go," Pohl said. "You can leave the locker open."

Motz nodded. Forensics would turn everything upside down. No need to cut the lock.

"You going home, dear?" Anita said around Ritter's shoulder. "That's a good idea. You need the rest. Don't worry about—"

Pohl guided Veronica by the elbow.

Anita's eyes got big. "You're not arresting her, are you?"

"I'm afraid so," Ritter said.

"But she didn't do anything!" Anita tried to get around him.

Ritter grabbed Anita by the shoulders. "We will be the judge of that. For now, she stays with us."

Anita called after Veronica. "Hang on, honey! I'm calling the lawyer right now!" As she went through her Rolodex, she gave Ritter the third degree. "You can't hold her!"

"Actually, we can," Ritter said. "We can hold you too. For forty-eight hours without charge."

Motz looked at Ritter incredulously.

"I'll have your badge!" Anita said. She found the card, whipped it out, and punched in the number on the large inclined office phone. "This is Anita Krenz in Herbertstrasse," she said into the receiver. "It's an emergency. Some fool just arrested Veronica Lühmeyer on a trumped-up charge." She switched her phone ear. "What?" She looked at Ritter. "What's the charge?"

"Involuntary manslaughter," Ritter said.

"Did you get that? Involuntary manslaughter. Do you believe that?" There was a pause. "But—" There was a longer pause. "I know, but—" Anita started moving things around on her desk. "But—" She stopped. "He said that? Are you sure? Did you speak with him per—" She was cut off again. "Yes, I understand. Thank you. Yes, of course. Thank you. *Auf Wiederhören.*" She hung up the phone.

"Our lawyer has instructed us to cooperate," Anita said with hatred. "For the time being."

Motz felt for her. The order definitely came from Willi.

■ ■ ■

"We need a list of all the people who entered and exited this house today," Ritter said.

Without a word, Anita turned her Day-At-A-Glance to face him. It looked like a busy doctor's schedule. Each two-page spread outlined one day of the week. The columns were labeled G1, G2, G3, G4, Black, and White, just like the phone. The pages were covered with matching colored marks.

Motz picked up a box of chalk next to the day planner. It was wrapped in cellophane. "This for the blackboard upstairs?"

"Yes," Anita said evenly. "The Innensenator, Herr Mertens, liked chalkboards."

"He did, huh?"

"It was part of his therapy with Mistress—Frau Lühmeyer."

"Mmm-hmmm," Motz said. Therapy, my ass. He tried to open the package, but it was sealed. "New pack?"

"Yes," Anita said. She looked tense, like she was expecting a punch. She'd obviously been questioned before.

"What's it doing down here?" Motz said.

"We ordered it too late." Anita's left eye was twitching. "It came after Herr Mertens arrived."

"How did it get here?" Ritter said, looking up from the day planner.

"Our gofer, Frederic."

"Who?" Ritter said.

"Frederic is a young man from Vienna," Anita said. "He runs errands for us."

"Like buying chalk."

"Like buying whatever I tell him to buy," Anita said. "That's why he's called a gofer."

Motz wanted to laugh.

"What else does he buy for you?" Ritter said.

"Medical supplies."

"Medical supplies?" Ritter said.

That sobered Motz up. They were talking about the White Room. The truly sick shit.

"Enemas, that sort of thing," Anita said. "You know." Her twitch was syncopated now.

"No, I don't know," Ritter said.

Me neither, Motz thought. The *Puffmutter* wasn't his kind of people after all.

"From the pharmacy." Anita arched her thick back. "We run a clean house here."

"Name, address, phone number," Ritter said.

Anita's twitch stopped on a dime. The hatred was back in her eyes. "Am I a suspect too?" she said, her voice strong and steady.

"I meant the gofer, this Frederic," Ritter said. "We need his complete name and contact information."

Anita grabbed her *Albatros Apotheke* notepad and wrote down Frederic's name and number from memory. "I don't know his address." She tore off a page. On the banner of the notepad, an anchor replaced the traditional snake symbol in the old A-shaped icon.

"Frau Krenz, why didn't you give the chalk to Frau Lühmeyer?" Motz asked.

"Oh, we never disturb Mistress Veronica."

"You sure about that?" Ritter said.

"So you think she's innocent!"

"We don't think anything," Ritter said. "We investigate—in all directions."

TWENTY-SEVEN

New Arrival

Andreas Scherf was humming as he nodded goodbye to the guard at HansaBank. The counting machines had confirmed that Senator Althaus had delivered the full amount, which was now safely tucked away into Andreas' new savings account. The empty briefcase felt light as a feather. Andreas had agreed to return the following day to discuss investment options. The assistant bank manager favored real estate in Japan.

The radials of the Mercedes made a singing noise across Jungfernstieg, the glistening brass doors of the shopping palaces reflecting the white stone of the pavilion. Beyond that, in the middle of the Inner Alster River, the fountain shot up high into the air, sending a misty rainbow Andreas' way. Up ahead on the right were the slate roofs and mirrored windows of City Hall, the stone palace of intrigue that had so fascinated him in his youth. He sighed happily. At long last, he had arrived.

A car horn brought Andreas back to the present. He let the HansaTaxi into the right lane and followed it along the inner canals of the Speicherstadt, where he had his recent photography class. The old brick and slate warehouses looked like working versions of City Hall. The taxi turned off at St. Michaelis Church.

As Andreas sped by, he saw two fat tourists get out of the back seat. The driver was undoubtedly telling them the clock tower of "The Michel" was Hamburg's trademark structure, the one that appeared on all desktop calendars. He probably didn't mention that it also marked the border between the wealthy city center and the "colorful" St. Pauli district. As always, the scum collected outside the former city wall. Up ahead, Andreas spotted an unleashed Rottweiler prowling the Reeperbahn.

He turned onto Davidstrasse—and wished he hadn't. Blue lights were flashing at the other end of the block. A police raid. Nothing unusual about that, even if it was a bit early in the day. Then he saw the blue-and-white police cars parked at extreme angles outside the west gate of Herbertstrasse.

Andreas' heart stopped. What if Mertens got caught in the raid? The cops wouldn't use kid gloves on his driver. Andreas' scrubbed record would get leaked to the press. Worse, Senator Althaus wouldn't have any more use for the photos and would want his money back.

It was too late to stop, so Andreas looked straight ahead as he drove toward the blue lights, like somebody trying not to rubberneck. He hoped nobody saw the city plates.

As Andreas got close enough to make out faces, the cops turned their backs to him. A police van pulled through the big red gate, made a sharp left, and headed his way. He pulled over to the curb with a pounding heart, but nobody seemed to notice him.

Andreas saw a flash of red in the back of the van. They had Mertens! Then he made out the long black hair, pale cleavage, and red latex. It was a domina, not Mertens. He exhaled loudly. That was close. Still, he wasn't out of the woods.

Andreas held his breath as he drove past the gate, praying that none of the cops turned around, and made a quick left onto Hopfenstrasse. Miraculously, no blue lights followed in the mirror.

The next few minutes felt like hours. At every turn, Andreas was convinced that somebody had seen—and would remember—the Mercedes.

By the time he made it to the Sex Workers United building, the back of his shirt was soaked with sweat. He was so happy to see the old red brick that he barely felt the bottom of the car scrape the driveway. Helen Patch's brown Chevy had never looked so good.

Andreas jumped out and ran up the stairs. At the landing, the back door was already open. That was new. Helen was normally a stickler for security.

Her unfriendly stare filled the doorframe—and stopped him cold. The cigarette in her wide mouth was shaking. Trouble was written all over her face. "Were you followed?" she wheezed, pulling him in and quickly shutting the door behind him.

"I don't think so," Andreas said. "But I saw a bunch of cop cars outside—"

"When did he tell you to be back?"

"Fifteen hundred hours, like always. Why? What happened?" Andreas wiped cold sweat from his brow.

"He never came back," Helen said, waddling back to her desk and crushing her cigarette in the overflowing ashtray.

"From where?" Andreas said as innocently as he could. "I thought the two of you were in a meeting."

"Oh, please!" Helen said. "Don't pretend you don't know about his proclivities." The last word sent her into a coughing fit.

Andreas' slick face flushed. "Are you okay?"

"Don't bullshit a bullshitter," Helen said, holding the desk with one hand and waving the air with the other. "I saw you down there with your big camera this morning, right after he left." She motioned to the back window between gasps for air. "I was wondering why the car was still there. Then I saw you aiming that bazooka lens at the back door. I couldn't believe it! You ungrateful bastard!"

Helen made dry gasping noises that reminded Andreas of a sea lion.

"After all he did for you!" she said. "Not to mention me!" She gasped some more. "I wanted to warn him, but he was already gone. Now it's too late."

"What are you talking about?" Andreas said. His brain was frantically doing the math. Knowing Helen, she'd want a cut of his take from Althaus. He figured she'd demand sixty percent. He'd offer her forty percent of nothing.

Helen stood up straight as though to spite him. "Don't tell me you didn't hear all the sirens! They raided the Herbert!" Incredibly, her wheezing was gone.

As if on cue, another siren blasted the street below. Andreas ran to the front window. More blue lights flew by.

"They're probably questioning him right now," Helen said, a bit hoarse but back in control. "But then you already knew that, didn't you, you little weasel!"

"Oh, my God!" Andreas said. "That's terrible!" He sat down on the nearest chair to collect his thoughts.

"And they're definitely searching for you." Helen was staring at him like a zoo animal.

Andreas sprang to his feet. "Why me?"

"Because I called them," Helen said.

"What?!" Andreas said. "Why?"

Helen's eyes flashed. She dipped her bull head like she was about to charge. "You set him up, didn't you?"

Andreas backed away from her, his arms outstretched to thwart any attack.

"Answer me, you ungrateful bastard!" Helen spit out the words, moving her bulk from side to side as she plodded forward. "You're working for Althaus, aren't you?" Each step shook the old vertical-beam flooring. "You fucking asshole!"

Andreas fled along the wall, scraping his shirt on the old brick. He flung open the iron door and ran down the grated steel stairs, which clanged in rapid fire after him.

Helen's tubercular cough followed him down to the parking lot.

Andreas looked around wildly. A car with city plates was

definitely out. So he headed back to the driveway. The fresh scrape marks under his feet seemed to mock him.

Andreas forced himself to slow down. Running would just attract attention.

Getting to the corner took an eternity. Waiting for the crosswalk light to turn green was even worse. When it finally did, he crossed the first two lanes of the Reeperbahn, the island, and then the other two. The moment he stepped up onto the far sidewalk, he spotted two cops hoofing it his way. He wanted to run, but his feet felt like concrete.

The cops pounded the pavement right past him. One of them caught up with an African kid in a hooded sweatshirt. A dozen cell phones skidded across the grimy concrete. One cop held the thief's arm at a painful angle. His partner slapped on the cuffs. Both were out of breath and angry about it. Neither paid any attention to Andreas.

Andreas stumbled over a metallic-red cell phone with a shattered display and limped around the corner into a blind alley. There he was hit by the stench of rotten garbage and human waste. Behind the first dumpster, a gnarled old man in a filthy sleeping bag gave him a toothless grin. "New arrival?" he said.

TWENTY-EIGHT

Kicking Ass

Konny, the owner of St. Pauli Auto Body, ran a big finger over the deep scratch zigzagging the white piping. "This is a real crime," she said. Her white flattop matched her deep baritone.

"You were right about that place," Laura said, from her perch on a stack of steel radials. "Little dicks with big wallets."

Konny knew a thing or two about crime. Like grand theft auto.

"Somebody really has it in for you," Konny said, patting the side of the Charger. It wasn't clear if she was talking to Laura or the car.

"When I find them, they're gonna wish they were never born!" Laura said. She took the banged-up wooden ball out of her jacket. It sounded like a shotgun ratchet when it hit the ground and bounced off the wall and back into her hands. *Ka-chunk! Slap! Ka-chunk! Slap!*

"Hey, cut that shit out!" Konny said, standing to her full height. She was a head taller than Laura now.

Ka-chunk! Slap! Ka-chunk! Slap!

Konny took a step toward her. "Hey! I mean it! You're fucking up my plaster!"

Ka-chunk! Slap! Laura kissed her new toy.

"What the fuck *is* that?" Konny said.

"My monkey ball." Laura rubbed her calluses against the wood grain. "Fights stress."

Konny laughed. "Don't fight it, kick its fucking ass!"

"Oh, this bad boy kicks ass," Laura assured her. "Already tested 'im in a sock." She whirled her arm at the elbow to demonstrate.

Konny sobered up. "Find the fucker did your car, I'll help."

"I'll find him alright," Laura said, throwing the ball up. "I got a pretty good idea who it was." *Slap!*

"Who?"

"Little weasel, runs errands for the Herbert." And slimes other people's Ibiza photos, she thought, squeezing the ball.

"He works with Veronica?" Konny seemed surprised.

"Nah, he's just a gofer. Pencil dick motherfucker."

"Why would a nobody like that scratch your baby?"

"Because he's a creep," Laura said. "And he knows I know he's a creep." Shoulda kicked his teeth in at the Herbert, she thought.

"You know where he lives? We can do him now."

"Nah, but I got a bead on the little fuck." Laura had already called in a marker at The Cage. Back payment for some stepped-on crank. She put the ball back in her pocket.

"Just say the word," Konny said. An unfiltered Roth-Händle flamed briefly in her hand. The Zippo cracked shut. "When did it happen?"

Laura rubbed her forehead with her slapping hand. "Dunno, about lunchtime." Way past my bedtime, she thought. Shit always happened when you did things for other people. Never again.

Konny coughed smoke. "What? You were down there at noon? I heard the Herbert was swarming with cops! Somebody said the mayor got whacked."

"Huh?" Laura said. "Cops?" She didn't see shit down there. Just workers eating lunch in their vans, like always.

"Yeah, cops. Didn't you hear all them sirens?" Konny took another deep drag.

"Sirens? When?" Laura said. Another DUI would violate her parole. Fuck that.

"Round about one." Konny smashed the cigarette into an inverted Rambler hubcap. "Musta been after you left."

"I didn't hear nothing," Laura said. Then again, she *was*

radically shitfaced at the time. Lucky she didn't run into any cops. She laughed. Lucky for them.

Konny chuckled with her. "We can't all live in Eppendorf."

"If you can call it living." Laura fingered the Ibiza photo tucked between her right thigh and the radial.

Konny's harsh features softened. "Oh, honey, you two have a fight again? You need a place to stay?"

Laura stared at the perfect sunset. "It's way bad this time. She applied to UKE."

"She wanna be a nurse?" Konny said. "I thought she had a choice gig at the Herbert."

"She wants to be a fucking doctor!" The word made Laura's throat ache. "You believe that shit?"

"No way!" Konny said.

"Yes way. She applied to fucking medical school!" Laura was having trouble seeing straight. She mopped her eyes with the back of her hand.

"That cunt," Konny said. "There's straight and then there's straight. Next thing, you gonna tell me she's gone hetero."

"I'd be the last to know." Laura didn't bother fighting the tears now. What was the use? "The cold bitch didn't tell me squat. You know what *that* means."

"Secrets are never good," Konny said.

Laura just waved her away.

"She never really came out, did she?" Konny said.

"Not Little Miss Priss." And here she thought she was protecting Veronica. Turned out it was all show, for the others. Laura didn't count.

"Honey, is it possible she did it?" Konny said.

Veronica must've planned her getaway for months, right under Laura's nose. "I could kill her," she said, thumbing the edge of the photo again. The corner was turning into a hinge.

"I mean, she works there and all," Konny said.

Laura looked up through her tears. "Huh?"

"You think maybe *she* scratched your ride?"

Laura shook her head three times. No, no, no. "Never! She's too perfect. She would never stoop to *our* level."

"Oh, honey," Konny said again. "I always told you she weren't our kind."

Laura pulled out the crumpled photo and tried to smooth it against her thigh, but it was hopeless. "What am I going to do?"

"C'mon," Konny said. "I got what the doctor ordered. Upstairs." The canvas tarp floated down gently over the Charger as she passed. "Good night, doll," she said.

Laura jumped down reluctantly. At the door, she looked back at her baby sandwiched between those tractor trailers.

Konny pulled down the steel door and locked it with a massive lock. The sign bolted to the outside said: "Sorry We're Closed."

■ ■ ■

Heavy metal *whomped!* the room like a big heartbeat. Laura snorted another long-ass line from the cracked mirror on the military footlocker. She pinched her nostrils as the meth burned its way down the back of her throat.

Konny grabbed the fifty-euro "straw" from her outstretched hand, bent down, and took a deep drag. The seat of the shit-brown couch was protected by a quilt decorated with cigarette burns. She rubbed her gums. "What you need is a vacation."

"Tell me about it." Laura laughed. Some crystals had gotten onto the sunset. It looked like it was snowing on Ibiza.

"That'a girl," Konny said, giving her a playful punch to the ribs.

TWENTY-NINE

Private Investigations

POLAS told Meike that Hasani called his father in Albania every Saturday night. Other than that, nothing. No calls whatsoever. Not even to family or friends in Germany—or his own casino. Obviously, Hasani didn't trust phones. Probably afraid of drones.

Willi Kaiser, on the other hand, was a lot more phone friendly. His phone records were a who's who of Hamburg's rich and powerful. One name jumped out at Meike. Innensenator Mertens. There were dozens of calls to Mertens' office in the past week. And an equal number of faxes. Kaiser made no attempt to cover his tracks. It was possible he wanted Organized Crime to know about his good contacts in City Hall.

Meike checked the third name on her list. In the past month, Norbert Grube had made hundreds of calls. That Grube favored the rich was not exactly news. He was, after all, the manager of a small but powerful bank on Jungfernstieg. The calls ended at thirteen thirty-one. The last entry looked familiar.

The reverse directory confirmed Meike's suspicion. Grube called Kaiser just fifteen minutes after Anita Krenz called Davidwache to report Mertens' death. Meike smelled blood and dug deeper.

POLAS told her that Norbert Grube was the son of the late Hubert Grube, his predecessor at HansaBank. Hubert was survived by one Hildegard Grube. Her assets were seemingly endless.

Meike had just seen one asset in person. Herbertstrasse 7b. Bingo. The crime scene.

Meike looked around the room, but none of her colleagues was there to tell. Excitedly, she opened a new file and started typing. Grube was Kaiser's straw man.

■ ■ ■

Her assigned work done, Meike decided to call an old one-night stand in Frankfurt. The picture in the ComVor personnel database looked a lot sterner than the one in her mind. She punched the number. If anybody would know how to unblock Ritter's file, it would be Vladimir Netsky, thick Slavic accent and all. He even had a tattoo of Vladislav III, aka Dracula, on his forearm.

He picked up on the fourth ring with a yawn. "Meike."

"And they say chivalry is dead," she said.

"Sorry, I just got back from Wiesbaden."

"Another POLAS seminar?" Meike said. Like she cared. But attention was Vlad's currency, so she gave it to him.

"CRIME," he said. "You know, the web-based subset. It was awesome. They have an HP MetroCluster made up of Proliant servers with HP Surestore disk arrays, XP512 data storage, Alcatel omniswitches—"

"That's awesome," Meike said. "The reason I'm calling—"

"—an RPC-based client–server system for NIS domains and a Nortel Alteon load balancer."

"Wow." Meike looked at her fingernails. The black polish was starting to chip. "The reason I'm calling—"

"That isn't the half of it!" The tiredness was gone from Vlad's voice. "You should see what they do with it! The virtual private database functions of Oracle 9i can handle—"

"Anyway, I need to ask you a favor."

"—a wide variety of web-based applications."

"We got a new squad leader," Meike said.

That stopped Vlad. "Yeah, so?" He sounded offended.

"I'm sorry," Meike said in her best blonde voice. "I just can't figure this out."

"Figure what out?"

"There's a block on his record in ComVor. I don't have, what do you call it, read access."

"You're in over your head, Meike."

Meike purred into the phone. "That's why I called you, Vlad. You're the expert."

"You don't understand." Vlad sounded older somehow. The geek hyperactivity was gone. "A blocked filed means BKA or BND."

Meike felt a shiver go down her spine. "Spooks?"

"Black files. Need to know."

"Oh." Meike paused and then went blonde again. "But I need to know!"

"We're talking about the big boys," Vlad said sternly. "They're notified within thirty seconds of login. I could lose my job!"

"If you can't do it, you can't do it," Meike said. A cheap shot directed at his weak spot. His vanity.

"Who is it, Meike?" he said. "I need to know what I'm getting into."

"KHK Thomas Ritter." Meike knew she was betraying her new squad leader. But she had to know if Ebeling had put a snitch on their squad. Lars and Motz routinely crossed the line in the name of justice. Meike herself was involved in at least some of their shenanigans. So Vlad wasn't the only one who had to fear for his job—or worse. The state prosecutor wouldn't hesitate to throw them to the wolves if Internal Affairs had a star witness in their ranks.

"*Our* KHK Thomas Ritter?" Vlad said.

"He's *our* KHK Thomas Ritter now," Meike shot back. "Word here is he's a snitch." Hearing herself say it out loud sent another shiver down her spine. Internal Affairs didn't plant somebody unless they already had something pretty incriminating.

Meike did a quick inventory of her infractions. Unlike Lars and Motz, she had never hit a suspect. Well, except for that time with the phone book. But this wasn't the first time she had used Vlad. And digital anything was traceable somehow.

"What's that have to do with you?" Vlad said.

"Ritter's my new squad leader," Meike said. "I need to know if I can trust him."

"We wondered what happened to him after the Rosenfeld hearing."

"Well, you don't need to wonder anymore." Meike remembered the clips of the Frankfurt Polizeipräsident before his arraignment. It wasn't a pretty sight.

"They should have given him a medal," Vlad said.

"I hear you," Meike said. She meant it. That's what made the next part so hard. "They say Ritter ratted him out."

"It was a closed hearing," Vlad said, suspicion back in his voice.

"Rosenfeld resigns, Ritter leaves town," Meike said. "Motive meets opportunity." She hesitated. "We think he may be working for Internal Affairs." Her heart and mind were now in open conflict.

There was an unpleasant pause at the other end.

"Vlad?" Meike said. The display told her he was still on the line.

"Jesus, Meike," he said finally. "What are you getting me into?"

"Nothing you can't handle. I've seen you do it before." She didn't bother dressing up the threat.

There was another, longer pause. "I can't promise anything. It will take a while."

"You're a doll!" Meike said with enthusiasm she didn't feel.

"I need to go low tech," Vlad said.

"Low tech?"

"Yeah. Go down to the IT center and tap into the Metro-Cluster."

"I knew that metro-thingy was good for something," Meike said, back in blonde territory.

"I need to invent a reason to go there." Vlad sounded like he had forgotten about Meike. "I have to sign in."

"But once you're in, you're in." Don't bother me with the details, Meike thought. Just do it.

"Right." Vlad's voice was far away.

"I knew you could do it. You always come through."

"Don't push it, Meike."

"You're the boss," Meike said cheerfully. "Call me when you get something." She hung up and exhaled loudly.

Well, that was that. She had just pulled the trigger. So why did she feel so bad?

THIRTY

The Shadow

The uniforms at the gate made way. POK Pohl was dragging some sleazeball in a purple polyester shirt. The two of them made their awkward way up Herbertstrasse to Haus 7b, where Ritter and Motz were waiting.

"Say hi to Stefan Vollbert," Pohl said. "The lingerie salesman who left the scene of the crime," he added. "Found him around the corner, on Talstrasse."

"Nice shiner," Motz said.

Ritter studied the bruise pattern around Vollbert's eye. "What happened?" he said. Maybe Pohl was the real reason the salesman ran away. The same reason the *Puffmutter* didn't want to give up Vollbert's name. She must know all about Davidwache.

Pohl jerked the salesman to attention. "He tried to run."

Innocent people didn't normally run from cops, Ritter thought. Unless the cops had a reputation for roughing up prisoners. "Herr Vollbert," he said. "Why did you leave the scene of a crime?"

The salesman looked scared. "Crime? What crime?"

Ritter winced at the Frankfurt accent.

Pohl hit Vollbert on the back of the head. "Don't pretend you didn't hear the sirens." He seemed to enjoy hurting the salesman.

"You had an appointment here at eleven," Ritter said to Vollbert.

"Yes, sir."

Sir. Ritter had to admit Pohl was effective. "Who with?"

"Anita and Tanja. Anita is the concierge."

The salesman was too talkative. His pupils weren't dilated, so it was probably just the fear. "What happened?"

"Tanja bought two bikinis, one pink, one black. I gave her a discou—"

"What else happened?" Ritter said.

"Anita went outside to open the gate for a BierShop truck."

"And?"

"Anita never came back. I think they had some kind of argument."

"Was the front door open when you arrived?" Ritter said.

"No, sir. Anita buzzed me in."

"Was the front door open when you left?" Ritter felt Motz tense up. This was the question that mattered.

Vollbert paused. "Yes, I think so."

Check your premises, Ritter thought. Scared suspects sometimes said what they thought you wanted to hear. "Think or know?"

Vollbert thought about it. "Know. I just walked through."

Motz wrote something down in his notepad.

"Anything strange happen while you were here?" Ritter said.

"Well, now that you mention it," Vollbert said. "A john ran down the stairs. He seemed pretty upset."

More writing.

A john. Vollbert was talking more like a witness than a suspect, Ritter thought. "How do you know he was upset?"

"Because he ran down the stairs."

Ritter didn't hear any irony in the salesman's voice. "You already said that."

"It was strange," Vollbert said. "The stairs didn't creak."

Now that was good, Ritter thought. It could indicate the size of the john. "Why was it strange?"

"The stairs always creak," Vollbert said.

Ritter liked that too. The salesman thought like a detective.

"Why do you think they didn't creak this time?"

Vollbert thought about it. "The john was light."

"Light or small?" Ritter said.

Vollbert thought about it some more. "Thin, light, fast."

This guy was a prosecutor's wet dream. Assuming he was telling the truth. "What did he look like?"

Vollbert closed his eyes. "Long black hair."

Unreal. Ritter hadn't seen anybody so cooperative since Kandahar. Of course, the jihadi had just taken a couple of rounds to his lower intestines. They dangled a Medivac in front of him. *Tell us what we want to know, and you might not die in agony.*

"How was he dressed?" Ritter said.

"Jeans, sweatshirt, sneakers."

The salesman was too good to be true, Ritter thought. Maybe that was it. These *milieu* types were great liars.

At Ritter's elbow, Motz was writing furiously.

"You see his face?" Ritter said.

"No, sir. I'm sorry."

Now the salesman was apologizing. As a rule, liars didn't do that. "You sure?"

"Yes, sir. He was just a shadow."

"How long did you see him?"

"Just a split-second."

"How come you remember so much?" Motz interjected.

Vollbert looked at him helplessly.

"In a split-second, you saw how he was dressed?" Motz said.

Vollbert straightened his shoulders. "Fashion is my business."

"Uh huh." Motz didn't sound convinced.

"So you didn't really get a good look?" Ritter said.

Vollbert shook his head. "No, sir."

If the lingerie salesman were to be believed, somebody fled the scene about the time of death. That was the best lead they had so far. "Okay," Ritter said. "We need your statement in writing."

He nodded to Pohl, who took Vollbert by the arm again.

The salesman offered no resistance.

■ ■ ■

After they left, Ritter began to prioritize tasks with Motz. "We need to find this shadow," he said. "He's our prime suspect."

"Maybe our artist can do a sketch of the jeans," Motz said.

"Your shadow sounds like the gofer," somebody said. It was Pohl.

"Where's Vollbert?" Ritter demanded.

"Outside, in the van," Pohl said. "Writing up his statement. Like you said." He sounded annoyed.

Good, Ritter thought. He turned to Motz. "What do we know about him?"

Motz consulted his notes. "Frederic Silbereisen. The gofer who bought the chalk."

"Chalk?" Pohl said.

"Yeah," Motz said. "For your girlfriend's blackboard."

Pohl took the jibe literally. "Veronica's into girls. Used to do a live show at The Cage. Double dildo."

Ritter ignored the banter. "The *Puffmutter* said the gofer is Viennese."

"Yeah, he's a real slimeball," Pohl said.

Pohl was getting too familiar for Ritter's taste. "You see him around here often?"

"Often enough. He's in and out of here all the time."

At least Pohl knew the locals, Ritter thought. But his attitude was grating.

"You know where Silbereisen lives?" Motz said.

"No," Pohl admitted. "All I know is he's a bigshot at Gamblers Anonymous."

"What?" Motz said.

Pohl grinned at him. "Yeah. Real weirdo. You can read all

about it on his Facebook page."

"Find him," Ritter said. "And keep your commentary to yourself."

"Yes, sir." The "sir" was predictably sarcastic.

"And take the lingerie salesman to the Präsidium," Ritter said. "He's a flight risk."

"What are the charges?" Pohl said.

"No charges. Protective custody."

"Yes, *sir*."

Ritter was visualizing an elbow to Pohl's mouth when his pocket vibrated. He took out his phone and saw the 040 area code. A local landline, probably Ebeling. He hit the green button. "Ritter," he said.

"Yes, you are." The girl on the other end giggled. She had a harbor accent.

Ritter forced himself not to look around. "Where are you?"

"That would be telling," she said.

Ritter heard the tinkling of a slot machine. It sounded like his one-night stand had talked some bartender into letting her use his phone. He could imagine the story she had told him. Knowing her, the truth.

"Have you forgotten my name already, Mr. Secret Agent Man?" she said.

Ritter racked his brain. All he could see was the fluffy Snoopy doll and the pert tits in his face. Then he remembered the name tag. "Jenny. Listen up."

"You remembered!" She sounded genuinely surprised and happy. "You get extra points for that, big boy."

Ritter grabbed the phone harder. "Listen to me, Jenny."

"I love the way you say my name, especially when you're mad."

"I'm very busy right now."

"I can *see* that," she said.

The uniforms were gone. Ditto for Motz and Pohl.

"There are a bunch of handsome men in dark-blue uniforms guarding that big red gate," she said.

Oh shit. His tormentress was at the entrance to Herbertstrasse. That was all he needed. And he had only himself to blame.

"I can tell you're busy." She was pouting now. "I'll call you back later."

"Jenny—"

The line was dead. Like Ritter's career, if he wasn't careful.

THIRTY-ONE

Private Office

"Let's go to my private office," Motz said as they walked through the big red gate. He admired the cleavage on the scantily clad redhead in the West cigarette ad. "Happy Birthday" was tattooed in gothic script on her left tit. She had a cigarette in one hand and a condom in the other. Her stockinged legs were crossed at the edge of a big red bed in a small red room that could have been in Haus 7b.

"Nice view," Pohl said with a dirty laugh. "Is she smoking before, during, or after?"

"All of the above," Motz said, staring at some uniforms, who jumped back from his Eldorado.

Pohl got a light from one of them and followed, trailing smoke.

"It's open," Motz said and lowered himself onto the hard bench seat.

Pohl took a hefty drag, flicked the glowing butt into the gutter, and dropped into the seat with enough *umph* for Motz to feel it. He brought the stench of nicotine with him as he slammed the passenger door.

Why not just dump an ashtray in my ride, Motz thought. It had been three years since he quit. Normally, smokers didn't bother him. In fact, he enjoyed cigarettes and perfume on attractive women. But Pohl just reminded him of what he wasn't missing. Wheezing and hacking every morning.

"So, what's up?" Pohl said. He opened his window far enough to spit out some stray tobacco.

Motz glared at him. That shit had better not be on the paint job.

Pohl gave him a blank look back.

"What's your take?" Motz said finally.

More blankness. "On what? Ritter?"

"No," Motz said impatiently. "Mertens, all this." He motioned back to the gate. "You hear things down here."

Pohl sniffed importantly. "Word on the street, Hasani is behind it."

Motz tasted something bitter. His jaw clenched involuntarily.

"I know, I know," Pohl said.

The hell he did, Motz thought. Pohl didn't know what it was like to lose a partner to a scumbag like Hasani. Or watch the bastard walk around free. Motz heard his own molars grind. He had to stop that shit. Sabine said it caused his earaches. "TMJ," she called it.

Pohl cleared his throat, a dry, rasping sound. "I don't like it either," he said.

Motz ground his teeth some more. Fuck TMJ. "That bastard killed Lars."

Pohl said nothing. He was noncommittal, like everybody else.

Motz was beginning to hate them all. Why was he always on his own?

"You know about the war between Kaiser and Hasani, right?" Pohl said.

"Who doesn't?" Motz said in disgust. He massaged his scalp. Now his headache was back. Goddamn Pohl.

There was some commotion at the gate. Outside Motz's window, uniforms stepped aside for a blue-and-white van.

Motz pressed his left ear with his palm and braced himself for the earth-shattering siren. It didn't come. As the van *swooshed* past, he looked up at the side window just in time to see Vollbert's right hand cuffed to a bar.

Motz shook his head. "Hasani is taking over the city, and we're going after lingerie salesmen from Frankfurt!"

Again, Pohl said nothing.

Motz's thoughts were interrupted by his own phone. He looked down at the screen. Meike. Maybe she had something solid, unlike some uniformed cops he could name. "Gotta take this," he said.

"And I gotta find Silbereisen," Pohl said, pushing open his door. He sounded relieved.

Motz didn't bother responding. "Okay, Meike, shoot," he said.

The passenger door slammed.

"What was that?" Meike said in Motz's ear.

"Car door." He watched Pohl mooch another light off a uniform. What didn't he just buy a Zippo like everybody else? Motz pulled himself together. "Okay, Meike, what've you got?"

"Had an interesting talk with Mertens' secretary," Meike said. Her voice was playful. She had something, and she was enjoying it.

Motz didn't have time for that. "And?" he said.

Meike ignored the warning in his voice. "You'll never guess who he met with this morning."

Motz knew she was inspecting the polish on her nails now. She always did that when she had something big. He forced himself not to snap at her. "Don't make it so suspenseful," he said.

"Senator Althaus," she said in triumph.

Motz forgot his headache. "No shit?"

"The one and only," Meike said. "Mertens' archenemy."

No wonder she was in such a good mood. "When?" Motz said. "Ten o'clock."

"Well, now, isn't that special," he said. "Two archenemies meet. One dies under mysterious circumstances two hours later."

"Hour and a half," Meike corrected him. "They were still arguing at ten thirty."

"Wish I coulda been on a fly on the wall," he said. "With a tape recorder running."

The passenger door squeaked open. Black jeans. Ritter.

"That Voss?" Ritter said, lowing himself onto the seat.

"Yeah, it's Meike," Motz said. He wondered how much Ritter had overheard through the crack in the window. Goddamn Pohl.

"I need to talk to her," Ritter said.

"I'm putting you on speaker," Motz said to Meike. "Somebody wants to talk to you." He put the phone on the dashboard between them.

Ritter pulled the door shut.

"Who's that?" Meike said suspiciously.

"Your new squad leader," Motz said.

Ritter addressed the dash. "What did you find on POLAS?"

The speaker rustled. "Anita Krenz, Veronica Lühmeyer, and Tanja Brüggemann are clean," Meike said. More rustling.

Ritter leaned forward expectantly. "But?"

"Lühmeyer's roommate is another matter," Meike said. "She's a real piece of work."

"Roommate?"

"Roommate, lover, whatever," Meike said. "One Laura Wesselmann. Thirty-three. Did time in Hahnöfersand."

A real suspect with a real record, Motz thought. Why didn't Meike tell him about that first?

"That's an island, right?" Ritter said.

"Alcatraz for women," Meike said. "Near Wedel. They just had their hundredth anniversary. But it's no Majorca." It almost sounded like she was flirting with Ritter.

"How long was Wesselmann on this, um, island?" Ritter said.

"Four years." Meike was reading now. "Aggravated assault. Beat some girl half to death."

Motz felt a rush of energy. The domina's girlfriend sounded like bad news. People didn't change, they just got more extreme.

Aggravated assault could have been practice for murder. They'd better have a talk with this girlfriend.

"Lovers' quarrel?" Ritter said.

Motz knew what he meant. Dykes did crazy shit in fits of jealous rage.

"That'd be my guess," Meike said. Again, the flirtatious tone.

If Ritter noticed, he didn't show it. "Where do they live?"

"Eppendorf," Meike said. "Nonnenstieg 13."

Motz whipped out his pad and pen. "Got it," he said.

Meike wasn't done. "Wesselmann owns a vintage Dodge Charger."

"What year?" Motz said. The girlfriend was getting more interesting by the second. She sounded like a St. Pauli original.

"Nineteen seventy-six," Meike said. "Green with white piping down the side. Fully restored."

"Sweet." Motz wondered how Meike got the details about the car. POLAS didn't usually record the good stuff off the street. Knowing Meike, she conducted her own private investigation.

"Wesselmann's real sweet, all right," Meike said. "Works as a dancer in The Cage."

Wait a minute, Motz thought. Didn't Pohl say the domina used to work in The Cage?

"This Wesselmann a domina too?" Ritter interjected.

"No," Meike said. "The Cage is a strip joint on the Reeperbahn."

"Live sex," Motz said. Like the Safari Club on steroids. They made monkey love look like teenage handholding. The Cage was all about S&M, double dildoes, golden showers. The entire staff had rap sheets as long as his arm. Hells Angels did security. Motz massaged the scar in his scalp. His stubby fingers fit right in the groove.

"What time does this club open?" Ritter seemed to assume Meike was thorough.

It was a good assumption.

"About eight," Meike said. "Show starts at ten."

"Twenty-two hundred hours." Ritter pulled up the sleeve of his sweater and checked his watch. "If we don't find Wesselmann by then, we'll brace her at work."

"If she shows up," Meike said. "I don't know how long we can keep a lid on this."

"We can't," Motz said. Besides, why should some pervert get special treatment just because he was rich and powerful?

Ritter leaned toward the phone again. "What about the victim's wife? Did she check out?"

More rustling on the line. "According to Ebeling, the widow had a tennis lesson at the time of death."

"According to Ebeling," Motz said. "Hope he and the widow got their stories synchronized." Working for that slimeball was like having both hands tied behind your back.

"Double-check the wife's alibi," Ritter ordered.

Motz did a double take. The new guy didn't trust Ebeling either.

"Already on it," Meike said.

Ritter adjusted his weight on the seat. "What about Mertens' driver?"

"Not home," Meike said curtly.

Ritter was just as short. "You put out an APB?"

"At Herbertstrasse, before I left." Meike sounded annoyed, like she was talking to Ebeling.

"What about Mertens?" Ritter said.

Meike paused. "That's where it gets interesting."

"Interesting how?" Ritter said.

"Mertens had a meeting with the president of Sex Workers United at eleven this morning," Meike said.

What the fuck, Motz thought. Mertens really had sex on the brain.

"Sex Workers?" Ritter said.

"Whores' union," Motz explained. "Part of Verdi."

"And?" Ritter said. "Why wouldn't he meet with a union boss?"

Meike intervened. "The meeting was scheduled to run until fifteen hundred hours."

"Sounds like a cover story for Mertens' wife," Motz said. Not to mention the entire Hamburg Senate.

Ritter spoke into the phone. "Tell Davidwache to bring in this union president for questioning."

"Why don't you tell them?" Meike objected. "You're still at the Herbert, aren't you?"

Ritter ignored her and turned to Motz. "I think it's time we braced the domina's girlfriend."

"Let's do it," Motz said and fired up the Eldorado.

"Keep us posted," Ritter said to Meike.

"Okey dokey," she said in a miffed tone.

Motz killed the phone and one-handed the Eldorado away from the curb. As they gurgled around the corner onto Davidstrasse, he spotted a black van with dark windows down the block. The driver was pretending to read a newspaper. "Friends of yours?" he said.

"Hardly," Ritter said.

Motz grinned. "That bad, huh? All the way from Frankfurt? Now I'm impressed." He didn't notice the girl getting onto the turquoise moped behind them.

THIRTY-TWO

U-Haft

"What do you mean I can't see her?" Anita yelled. "I brought her homemade chicken soup!" She held up the Tupperware for the guard to see. It was her special recipe for girls with heartache. It wasn't like this was the first time she'd seen one of her girls behind bars. But this time the charges were ridiculous. Involuntary manslaughter. What a joke.

"Sorry, ma'am," the guard said. "No one is supposed to see her until the hearing." His voice was muffled by the thick glass. He had crumbs on the front of a navy-blue shirt that stuck out over his belt. "JUSTIZ" was stenciled on the right patch pocket.

"Says who?" Anita yelled back. She'd bet the fatso hadn't seen his own dick in decades. One of those pricks who got off on saying no. She spotted a cream pie on a corner desk. It was missing three wedges. Each was a calorie bomb in the fool's stomach. He probably used his swivel chair to walk.

"Special instructions from Kriminalhauptkommissar Ritter," the guard said, reading from a clipboard. "Davidwache gave me the order in person. It says no visitors."

Ritter, the mean one with the cold blue eyes, Anita thought. "Just you wait until I talk to my lawyer!" she yelled. She set the Tupperware on the narrow counter and reached for her phone. She held it up for the guard to see.

"Her lawyer is with her right now," the guard said, brushing crumbs off his belly.

"What?" Anita yelled. "I thought you said no visitors!"

"He's a lawyer," the guard said. "That's different."

"But I'm her mother!" Anita meant it. Most of her girls didn't have real mothers. She took them under her wing like lost birds. She took good care of her girls.

The guard shook his head. "You're Anita Krenz. They told me about you." He was smirking now.

"Who's *they*?" Anita said. And wipe that smirk off your lard-ass face.

"Kriminalhauptkommissar Ritter."

Goddamn that Ritter, Anita thought. He was dangerous.

A strange honking noise came from the sliding aluminum tray at the base of the glass. It was the guard laughing at her.

"If you know who I am, then you know who I work for," Anita said. And what he'll do to you and your dumpy, pie-making wife if you don't open that fucking gate, she thought.

The honking stopped.

"Are you threatening me?" the guard said, sucking in five centimeters of gut.

"I don't have to," Anita said. "My lawyer does that for me." And if that doesn't work, we'll pay a visit to your shithole house in the suburbs.

"Speaking of the devil," the guard said, looking at a monitor. "Here he comes now."

At the other end of the oval-shaped hall, there was loud buzzing and clanging. Anita could feel locks being turned with those big keys.

The first time she saw them, she was impressed. All that steel between her and freedom. After a while, she got used to it. The one thing she never got used to was the smell. Instead of Lysol, they used some sort of industrial disinfectant. She never knew how people were able to eat under those circumstances. And those aluminum toilets without lids. It was grotesque.

"Frau Krenz." The dignified voice belonged to Willi's lawyer. He extended a bony hand. "Are they giving you some kind of trouble?"

Despite his age—what was he now, ninety?—his voice was as strong as ever.

"They won't let me visit Veronica." Anita always felt like a little girl in his presence. He even smelled like a gentleman. Old Spice. Everything was going to be okay.

"Ah, yes," the lawyer said, setting down his thin briefcase. "That's just a little formality."

Anita could all but see her own reflection in his wingtips. You could tell a lot about a man by the way he treated his shoes.

"Frau Lühmeyer will be able to see visitors after the hearing, first thing in the morning," the lawyer said.

"But she's cooperating!" Anita said.

The lawyer blinked at her kindly. "Nothing to worry about. We'll take care of it."

Anita wasn't so sure. Veronica hadn't looked too good when they dragged her away. One night alone in this place could be one too many. "How is she?"

"She's fine," the lawyer assured her. He looked at the Tupperware. "Is that chicken soup? That's almost worth getting locked up for."

The Old Spice feeling was gone. All Anita smelled was disinfectant.

■ ■ ■

After Kaiser's lawyer left, Veronica began pacing her cell. Ten paces long, two wide—if you didn't count the cot and toilet. She stopped and lined up the hard mattress with the steel support. Straight lines. Ninety-degree angles. Order.

Twenty-four hours, the lawyer had said. They were having the hearing the next day. *This is a high-profile case. No delays. That is good for us.*

He wasn't so positive about UKE. *Let's just take this one step at a time.* Veronica began pacing again. Her dream career was over before it began. No medical school would take a candidate who had been arrested for manslaughter, voluntary or not.

Veronica laughed out loud. It was ridiculous. Everybody kept telling her everything was okay. Nothing was okay. Everything was wrong. Like that yellow card.

She stopped pacing. The yellow card. How did that get in her purse? She had intentionally left it at home. The only person—

The steel flap in the door fell open. A tray wrapped in aluminum foil slammed onto it. "Dinner!" the guard barked.

Veronica laughed again. *Dinner.* Come and get it. What were they serving the distinguished residents of U-Haft tonight? *Soupe à l'oignon? Pulpo a la gallega?* Monkey brain tacos? Her laugh turned into a sob. Laura.

Veronica grabbed the tray and threw it against the wall.

"Hey, quiet in there!" somebody yelled.

Footsteps followed.

The flap flew open. "What the hell are you doing?" the guard yelled.

Veronica stifled her sob. "Eating my dinner."

"We're not cleaning that up for you," the guard said. "Enjoy eating off the floor."

The flap slammed shup.

Veronica shook her head. The green stripe on the wall was splattered with beef stroganoff, like modern art. The aluminum foil was crumpled into an abstract sculpture atop the bent tray. The knife was resting on the fork, like somebody had taken a pause in eating. The whole thing smelled like wet cardboard heated in the microwave.

■ ■ ■

"Hey there!" somebody whispered loudly.

Veronica stopped scraping.

"Hey!" It was the next cell.

Veronica resumed scraping.

"Hey!"

Scrape, scrape, scrape. She stopped and examined her work. Compared to the other graffiti cut into the wall, hers was child's play. No obscene words or images, no threats to public order, no phone numbers for a good time.

Twenty minutes later, she tested the blade on her thumb. The blood tasted good and warm. She was ready. Even the voice in the next cell had given up.

Veronica laid down on the cot. It was no harder than her bathtub, really. She closed her eyes and twisted the ceramic knobs in her mind. She waited until the water was hot to the touch and then dropped the plug. The bubble bath steamed up around the candles. She eased herself down into the delicious warmth and took her first sip of Cabernet.

The steam took the sting out of the first cut. She didn't even feel the second. She cut slowly and carefully. Lengthwise, that was key. Open the arteries all the way. Let it flow. Let it all out.

The bubbles tickled her chin. She was floating now.

> *Dear Veronica Lühmeyer,*
> *We are pleased to inform you....*

Her hair spread out on the surface of the warm dream. She was an intern now, working the emergency room on seventy-two-hour shifts, earning her stripes. Knife wounds, heart attacks, strokes, she was always there, always ready.

Another siren was blaring outside. Red lights were flashing. The patient on the gurney had blue lips. The paramedics said asphyxiation. They had written him off for dead.

Frau Dr. Lühmeyer pushed them aside. She turned the patient on his side, cleared his tongue, put the resuscitator over his nose and mouth, and started pumping the red ball. Everyone said to give up, it's over, he's dead, his heart has stopped. She ignored the naysayers. She pumped and pumped and pumped and pumped.

You had to believe. You pumped and believed until his heart pumped and believed. You breathed life into him.

The patient moved under her hands. The mask fogged up. He was alive! She had done it! He was breathing on his own!

The bubbles tickled her nose. She smiled as she let go, sliding down all the way into the warm dream, her golden hair swirling after her. It was heaven.

THIRTY-THREE

Nunnery

Just before Klosterstern, the Eldorado turned off Rothenbaum-chaussee onto Abteistrasse and then left onto Nonnenstieg. As in nuns' stairway, Ritter thought. "There a nunnery around here?"

"Used to be," Motz said. "Let's hope the dyke hasn't taken a vow of silence."

As they made their way up the narrow street, Ritter took in one villa after another. Most were made of stone, with high windows. Out front were luxury armored personnel carriers with designer hood ornaments to protect overprivileged families. Or the occasional electric car for the environmentally conscientious single.

"No pimped-out green Charger," Motz said. "Here, it would stick out like a sore thumb."

Like a vintage Cadillac with futuristic tailfins, Ritter thought.

Motz double-parked next to a utility truck in front of a Victorian walk-up. "This is it," he said and killed the engine.

Ritter double-timed it up the wide stone steps to the front door, which stood wide open. He examined the name plates on the brass board. "Lühmeyer/Wesselmann" was engraved in a tasteful serif.

Motz clomped up behind him.

"Second floor," Ritter said and led the way. Inside was a narrower carpeted stairway.

After the second landing, they found the right door. Ritter rang the buzzer. No answer. He knocked, loud. Nothing. He turned to Motz. "You hear somebody screaming inside?"

Motz backed up and kicked the door hard with what had to be a steel shank. The bolt broke free from the doorpost.

Inside, they found a half-empty case of Astra, an overflowing ashtray, and a splatter stain over the mantle that reeked of beer.

"Watch your feet!" Ritter yelled. Shards of blue and brown glass stuck up menacingly from white carpet. But no Laura Wesselmann.

While Motz checked the bathroom, Ritter hit the bedroom. The waterbed was unmade. Somebody had slept in it recently. He ducked his head into the kitchen, which had small shoulder-high tiles with blue inlays and a rustic country look that had cost somebody a lot of time and money. "Clean!" he yelled and walked back into the living room.

"She's long gone," Motz said from the doorway.

Ritter stepped over the glass shards and peered down at bits of smashed wood that could have been a flower vase. Or a drug stash. There was a hammer on the ground next to the pieces, along with a stretched-out white sports sock. The shattered blue bottles looked like the source of the glass crumbs on the sock.

Ritter picked up a broken picture frame with a gloved hand. The Plexiglas front fell to the ground in two pieces.

"Wonder what was in there," Motz said.

"Or who," Ritter said. The beer stain had a dry rectangle in the middle about the size of the frame. He stepped over the glass shards again and held the frame against the wall. A perfect fit. He called the Präsidium.

Meike picked up on the third ring. "Voss." She sounded out of breath.

"Put out an APB on Laura Wesselmann," Ritter said.

"The domina's girlfriend?" Meike said.

"That's right."

"She a material witness?"

"No, a murder suspect." Ritter hung up and bagged the frame.

"What makes you so sure?" Motz said.

Ritter held up the bag. "I don't like coincidences."

Motz nodded and pulled out his phone. "We need a full Forensics crew at Nonnenstieg 13." There was a pause. "Yeah, the domina. The place is a wreck. Looks like somebody went ape-shit." He hung up.

Ritter looked at his watch. Eighteen twenty-three. "Lühmeyer should be processed by now. Let's give her another go."

"Lead the way," Motz said. Outside the apartment, he lifted and pulled the broken door shut after them.

Ritter slapped a seal across it and the door jamb. He initialed and dated the seal. "Let's get this done," he said.

■ ■ ■

Outside the windows of the Eldorado, Ritter saw the boutiques of Eppendorf become seemingly endless villas, TV studios, and wellness centers on Rothenbaumchaussee. *MOPO* said the leafy Harvestehude and Rothenbaum districts had the most millionaires in Germany.

Ten minutes later, they eased to a stop opposite a miniature version of the central train station called Bahnhof Dammtor. When the light finally turned green, they veered to the right and under an old rail bridge. Coming up on the left was a white-stone palace. The sign under the red clock up top identified it as Casino Esplanade. Ritter had to wonder what Motz was thinking.

Without warning, the Eldorado made a right at an old war memorial. A block later, another right led to the gated entrance of a huge park. A left brought them toward a massive white warehouse complex with a dozen half-domed roofs. The convention center, if Ritter wasn't mistaken. Through the sliding gates, it looked like a film studio.

A hard left pulled them away from the studio. An old brick building appeared in the windshield with a double-reinforced gate.

The detention center holding Veronica Lühmeyer. The gate was framed in white stone.

"This really U-Haft?" Ritter said. "It looks ancient, nothing like ours."

"We're more traditional here," Motz said and tooted the horn. "Still got bullet holes in the back wall, next to the guillotine."

"Nice," Ritter said.

"The cons call it *Mutter*," Motz said.

"The names in this town."

The double doors opened in front of them. The Eldorado drove in and the doors closed.

Ritter had a funny thought. "They keep men and women here?"

"We're equal opportunity," Motz said.

■ ■ ■

At the front desk, Ritter signed the clipboard and handed it back through the opening under the glass.

The fat guard looked at the entry. "Lühmeyer?"

"Yes," Ritter said, annoyed. His handwriting wasn't that bad.

"And you're Ritter? The Kriminalhauptkommissar who ordered solitary?"

"Yes," Ritter said impatiently. Remains of cream pie were getting stale at the tub-a-lard's dimpled elbow. Where did they find these clowns?

"She's not here," the guard said.

"What the hell you mean she's not here?" Ritter could see his own breath against the glass. "Davidwache brought her up here a couple of hours ago!"

"She's on the way to the morgue," the guard said.

"What?!" Ritter and Motz yelled in unison.

The guard looked at them evenly. "Suicide."

Ritter felt the ground move. "She's dead?"

"Saw them cart her out a little while ago," the guard said. "Sheet over her head, label on her big toe."

"What the fuck!" Motz yelled. "How is that possible?"

The guard shrugged. "She used a bread knife."

Ritter grabbed the slippery aluminum counter. "Didn't you watch her?" he said, trying to blink away the dizziness.

"Nobody said she was suicidal," the guard said. "Just no visitors." He looked at Ritter with meaning. "Besides, we got a full house."

"You can kiss your cushy desk job goodbye!" Ritter said. Of course, he knew that would never happen. The bloated asshole was a CYA expert. *The Kriminalhauptkommissar who ordered solitary.*

The guard shrugged again. "That's what they all say."

Ritter turned to Motz. "You believe this shit?"

"Welcome to my world," Motz said.

THIRTY-FOUR

Big Board

An hour later, they were all gathered on the sixth floor of the Polizeipräsidium. Motz looked at the clock impatiently. Seven twenty-one. The second hand thudded like a hammer over his left eye. *Chunk, chunk, chunk.*

What a waste of time. Hasani was making his move, taking over St. Pauli and buying off half the senate, and they were holding a meeting. He should make a motion to shoot Hasani and all known associates. I second the motion. Meeting adjourned.

"Next up is Frederic Silbereisen," Ritter said, "the gofer for Haus 7b." He was pointing to the white board with his black marker.

All kinds of important lines connected photos of the victim and his wife and his domina and her girlfriend and now some long-haired loser who looked like he'd been neutered.

"The what?" Ebeling said.

"The gofer," Ritter said. "He makes special deliveries."

"Is this the person who had an argument with the *Puffmutter*?" Ebeling said.

Motz adjusted his chair noisily.

"No," Ritter said. "That was the beer truck driver."

"So, what do we know about this, um—"

"Gofer," Ritter said.

"—about this gofer?"

Motz looked at the clock again. Seven twenty-two.

"Two witnesses place him at the crime scene just before and

after the killing," Ritter said. "The beer truck driver and a lingerie salesman from Frankfurt."

"Motive?" Ebeling said.

"The gofer's possible motive is murky," Ritter said. "Like his character."

Like this meeting, Motz thought. He wondered if Pohl had found the gofer yet. Sitting here listening to this bullshit was torture. There was a hundred percent chance Hasani was going to hit Kaiser while he was down. He couldn't help himself. Like a dog licking his balls, he'd do it because he could.

"POLAS says Silbereisen did time in Vienna for embezzling money from an old lady," Meike said. "Now he lives with a transvestite hooker in St. Pauli."

"Sounds like a killer lead," Motz said, yawning.

"POLAS says this gofer lives with a transvestite?" Ebeling said.

"No, the girl at Wäsche-Engel," Pohl said from the doorway.

What the fuck, Motz thought. Pohl was supposed to find the gofer, not score points with the chairman of the board.

"Is that a dry cleaner?" Ebeling asked.

"Yes, sir," Pohl said. "They clean the sheets for all the houses in Herbertstrasse."

"Hope they wash at ninety-five degrees," Motz said.

"This is all very interesting," Ritter said. "But being a creep isn't a motive."

"It is for me," Meike said.

Ritter shook his head. "That's not good enough."

Motz looked down at his spiral pad. He had drawn a box around "Hasani" with a dozen pen strokes.

"Yes, it is," Meike countered. "The lingerie salesman saw him leave the Black Room."

"Did he?" Ritter said. He sounded like the captain of a debating society.

Motz had heard enough. "He told *both of us* he saw the gofer run downstairs right after the killing."

By way of answer, Ritter unpinned the picture of the domina's girlfriend and pinned it next to that of the gofer.

Meike stood up and walked to the board. "They could be twins."

"Fraternal twins," Motz said. He bracketed the corners of Hasani's box.

"The lingerie salesman's description fits both the gofer and the girlfriend," Ritter said. "So, the lingerie salesman may have actually seen the girlfriend."

"Or the gofer," Motz said.

"See the problem?"

"Where does that leave us?" Ebeling demanded.

Nowhere, Motz thought.

"With two high likelies." Ritter said.

"In other words, nowhere," Ebeling said.

When you're right, you're right, Motz thought.

"I wouldn't say that," Ritter countered. "We will find them."

"We've been looking all day," Meike said.

"Don't look for them," Ebeling said. "Find them."

Motz finally caught Pohl's eye.

The street cop shook his head. His guys still hadn't found the gofer.

■ ■ ■

"KOK Beck, what about your other suspect?" Ritter said. "This Albanian?"

It took a moment for the question to register. Did Ritter consider Hasani a suspect? "I'm working on it," Motz said. "Hasani could be testing Kaiser."

"Now is not the time for your private vendetta, Beck," Ebeling said. "Organized Crime is working on it."

"Organized Crime is investigating Hasani? Since when?"

Motz said. And why the fuck didn't you tell us about it?

"They're investigating both." Ebeling had a funny look in his eye.

"What? They're investigating Kaiser too? Why?" Motz's mind was reeling. Was *that* the black van he saw at Kaiser's restaurant this morning? Jesus. If he saw them, they saw him—making a payoff to a gangster.

"Evidently, Hasani and Kaiser share the same accountant in Rothenbaum," Ebeling said.

"What?" If Willi got wind of that—

Ebeling held up his hand. "That's all I'm at liberty to say. It's need to know."

Need to know. Ebeling and his old boy fucking network, Motz thought. They probably had magic rings and secret handshakes.

"What can *you* tell us, KOK Beck?" Ritter said.

Motz tore his eyes away from Ebeling. "My sources tell me there's a war brewing between the Hasani and Kaiser gangs."

"Which sources?" Ebeling said.

"Confidential sources," Motz said. "Mertens may be the first casualty."

"The Innensenator is more than a casualty," Ebeling said.

Motz ignored him. "Davidwache has eyes and ears all over St. Pauli."

"Trust the man on the ground," Ritter said.

"Exactly."

"If Mertens is the first casualty in this gang war," Ritter said, "who was behind it? Kaiser or Hasani?"

"Hasani."

"KOK Beck—" Ebeling said.

"Motive?" Ritter said.

"Well," Motz said, "like I told you this afternoon, Hasani wants to raze Herbertstrasse and built condos."

For once, Ebeling agreed with him. "It has to do with mass," he told Ritter. "Imagine a skyscraper in St. Pauli."

"Hasani has done more than imagine," Motz said. "He's ready to build."

"How would he finance it?" Ritter said.

"The usual. Drugs, prostitution, gambling, extortion. Not to mention killing cops who get in the way."

Ebeling held up his hand. "That was never proven. All we know for sure is that he runs the Casino Esplanade."

"For money laundering," Motz said.

"That's Organized Crime territory."

"That got Lars killed!" Motz yelled, spittle on his lip.

"*That* case is closed, Herr Oberkommissar."

"Lars is not a case, Herr Inspektionsleiter!"

Ebeling shook his head. "I'm sorry, Beck. We all are. But the case is closed."

"So, we have a strong motive for Hasani," Ritter said. He wrote "real estate" under his photo. "Do we have any evidence?"

"No," Ebeling said. "We have nothing."

Motz wiped his lip with the back of his hand. "That's always the problem."

"Then we have to call Hasani a maybe," Ritter said.

"Hallelujah," Motz said. About fucking time.

Ebeling shook his head but said nothing.

◼ ◼ ◼

"It's going to be a long night for all of us," Ritter said. "Our top priorities are finding the girlfriend and the gofer. After the press conference, KOK Voss and I will pay a visit to The Cage."

Meike looked surprised.

"What makes you think the girlfriend will show up for work?" Ebeling said. "She's wanted for murder."

"It won't help us not to try," Ritter said.

Motz liked that.

"KOK Beck will continue pursuing the Hasani angle," Ritter continued. "We need solid evidence we can hang him with, Herr Kriminaloberkommissar."

Motz liked that even more. "You can bet your life on it," he said.

For the second time, Ebeling didn't reprimand him. The pressure from City Hall must be intense.

"I need for Davidwache to find the gofer," Ritter continued.

"Yes, sir," Pohl said.

"Little shit has a meeting at eight o'clock," Motz said. "Gamblers Anonymous."

Ritter looked at his watch. "That's in fifteen minutes."

"I'm on my way," Pohl said.

"The rest of you will continue searching for Mertens' driver," Ritter said. "Scherf is somewhere out there. Find him."

There was a rumble of assent.

"Okay, then," Ritter said. "Heads up out there."

As everybody stood up, Ritter followed Ebeling out of the room.

THIRTY-FIVE

Sparta

Lights flashed as Ebeling and Ritter walked into the press room. The state prosecutor was already seated in a form-fitting navy-blue suit, matching nylons, and oversized black glasses. Her silver-blonde hair glistened. She crossed her perfect legs the other way and examined Ritter from head to toe.

Bold, Ritter thought. At least under cover of cameras. Behind closed doors, she was probably "professional." He took the third seat on the platform.

Next to him, Ebeling tested the mike. Then he plunged in. "Ladies and gentlemen, my name is Dr. Klaus Ebeling, Inspektionsleiter of LKA 411."

More lights flashed.

"Why LKA 411?" someone yelled. "Was it murder?"

"There will be time for questions later," Ebeling said. "Please refrain from interrupting our formal statements. That goes for Radio Hamburg too."

The yeller thought better of a second attempt.

Ebeling turned to his left. "This is Frau Dr. Stefanie Singer from the state prosecutor's office."

The prosecutor nodded. She had a concerned expression trained on the flashing cameras.

Hollywood perfect, Ritter thought. The type who threw dedicated detectives and police presidents under the bus.

"And this is Kriminalhauptkommissar Thomas Ritter, who is leading the investigation."

Ritter looked briefly into the lights.

Ebeling went back to his script. "Innensenator Carsten Mertens is dead."

The room exploded with voices.

Ebeling held up his hand until it quieted down. "Thank you," he said. "The coroner has put the time of death at just after noon today. Cause of death was asphyxiation. The investigation is in high gear. I don't need to tell you that the Polizei Hamburg is pursuing every possible lead. KHK Ritter will provide you with a brief status report."

"Thank you," Ritter said. He consulted his notes briefly. "At thirteen sixteen hours, officers from Davidwache notified LKA 411 of Innensenator Mertens' death. Davidwache secured the crime scene and immediate vicinity. Detectives, technicians, and the coroner arrived shortly afterwards. The coroner established the time and cause of death. At the crime scene, Forensics gathered important physical evidence, which is currently being analyzed. Together with Davidwache, LKA 411 conducted a canvas of the immediate vicinity, interviewing dozens of witnesses. As Inspektionsleiter Ebeling just told you, we are pursuing every possible lead."

"Now, are there any questions?" Ebeling said.

"Was it murder?" It was the yeller again.

Ebeling ignored him and pointed to an attractive reporter on the other side of the room. "HTTV?"

"Herr Inspektionsleiter," she said. "Why was Davidwache the first to the crime scene? Normally, that's the job of KDD, isn't it?"

Here we go, Ritter thought. If Anita Kranz had placed an emergency 110 call, the on-call uniforms would have been the first to respond.

"It just worked out that way," Ebeling said. "Davidwache happened to be closer."

"So, the murder occurred in their precinct," the HTTV reporter persisted. "Where exactly in St. Pauli, Herr Inspektionsleiter?"

Ritter stared at his muted mike. Ebeling would have to earn his money now.

"I didn't say it was murder," Ebeling said. "And that's a second question. Let's give someone else a chance." He looked around for other hands. "How about *MOPO*?"

"Yes, thank you," the *MOPO* reporter said. "Where exactly in St. Pauli did the, um, killing occur?"

"We're not at liberty to say," Ebeling said.

Good answer, Ritter thought.

The *MOPO* reporter was outraged. "All afternoon, the Polizei blocked the area around Herbert—"

"That's not a question." Ebeling pointed to a bald guy in round black glasses. "Let's give *BILD* a chance."

Ritter was impressed. Ebeling didn't deny the obvious, he simply ignored it.

"Is it true that Innensenator Mertens was found dead in a bordello?" the bald guy said.

"As I just said, we're not at liberty to say at this point," Ebeling said. "As you know, LKA 411 withholds certain key facts from the press in the early stages of an investigation. We don't want the perpetrator or perpetrators to know what we know."

Ritter looked past Ebeling. The state prosecutor's face was blank. Her body language telegraphed to everyone in the room that she took no responsibility for anything the cops said. Ritter and Ebeling were already under the bus.

"So that's a yes?" the bald guy said.

"No, it's a no comment," Ebeling said. "As you well know." He looked away from the round glasses. "Someone else."

A mousy woman spoke up. "*Hamburger Abendblatt*. I have a question for KHK Ritter."

"By all means," Ebeling said.

Ritter heard the warning in his voice. Keep a tight lid on this.

"Herr Kriminalhauptkommissar," the mouse squeaked, "how

optimistic are you at this stage of the investigation?"

Ritter relaxed. The question was ridiculously harmless. Maybe Ebeling planted it. "We are very optimistic," Ritter said. "We have strong leads and the best police force in Germany."

Ebeling nodded sagely, like Ritter had said something of substance.

Even the state prosecutor's face softened for a moment.

The mouse scribbled furiously on her pad.

"The Polizei Hamburg will not rest until justice is served," Ritter concluded. "You can quote me on that."

Instead of thanking him, Ebeling pointed to the yeller. "I almost forgot Radio Hamburg. Did you have a question too?"

The yeller picked up where he left off. "Is the Polizei Hamburg covering up for Innensenator Mertens?"

Ebeling was ready. "I don't know what they taught you in journalism school, but I was raised not to speak ill of the dead."

Good for him, Ritter thought.

"Especially when the dead is your former boss," the yeller said.

Ebeling slammed the table with his fist. "Enough!"

The state prosecutor flinched.

"The Polizei Hamburg is pursuing this case like any other," Ebeling said. "Carsten Mertens always said he was a citizen first and a senator second. He deserves the same courtesy and respect as every other citizen of this fair city-state."

Ebeling should have been an actor, Ritter thought. His outrage was almost believable.

■ ■ ■

After the press conference, Ebeling poured Ritter a cup of Earl Grey at his desk. "Milk, Herr Kriminalhauptkommissar?"

"Is Beck being followed by Internal Affairs?" Ritter said. "We keep seeing unmarked vans out there."

Ebeling had trouble controlling the tea pot. "Excuse me?"

You heard me, Ritter thought.

Ebeling wiped droplets from his school tie. Seeing it was useless, he threw down the linen cloth. "That was probably Organized Crime."

Ritter was confused. "Why would Organized Crime follow Beck?" Sure, he had a big mouth, but that was no crime.

"As I said in the team meeting, Organized Crime has been investigating Hasani and Kaiser for some time," Ebeling said.

No, you didn't, Ritter thought. You said *are* investigating. That's not the same thing.

Ebeling's eyes were wary. "This is strictly confidential."

Just say it, Ritter thought.

"Their surveillance intensified after KHK Hanson's accident," Ebeling said.

Ritter was stunned. "So Beck is right!" About you too. Thanks a lot, Rosenfeld.

"Beck doesn't need to know that." Ebeling was smiling.

"He doesn't?" What kind of sick game was Ebeling playing now?

"It's not what you think." Ebeling showed Ritter green teeth. "Beck does his best when swimming against the current."

The room swayed.

"You're a man of education," Ebeling said. "You know about ancient Sparta."

Ritter clutched his armrests. "The Spartans paired lovers as soldiers," he said. "They fought to the death."

Ebeling nodded in approval. "Partners are like lovers, Beck and Hanson especially. I wouldn't want to be in Sulejman Hasani's shoes right now."

Ritter's knuckles were white. The electrical *zap-zap* was replaced by high tinny buzzing. "So, Beck is bait for Organized Crime?" Maybe Ebeling *wanted* Motz to go after Hasani to provoke an incident that would force Organized Crime to swoop in and nab the gangster. It was possible that Organized Crime was in on this dirty deal. Maybe they, not Internal Affairs, were the ones in the black van outside Herbertstrasse earlier in the day. Maybe they were just monitoring their unknowing "asset." That would mean Motz was expendable.

"Let's just say it's a win–win situation." Ebeling sipped some more Earl Grey. "Please, drink it while it's hot."

The room righted itself, but Ritter didn't loosen his grip. The tinny sound was filling his head. "This doesn't have anything to do with the Mertens killing, does it, sir?"

"You're new in town," Ebeling said. "This has everything to do with the Mertens killing."

THIRTY-SIX

The Third Man

Meike was querying her computer for the best route to The Cage when her cell phone rang—a suppressed number.

"Yes," she said.

"Meike, it's me," a thick Russian accent said. Vladimir Netsky, her hacker in Frankfurt.

"Vlad!" Meike said. "What have you got for me?"

"I moved heaven and earth," he said. "Do you have any idea how hard it is to hack through a BND firewall?"

"You're right," Meike said. "I have no idea." She'd read somewhere that a seventeen-year-old had done just that—and was now serving time.

"It takes elephant balls," Vlad said. "And brains. I know you like both."

Meike wrinkled her nose at the image. "How did you get in?"

"I had only thirty seconds," Vlad said. "In and out."

"Wow," Meike said. Sounds familiar, she thought.

"I wrote a program to download his entire file in twenty."

"Won't they notice?" Meike couldn't imagine spooks letting any breach of security go, if only for twenty seconds.

"Only after thirty seconds." Vlad sounded annoyed. "Aren't you listening?"

"Of course," Meike said. "There's just a lot going on right now. You know how it is."

"I know," Vlad said. "But try to stay focused."

"I will. Go ahead."

"You remember the Rosenfeld hearing, right?"

This is it, Meike thought. "Of course. I called you about that, remember?"

"Yes," Vlad said. "And you told me KHK Ritter was the snitch, right?"

"Right," Meike said. She knew better than to second-guess Vlad now. He always put her in her place before dropping a bombshell.

"Wrong," Vlad said.

"Wrong what?"

"Ritter wasn't the snitch."

"Say that again." Meike was sitting up straight now.

"Ritter didn't rat out Rosenfeld," Vlad said. "He worked for him."

"What! Ritter worked for the Frankfurt Polizeipräsident?"

"That's right. And you'll never guess what his special assignment was."

"I'm sitting on the edge of my seat," Meike said. That was no lie.

"His job was to interrogate the kidnapper."

"Ritter was the third man?" Meike couldn't believe it. "I thought that was just a myth."

"That's what you were supposed to think," Vlad said.

"But Rosenfeld confessed to torturing the kidnapper," Meike said. "They said Ritter snitched on him."

"Who's *they*?"

"Everybody," Meike said. "Half the department."

"Don't believe everything you hear. The snitch label is Ritter's legend."

"His what?" Meike said. "That sounds like spy talk."

"That *is* spy talk. BND is a spy agency, remember?"

Meike took a deep breath. Something was wrong. "What exactly did Ritter do?"

"That's where the details get a little fuzzy. Something to do with a toilet. Ever hear of waterboarding?"

"Oh, shit." Meike tried to picture Ritter holding a child molester upside down over a toilet. It was easier than she expected.

"That would be my guess," Vlad said with a chuckle.

"Your guess?"

"My *educated* guess."

"Just say it, Vlad."

"You take all the fun out of it, Meike."

"Vlad!" Meike warned.

"Ritter was in Tora Bora right after 9/11. GSG-9."

Meike gasped. "Afghanistan? Special forces?" She'd heard GSG-9 helped the *Amis* hunt for bin Laden in Hindu Kush.

"Actually, it's not that surprising," Vlad said. "His father is a brigadier general with the Bundeswehr. He works with the Luftwaffe and NATO."

"Jesus," Meike said. "Ritter's an army brat?"

"So to speak," Vlad said. "One other thing."

"Yes?" Meike said. She had had enough surprises for one day. The line went dead.

"Vlad?" Meike said.

Vlad came back on the line, breathing audibly like a prank caller.

He was interrupted by three loud bangs.

"Vlad?" Meike said again.

"Vladimir Netsky!" a gruff voice yelled in the distance.

"Oh, shit." Vlad's voice was barely audible. "There are two suits outside my door." It sounded like he was walking. "I'm keeping the line open."

Uh oh, Meike thought. That must be Internal Affairs. Or BND.

Something crashed on the other end of the line. Not good.

"Vlad?"

"Wait a minute!" Vlad said in the distance. "You can't—"

Another crash.

"Who are you?" Vlad yelled.

"Get dressed!" the gruff voice said. "The boss wants to talk to you."

"Who the hell are you?" Vlad said.

"You seem to have a special interest in our computer records," another voice said. It sounded more intelligent.

Oh, shit, Meike thought. It really was BND.

"We don't have all day," the gruff voice said.

Something scraped the line.

"Hello?" the intelligent voice said in Meike's ear.

She killed the phone. Her heart was pounding. If BND had Vlad, it was only a matter of time before they showed up on her doorstep.

Her desk phone rang.

She almost jumped out of her chair.

An inside line. The central operator. Maybe BND was already here.

"KOK Voss," Meike said, her heart pounding in her ear.

"We've got a call from a witness," the operator said. "A Frau Spiess. Something to do with KOK Beck. She seems kind of confused."

The pounding picked up speed. "I'll take it," Meike said, bracing herself. BND never announced itself.

"She's all yours."

Something clicked.

"Frau Spiess?" Meike said. The whole room was pounding now.

"I'd like to report a grave robbery!" a shaky voice said.

"A grave robbery?" Meike said, almost laughing. The old lady sounded like a crackpot, not a BND operative.

"And I know who did it!" the old lady said.

"You do?" Meike said, cupping her head in her other hand. The paper mat on her desk had coffee stains she hadn't noticed before.

"It's that Dietmar Beck! I'd recognize that stinker anywhere!"

Meike didn't know whether to laugh or cry. Nobody called Motz by his real name. He sure knew how to pick them. Today of all days. "Frau Spiess, let's start at the beginning, shall we?" The stains formed concentric circles around miniature calendars of August and September.

"Hmmph!" the old lady said in her ear. "That Dietmar was the worst third grader I ever saw! Always getting into mischief, always talking out of turn."

That's our Motz, Meike thought, rubbing her forehead. At least her pulse was down to the low hundreds.

THIRTY-SEVEN

Gamblers Anonymous

Motz pulled up to the curb outside Gamblers Anonymous.

Pohl was crouched next to someone in the gutter, a bloody handkerchief in his hand.

Motz slid over and pushed open the passenger door. "That him?"

"Yeah," Pohl said. "Say hello to Frederic Silbereisen."

The gofer looked up at Motz hopefully. His nose was misshapen, like it was broken.

Motz got out and slammed the door. "What happened?"

Pohl grinned. "He fell down the stairs."

Nearby, an oversized transvestite dressed like a bad '70s remake was examining the glitter on a fingernail.

"Those the stairs?" Motz said.

Pohl laughed. "Big steps."

Motz walked over to the transvestite. Her hands were bigger than his. "Take a walk, sister," he said. "We'll take it from here."

She didn't seem to mind the rough language. Motz had the queasy feeling she liked it.

"Give him the rubber hose treatment, Herr Kommissar!" The transvestite snatched up a white Chihuahua. "Come with Mommy, Blanco. We're going home—without Daddy." She looked at the gofer with contempt. "Daddy has been a very bad boy. He gambled away our rent money."

Motz watched the transvestite maneuver the cobblestones with her mammoth silver platforms. You could never be too careful in this neighborhood.

After she and the mutt rounded the corner, Motz got on his haunches next to the gofer. Up close, Frederic Silbereisen looked like a rabid weasel. His eyes were jumping around manically, like he was off his meds. Blood had crusted around his nostrils. "Does it hurt?" Motz said.

Frederic flushed. "Yes."

Motz believed him. But the transvestite obviously hadn't hit him with a closed fist. Otherwise, his nose would be mush. That probably counted as love between those two freaks. "Do you want it to hurt more?" Motz said.

Frederic's flush darkened. "No, of course not!"

Motz shook a latex glove out of his pocket and squeezed his hand into it. Then he grabbed the weasel by the collar. "Did you kill Mertens?"

"Who?" Frederic said, terror in his eyes.

Motz slapped him hard across the mouth. "Lose the attitude!" He could hear Pohl laughing.

Frederic whimpered.

Motz looked at the blood on his glove in disgust. Probably HIV positive. He let go of the collar. "Tell me what happened today."

"Today?" Frederic said.

Motz slapped him again, this time on the back of the head.

Pohl looked like he was crying.

The gofer flinched, like he expected more.

"In Herbertstrasse 7b," Motz said. "Tell me exactly—and don't leave anything out."

"Well." Frederic tried to sit up straight. "This morning, Anita Krenz, the concierge, called and asked me to deliver some chalk."

Chalk. That confirmed the *Puffmutter's* story. Motz pulled off the glove so it was inside out, dropped it in the gutter, and pulled out his notepad. "When?"

"About eleven fifteen."

Motz wrote down the time. "Then what?"

"I bought the chalk at the stationery store. Mistress Veronica is very picky. She only accepts Pelikan in the blue box."

Mistress Veronica. Motz paged back in his notepad. The *Puffmutter* said the gofer arrived shortly after Mertens. "When did you deliver it?"

"Just after noon."

"Receipt?"

Frederic thought about that. "I gave it to Anita."

"Personally?" Motz said. He and Ritter had forgotten to ask the *Puffmutter*. With a little luck, it would have a timestamp.

Frederic thought again. "No, she had me put it on her desk, when I picked up my payment."

Motz tensed. "Was the front door locked?"

"No," Frederic said. "It was wide open."

Motz underlined "open." That hardly narrowed the list of possible suspects. Still, it didn't help the gofer. The weasel went in without supervision. That changed things. Motz was no shrink, but suffocating a bound-and-gagged victim sounded like something a weasel would do. On the other hand, the *Puffmutter* didn't strike him as naïve. "Does Anita always let you just walk in?"

"No, never!" Frederic was adamant.

She was no fool, Motz thought. "What was different today?"

"She was fighting with the BierShop driver," Frederic said.

Motz remembered the lingerie salesman's words. *I think they had some kind of argument.* "Where?"

"Out in front. His truck blocked the path to the door."

"They fought about the truck?" Motz said.

"No, I don't think so."

"Why don't you think so?"

"Because. I don't know."

"You don't know." Motz looked at Pohl, who was wiping his eyes.

"It was chaotic," Frederic said. "Besides, I think she's having a midlife crisis."

Oh, boy, what a nut job, Motz thought. "Are you trained in psychology?"

"I've taken a few courses. Online."

Great, Motz thought. The fucking Internet. That's all this idiot needed. An insanity booster. "Ever been to a psychiatrist?"

"No, never!" Frederic said, pressing himself against the wall.

"Why not?"

Pohl was laughing again.

"They can't make me go!"

Motz looked into the little rat's eyes. "We can make you do whatever we want. What haven't you told me?"

Frederic's wide pupils jumped around, but his face stayed put. "The car. It was parked outside."

Motz jerked him up by the lapels. "Look at me."

Frederic tried to sink into his jacket. "Don't hit me again. Please."

Motz didn't have time for this shit. "What car?"

"A hotrod, like pimps drive. I think it was green."

Wesselmann's car was green. Motz decided to test the little shit. "Four-door Lincoln. Spoiler in back?"

"I think so, yes," Frederic said.

Wrong answer. Nobody would trick out a town car like that. "You don't even know what a spoiler is, do you?"

Frederic looked Motz in the eye. "The car belongs to Mistress Veronica's girlfriend."

Motz wanted to smack the smirk off his face, but the sudden attitude meant he knew something. "How do you know it belongs to Mistress Veronica's girlfriend? You know her?"

Frederic nodded vigorously. "I saw her in the photo."

"What photo?"

"The one in Anita's office."

Motz remembered the tan bimbos on the board—and the bagged photo fragment in his pocket. "Who was in the picture?"

"Mistress Veronica and her girlfriend," Frederic said triumphantly.

That had to be the missing photo. The bulletin board had pictures of lots of girls and lots of vacations, but no Veronica Lühmeyer and no Laura Wesselmann. Maybe something about the missing photo, not the yellow card, was what really spooked the domina. She might have even torn it down herself. He'd have to ask Forensics about that.

"She gave me my money," Frederic said.

Motz was disoriented. "Who gave you money?" He'd heard insanity was contagious.

"Mistress Veronica's girlfriend," Frederic said. "She paid me for Anita."

"What?"

Frederic straightened himself. "For the chalk."

"Why would Mistress Veronica's girlfriend pay you for chalk?"

Frederic shrugged. "She was just there. In Anita's office."

Motz looked at Pohl. The gofer had just put the domina's girlfriend at the place and time of the killing.

Motz turned back and smoothed the gofer's lapels. "When?"

"When I got there." Frederic frowned. "She wasn't very nice."

"What do you mean she wasn't very nice?"

"She didn't say anything."

"What?" Motz was losing his temper again. This crazy shit really was contagious.

"Like I was air." Frederic seemed hurt by the slight. "She just gave me ten euros from the envelope."

"And then what?" Motz said.

"And then nothing. No goodbye, no nothing." The gofer sounded bitter.

"Did she seem upset?" Motz said.

Frederic bristled. "She seemed hostile. She's a dyke, you know." He said it like Motz would understand.

"How do you know?" Motz said.

Frederic gave him a sly look. "She drives a green Dodge Charger."

"Son of bitch," Motz said. The gofer was playing him. "You just said it was a Lincoln."

"No, you did," Frederic said.

Motz wanted to punch the little weasel for real, but he wasn't wearing a glove. Then he had it. "What did you do to the car?"

Frederic looked proud. "I scratched it."

Motz liked that. The weasel was incriminating himself. "How did you scratch it?"

"With my house key."

Motz nodded, like that was a good choice. "Show me the key."

Frederic took a small key ring out of his jacket pocket. It had a pair of dice dangling from a silver chain.

Motz tried to ignore the body warmth on the metal. The third key had tiny fragments of green and white paint on it. He dropped the ring into the evidence bag Pohl held open for him.

While Pohl labeled the bag, Motz turned back to the gofer. "What else did you do?"

"That was it."

Motz patted his narrow back. The bony frame gave him the creeps. "See how easy that was? Now you get to write it all down."

■ ■ ■

Motz handcuffed the gofer to the overhead handgrip in the back seat of the Eldorado, giving him a front-row view of baby turds on the sidewalk, about the size you would expect from a white Chihuahua. Then he motioned Pohl over to the doorway of Gamblers Anonymous, out of hearing range. "Take a statement and put him in a cell for safekeeping."

Pohl looked at the car. "What are we holding him for? Vandalism is barely a misdemeanor."

"That and being a slimeball."

"We can't do that," Pohl said.

"He doesn't know that."

Pohl surprised Motz. "I'll bet he'll like it. It'll make him feel important."

"You work with what you've got," Motz said. "He's cooperating now."

"Do you believe him?"

"I believe he believes himself."

Pohl looked confused. "Was that a yes or a no?"

"He's a borderline personality."

"A what?"

"Been seeing this shrink," Motz said. "I get a lot from therapy."

Pohl didn't look confused anymore. More worried.

"What?" Motz said.

"I forgot to mention." Pohl sounded far away. "Just before you got here, I saw some guys in a black van."

Oh shit, Motz thought. Internal Affairs. "Where?" he said, looking around.

"Across the street. I had the impression they were watching Silbereisen."

"Oh," Motz said, relieved. "That's just Organized Crime." Pohl didn't need to know about the rat squad.

Pohl shook his head. "It wasn't one of ours. I checked the plates. Plus, they looked wrong."

"How wrong?"

"Way wrong, like outsiders," Pohl said. "You know, southerners."

The old code word for *them*. "Albanians?" Motz asked.

"Could've been."

Motz turned to the rear seat of the Eldorado. "Maybe Hasani

wanted to talk to our friend."

"You mean the guys with the blowtorch?" Pohl said.

Motz nodded grimly. "You might have saved the little shit from spot welding," he said.

The gofer appeared to be talking to himself.

Motz shook his head. "God protects drunks and fools."

"You mean Davidwache protects drunks and fools," Pohl said.

Motz had to laugh. Like everybody down here, Pohl was only half dumb. St. Pauli did that to you.

■ ■ ■

Motz walked back to the Eldorado. "Why is the Albanian mafia after you?"

Frederic looked pleased. "The Albanian mafia is after *me*?"

"I said *why*."

"I'm one of their best customers," Frederic said.

"Customers?"

Frederic looked proud and ashamed at the same time. "I have a little gambling problem. Roulette."

"You sick fuck," Motz said. "The last guy crossed the Albanians got his face blowtorched off."

"B-blowtorched?"

"They used a stitch welding torch," Motz said. "You know, the kind Blohm and Voss used to weld the *Queen Mary 2* back together on Dock 11."

Frederic looked like he was going to be sick.

"Not on my back seat!" Motz yelled.

Frederic swallowed obediently.

"You stealing from the Albanians?" Motz said.

"Not that I know of."

Motz looked at Pohl. "Not that he knows of. You believe this shit?"

Pohl shrugged.

Motz opened the door and unlocked the cuffs. "Stand up!"

"What?" Frederic said.

"You heard me, asswipe."

Frederic pulled himself out of the car slowly.

He wasn't moving fast enough. Motz yanked him out and slammed him into the wall below the Gamblers Anonymous sign.

Frederic slid to the ground like a slug. Then he curled into a fetal position, with his back in the corner. He obviously had experience getting beaten.

Motz crouched back down on his haunches. "Why were the Albanians looking for you?"

Between his hands, Frederic said, "I don't know. I get along with everybody."

Motz grabbed his collar again.

"Like that Afghani this afternoon," Frederic said.

Motz stopped.

Frederic was somewhere between sitting and standing.

"Afghani?" Motz said.

"Yes." Frederic's jacket was serving as a sort of noose.

"Where?" Motz said.

"At Casino Esplanade."

Motz's neck hairs bristled. "What makes you think he was Afghani?"

"He had on one of those funny hats," Frederic said. "Like that president. I watch the news."

Motz held Frederic against the wall. "Think carefully. This Afghani, he say anything?"

Frederic made a show of thinking. "No, he didn't say anything. But his bodyguard mentioned Anton."

An–ton. Motz felt an electric jolt. That was Lars' last word under the train bridge, next to the downed chopper and flashing blue lights. "Anton? Are you sure?"

"Yes." Frederic nodded vigorously. "My old hamster was

called Anton."

Motz took a deep breath, forcing himself not to pound the little shit's head into the wall—or think about what he and his transvestite "roommate" would do with a hamster. "Could he have said Antonov? Like the Russian name."

"Yes," Frederic said. "I knew it was Russian!"

Motz's head was pounding from too much restraint.

"Antonov is a Russian name," Frederic said.

Hot light jabbed Motz's eye. He let go of the collar.

Frederic slid to the ground again.

Motz stood up and walked over to Pohl, cradling his eye with his palm. "Son of a bitch! That crazy fuck will say anything to anybody about anything!"

Pohl looked at Motz with concern. "What was that about Antonov?"

Motz was breathing hard now. "Customs told Lars they suspected Hasani of smuggling heroin into the harbor from Afghanistan via Turkey." The jabs of light were getting unbearable. "They checked every ship on that route in the past six months. A Russian-flagged ship named *Aleksandr Antonov* operated in Turkey in that timeframe."

"Does that mean Hasani is planning another shipment?" Pohl said.

"Yeah." Motz pressed his burning eye. "But our sick friend here doesn't know that."

THIRTY-EIGHT

The Cage

Meike sat with Ritter in her cramped car outside The Cage. Things were beginning to pick up. There was a growing line out front. Mostly straight couples with money to see the animals in the zoo. She could feel the beat from the club in her leather seat.

They got out and scanned the block for the Charger one last time. Nothing. Walking back up to the club, they elbowed their way to the front of the line and badged an oversized bouncer with a shiny skull and neck tattoo. He moved back one centimeter to let them through.

Inside, the beat was keeping pace with the blue lasers bouncing against the brick walls of the former machine factory. The black iron window frames contained thick frosty glass that blocked the view of nonpaying curiosity seekers on the street. The pit in front of the stage, overlooked by an iron walkway that ringed the factory floor, was filling up fast. A large biker with greasy hair, a black leather vest, bulging muscles, and an indoor tan was handing out tissues from a motorcycle helmet.

Ritter pointed upstairs. Meike followed him up the grated steel steps. Twice, they had to step around couples making out. Ritter headed for a corner of the walkway that had a good view of the stage and easy access to the stairs. Through the grating, Meike could see people milling around underneath her rain boots. Despite the unmistakable stench of hemp, the crowd looked surprisingly respectable and fit. Most were over thirty. Probably teachers from Eppendorf and dentists from Winterhude.

It was too loud to really talk, so they just gestured. Meike took the opportunity to lean into Ritter and cup his ear a few times. Mostly, he nodded back, but she enjoyed it just the same. The looks of more than a few women spoke volumes.

After twenty minutes of false intimacy, the music died, and the strobes dimmed. Then two minutes of nothing. The crowd became impatient. Some people called out for the show to begin. The longer it didn't, the more restless they became. The walkway began to shake from the stomping. Meike held onto the railing. She knew the factory had been built to withstand the weight of countless diesel engines, but she wondered about hundreds of people jumping up and down. A large square object rose from the floor below. It stopped at about the level of her feet. It was swaying.

A throbbing beat began to fill the hall. A spotlight hit the swaying object, an iron cage hanging from an industrial hook attached to the track of an I-beam. The crane-like machinery had picked up the cage and moved it over the heads of the best seats. In opposite corners stood two nearly naked women, both glistening with oil like gladiators. The tall one with the white-blonde ponytail wore leopardskin torn to reveal dangerous curves. Sandals were lashed to her lower legs and feet. The other corner contained a small dark woman with razor-cut straight black hair held at an extreme angle by a blue bandana. Her sinewy body was covered with tattoos. She wore nothing but pole-climber boots, a thong, and a much-too-small tank top.

Meike cupped her hand to Ritter's ear. "That's the girlfriend."

Ritter nodded but didn't take his eyes off the cage.

Slowly, the white light dissolved. It was replaced by needles of blue light that appeared for a split-second in different corners of the factory. As the beat picked up, the needles grew in diameter and duration. The cage began to sway as the two dancers circled each other like mortal enemies, kicking and scratching and slapping. Each time they made contact, the sound of an electronic whip slapped the factory walls. The play fighting grew in intensity until they had each other by the hair and began bouncing off the walls of the cage.

To break the standoff, the small one dropped to the floor, pulling the blonde over her head like a TV wrestler. They writhed on the steel mesh, each trying to get a hold on the other's oily legs and arms and breasts. The smaller one was the more skilled wrestler. She managed to pin the blonde's shoulders with her legs. Try as she would, the blonde couldn't get out of the thighs that locked her head in place. So she kicked around with her long legs until she managed to do the same to the small one. Now, each wrestler's face was locked in the other's crotch.

Slowly, the blue bandana began to move up and down, up and down. The crowd gasped. The small one was licking the blonde like a dog. The repetitive movement wasn't lost on the long legs, which began to flail. The whipping sound was gradually replaced by moans and groans that sounded very real.

Even from where she was standing, Meike could see the blonde's toes were curled. She realized she herself was breathing hard.

Under the hot glare of hundreds of eyes, the moaning picked up, seeking release from its rhythmic torment. When the licking became unbearable, the room was filled with an ear-splitting scream of ecstasy punctuated by convulsing legs and spastic toes.

After a brief pause, the blonde went to work on the small girl, who rode her face like there was no tomorrow. The small one lifted her ass and let out strange yelps as she came in short squirts all over the blonde's face.

Meike saw blue-ish tissues mopping faces down below.

From one moment to the next, the room went black and silent. The factory was filled with a steamy mixture of awe and shame.

Meike began fanning her face with both hands.

Somebody down below clapped. The sound was echoed by somebody upstairs. After hesitating, the factory floor exploded in a thunder of clapping and stomping and whistling.

Gradually, the blue needles started their dance again. This time, they kept in the background, providing just enough light for people to find their way out.

Meike felt Ritter's hand on her ear.

"That was no act," he said.

Meike nodded vigorously. This was like a twisted version of the Safari Club, the legendary live-sex club around the corner from Herbertstrasse.

Ritter led Meike down the wide stairs, past the same couples, who now had that special glow. Downstairs, they walked against the current.

Ritter jumped onto the stage and pulled Meike up after him. Now they saw how big the cage was. The air behind the thick curtain was refreshingly cool.

"Either the girlfriend has a clear conscience or no conscience," Ritter said. "I'd put my money on no conscience."

Meike just gaped at him. It was scary how quickly he got down to business. She wondered if he was like that *after*.

Ritter said "Polizei" and badged the biker with the greasy hair.

The biker didn't budge.

Ritter casually slammed him into the wall and kept moving forward.

The biker touched the back of his hair and came up with blood.

"Coming, Voss?" Ritter said.

"Yeah, sure."

The biker looked at her in disbelief.

Meike shrugged. "Can't take him anywhere."

■ ■ ■

They found the girlfriend in the locker room. Somebody else was singing in the shower. A *MOPO* lay face down on the wet tile floor.

"Laura Wesselmann?" Ritter said.

"Who wants to know?" Laura shot a look at a frosted-glass window.

Meike stepped in front of the window, one hand on her P6 and one eye on the tile opening to the shower room, which was beginning to emit steam.

Ritter flashed his ID card. "Polizei."

Laura spit on the tile next to his boot. "Just because I have a record, you think you can razz me whenever you want."

Ritter kept his eyes on hers. "We want to talk to you about love."

Meike was impressed.

"What?" Laura looked back and forth between the two detectives.

"You weren't just acting up there." Ritter's tone implied that she had just agreed with him.

"I'm a good actor," Laura said.

"Or you're getting revenge."

Laura planted her feet like a boxer. "Revenge? What for?"

Ritter nodded again, like they were in perfect agreement. "Jealousy is a powerful thing."

Laura squared up. "The fuck you talking about?"

"Betrayal." Ritter sounded sad.

Laura balled her fists. "Fuck *is* this?"

Ritter nodded some more. He really understood her. "Is that why you killed Mertens?"

"What?" Laura's eyes jumped back to the window.

Meike shook her head. Bad idea, girl.

"We know you were in the Black Room today," Ritter said.

Laura's eyes went wide for a second. Then her tone became casually dismissive. "Oh, that." She cracked a knuckle on her bird finger.

"Yeah, that."

"What's the big deal? It was a little gag."

"A little gag?" Ritter said. "So you admit doing it?"

"No harm, no foul, right?" Laura said.

Ritter was right, Meike thought. The hardcase in front of them had no conscience. None.

"The man choked to death," Ritter said.

"What?" Laura said. "You're lying!"

Meike held up the *MOPO*. The dripping cover screamed: "Top Cop Dead in S&M House!"

The wet paper came apart as Laura ripped it from Meike's hand.

"Fuck me!" Laura said. "That really Mertens?"

"Yes," Ritter said. "You killed the Innensenator."

"But—but he was alive when I left!"

"When was that?" Meike said.

"I dunno," Laura said. "Noon-ish."

"The coroner says it took him five minutes to die," Ritter said. "Slowly, in agony."

Laura's eyes jumped around the room again. "You can't pin that on me! It must've been the creep."

"The creep?" Meike took half a step forward.

"Yeah," Laura said. "That creepy little gofer fuck."

Meike was almost close enough to grab her. "Why do you say that?"

"He was sliming all over the picture board when I got there."

"The picture board?"

"In Anita's office," Laura said. "He was sliming all over our picture!"

Meike remembered Motz studying all those big-titted photos. She had assumed it was just a big pinup collection to him. Maybe there was more to it.

Ritter reached into his jacket and pulled out a bagged picture frame that appeared to be broken. "This picture?"

Now Meike was really impressed. Ritter hadn't mentioned the frame to her.

Laura stared at the splintered wood.

"Where's the picture?" Ritter said.

"Where'd you get that?" Laura demanded.

"From your apartment."

"Fuck you doing in my apartment?" Laura looked ready to pounce.

"We've got some bad news." Ritter sounded genuinely sad. "Your roommate, Veronica Lühmeyer, committed suicide this evening."

Laura screamed and lunged at Ritter. He stepped back quickly. Laura tried to kick him in the groin. He sidestepped her boot and put his own in the back of her knee. She went down hard, face-first. Ritter dug a knee into her right kidney and cuffed one of the tattooed hands, while Meike struggled with the other. It was slippery with all that oil. Laura tried to bite Ritter's hand. The heel of his other hand hit her on the temple with a sickening, wet sound. She was out cold.

Feeling somebody's eyes behind her, Meike whipped around to the shower room, P6 in hand.

The blonde screamed and dropped her towel. Her perfect body was red from the hot shower but shaking in fear.

THIRTY-NINE

Black Hand

As POK Pohl led the gofer from the Eldorado to a waiting patrol car, Motz's phone rang. It was the last person he expected this time of night. Loni Hanson, Lars' widow. Not a good sign. "Loni?"

"They were here!" she said.

"Who?"

"You know who!" she said. "The Albanians!"

The phone almost cracked in Motz's hand. Maybe Willi hadn't made the payment after all. "When?"

"Just now!" Loni said impatiently. "They woke me up!"

"Is Sabine with you?" Dear God, he thought, please tell me she's at home with the girls.

"What? No! Of course not!" Loni said. "She left hours ago."

Motz tried to keep the relief out of his voice. "Right."

"Those guys were really scary, Motz." Loni's voice was shaking.

"I know, Loni," he said, trying to calm her down. "Just tell me what they said."

"Something about counterfeit money. Did you—"

"What?" Motz's mind raced. Did Lars bury bad money? Did he himself hand it on to Willi? Why didn't he at least run a counterfeit detection pen over it?

"Motz, please tell me you didn't—"

Something clicked in Motz's brain. "Fucking Willi."

"Motz?" Loni said.

"Son of a fucking bitch! Willi must have switched the money!"

"Willi Kaiser?" Loni sounded confused. "I thought you two were friends."

"It's more complicated than that," he said. Like a gangster squeezing an old man to "protect" his bar until he has a massive stroke, then getting his widow a slot in an upscale "senior residence" in exchange for the deed.

"Like you and Lars."

There was reproach in Loni's voice.

"That's different, Loni."

"Is it?"

Her words felt like ice on his heart.

"They said I owe them fifty thousand," Loni said. "They said it doubles in a week."

"Son of a bitch," Motz said. Willi went too far this time. The gangster had to know Hasani would go after Loni if he paid off Lars' debt with counterfeit money.

"They said they'd be back in the morning."

"I'll take care of it," Motz said.

"They painted a Black Hand on the door," Loni said.

Motherfuckers, he thought. This shit stops now. "I'll take care of it, Loni."

"That's what Lars always said."

Lars said a lot of things, Motz thought.

"What's going on, Motz?"

"Nothing I can't fix." Motz wished he believed it.

"You know how those animals are. They killed Lars."

"I know, Loni." If Motz didn't stop them, Loni would be next. "I will take care of it."

"I'm scared, Motz."

Me too, he thought. More than you know. "Are you in a safe location? Don't tell me where," he added quickly.

"Yes," Loni said. "I was married to Lars before you met him."

"Good," Motz said. "Sit tight. I'm paying those animals a visit right now."

"Be careful, Motz."

"Always." He already knew it was the dumbest thing he would ever do.

▪ ▪ ▪

"Everything okay?" Pohl said.

"Not really," Motz said. "That was Loni Hanson."

"Oh, what's wrong?"

"Nothing I can't handle." Like taking on the Hasani clan by myself, he thought.

"Motz, you know you can trust me," Pohl said.

The look in his eyes confirmed what Motz was already thinking. Nobody in his right mind went up against somebody like Hasani without MEK tanks, armored helicopters, and automatic weapons. But this was different. The die was cast. When somebody kills your partner and threatens his widow, you have to do something. "I think it's time I had a little chat with our friend Sulejman," Motz said finally.

"Hasani?" Pohl looked alarmed. "That doesn't sound like a good idea."

"No, it sure doesn't," Motz said. More like suicide by gangster. But he'd mourned enough. Now it was payback time.

"Did Hasani threaten Loni?"

"Don't ask," Motz said.

"Oh my God," Pohl said.

"I gotta go." Motz was already thinking about the ankle holster.

Pohl grabbed his arm. "Motz, wait!"

Motz shook himself free. "Back off, Ralf!"

"Shouldn't we at least call it in?" Pohl said, holding up his hands at chest level.

"No, that would spoil the surprise." God knew how many cops Hasani had on his payroll. If he could get to Lars, he could get to anybody.

"What are you going to do, Motz?" Pohl looked scared.

"Stir the pot, see what falls out," Motz said. Sometimes crazy was the only defense.

"But you need backup," Pohl said.

Motz laughed bitterly. "Who, Ritter? Ebeling? Forget it."

"I could cover your back."

"You could get suspended," Motz said. Or get a blowtorch tan.

"So could you."

Tell me something I don't know, Motz thought. He felt his legs wobble.

"You okay?" Pohl said.

"Just take the gofer to the Präsidium," Motz said. "You've done enough."

Pohl shook his head.

Motz opened the heavy door and dropped into the seat. On his second try, he got the door shut and keyed the engine.

The Eldorado gurgled to a start. He laid rubber on cobblestone. He had already forgotten about Pohl. It was do or die.

FORTY

Ibiza

In the property room, Meike emptied Laura's sports bag onto the table. She picked up the crumpled photo of Ibiza with a gloved hand. "Nice," she said. "Wish I was there."

Ritter held up the broken frame. "We've got a match."

"She break that?" Meike said.

"That would be my guess," Ritter said.

Meike pointed to white crystals clinging to the palm trees. "Coke?"

"Forensics can tell us for sure," Ritter said, "but I'd put my money on crystal meth."

"She does look like a meth head, doesn't she?" Meike slipped the photo into the bag Ritter held open for her. The bag disappeared into his side pocket.

■ ■ ■

The guard opened Laura's cell cautiously. "Watch yourselves," he said. "She likes to bite."

"Been there," Meike said.

Ritter was already talking to Laura in hushed tones. She was listening attentively.

"Your partner a psycho whisperer?" the guard said under his breath.

Your partner. Meike liked that. "Looks that way." Ritter seemed to have really bonded with Laura.

"Are you ready?" Ritter said to Laura as Meike and the guard walked up.

Laura let out a loud blast of air, like an athlete about to do the impossible.

Ritter led her by the hand out of the cell and into the corridor.

The guard was in awe. "Where'd you find this guy?"

"Frankfurt," Meike said. Via Tora Bora, she thought.

Ritter was breaking the police seal on a cell door down the hall. Laura was standing at his side.

Meike and the guard caught up with them and looked inside.

"Is this—?" Laura said.

"Yes," Ritter said. "Let me know when you're ready."

After a moment, Laura nodded.

Ritter walked to the far end of the cell, under the window, and turned around.

"Is that where—?"

"Yes."

Meike could feel Laura shaking. No more in-your-face bad girl. She was behaving like normal next of kin—except for the crank jitters.

Laura put both hands to her mouth. She was staring at Veronica's leather jacket, neatly draped over the desk chair.

Ritter pulled out the photo of Ibiza and placed it on the desk. "Sometimes, we hurt the people we love the most."

Meike watched attentively from the doorway. That seemed to be Ritter's big line. Maybe he meant it.

Laura knelt and rubbed her face against the jacket. A strange gurgling sound turned into a heart-wrenching wail.

"I know what it's like to lose someone," Ritter said. "My little sister disappeared on her way home from first grade. I was thirteen. They never found her."

Oh, Meike thought. That wasn't in Ritter's file, the one she "borrowed" from Ebeling's desk. Even Vladimir Netsky didn't mention it. Instinctively, she knew Ritter was telling the truth. She'd heard similar stories from family members during her short stint with Child Services.

Laura held herself and rocked gently. It seemed to have a calming effect on her.

"The hardest thing was letting go," Ritter said. "I will never forget her, but in my heart, I know she's gone."

Meike saw the pain in his eyes. This was no act.

"I didn't want to hurt *him*," Laura said. Her dark face was streaked with tears. "I just wanted to hurt *her*."

Ritter nodded.

Laura sniffed up a nostril of snot. "She didn't tell me."

"She didn't tell you what, Laura?" Ritter's tone was gentle.

"About UKE." Laura paused and collected herself. "We used to do a show together. You should have seen us. We brought down the house!"

"That I believe," Ritter said. "People know when love is real."

Him with the love talk again, Meike thought. She wondered if he was that way in private. Probably not. Just strong and silent.

Laura broke into a big smile. "That's what we always said." She wiped her nose with the back of her hand and part of her arm.

"Did you kill him, Laura?" Ritter said.

Meike's eyebrows went up. Damn, she thought. That was killer.

Laura's hand stopped halfway through the spider tattoo. "Who?"

"The man in the Black Room," Ritter said.

"Oh, him!" Laura rubbed her nose the other way. "He was just hanging out." She laughed at her own joke. "I was just funnin' him."

Meike braced herself. Ritter had his weapon side away from Laura for a reason.

"Why did you kill him?" Ritter said.

Laura jumped up. "He wasn't dead when I left!"

Meike hear the guard unbuckle his holster. She shook her head. *We have this under control.*

"I believe you," Ritter said. "You just wanted to teach Veronica a lesson."

Laura's head dropped. Muscle by muscle, the fight went out of her body. Even her fists unclenched as she staggered toward the chair. One of her hands caressed Veronica's jacket.

Meike heard the holster snap shut. Told you, she thought.

"How do you know he was still alive?" Ritter said.

Laura was staring at the jacket. "He was moving his head back and forth and making strange noises, like he was trying to say something."

That was it, Meike thought. Laura watched Mertens die. The love talk was just an act. She was a stone-cold killer.

"What did you do then?" Ritter said.

"I told him nobody could hear him." Laura laughed. It was not a nice sound. "The fool had a red ball in his mouth."

Meike wanted to slap cuffs on the bitch right then and there. Enough was enough.

"Did you put something in his mouth, Laura?" Ritter's tone was still gentle.

Meike knew Ritter was right, of course. Make her say it.

Laura nodded once.

"What did you put in his mouth?" Ritter said.

"Veronica's test scores." Laura sounded like a little girl now.

Now we got her, Meike thought. The little psycho just confessed to premediated murder.

"What kind of test scores?" Ritter said.

"From UKE," Laura said. "She wants to go to medical school."

Meike felt her shoulder muscles relax. Laura was giving it up now. They usually did that *after*. Meike stretched her neck to the left and then to the right, enjoying the gritty cracking noise at the base of her skull.

"So you put the test scores in his mouth," Ritter said.

Laura nodded.

"That sounds like poetic justice."

That sounds like bullshit, Meike thought.

Laura swallowed hard.

"Thank you," Ritter said. "I know that wasn't easy."

Laura shook her head.

"Now we need you to write it down," Ritter said. "You can do that for us, can't you, Laura? It would be a big help to Veronica."

"Where is she?"

"In a better place." Ritter made it sound like the most natural thing in the world.

You mean a refrigerator at the morgue, Meike thought.

"Can I see her body?" Laura said.

"After you write down your statement. Then we'll go see her together."

Meike admired the sincerity of the lie.

FORTY-ONE

Monopoly Money

Motz found a space big enough for the Eldorado outside the Cinemaxx, just around the corner from Casino Esplanade. He killed the engine and pocketed the key.

Leaning across the bench seat, he popped the glove compartment. The snub-nosed Smith & Wesson was under "Purple Haze." He struggled out of his right boot and strapped the holster onto his ankle with fingers that didn't want to cooperate. The .38 shells were already in place. He spun the cylinder for good luck and slammed it shut. The gun slipped back into the holster. He pulled the boot back on carefully.

His left shoulder bumped the wide door. His boot caught it on the way back. He used the roof to swing out of the seat and onto shaky legs. He stomped life back into them and headed to the back of the car. His left hand helped steady the key. The trunk swung open. He jerked up the spare whitewall and grabbed the green ammo box. Three 9-mm cartridges went into his jacket pockets.

He slammed the trunk and grabbed his phone. The battery was at twenty-seven percent. More than enough. After putting the phone on mute, he hit Record. The pulsing red light matched the pounding in his head. He was locked and loaded.

His heartbeat filled the air as he rounded the corner. The gambling palace loomed above him. It made him feel small and insignificant, like nobody would ever miss him. What the hell was he doing?

He knew that was the fear talking. He had a good plan and the will to see it through. In just a few minutes, he would be back outside, laughing the jitters away.

He inhaled a rush of resolve, badged the oversized muscle at the door, and brushed past his twin at the turnstile.

Entering the glass-walled elevator, he saw the second guard talking into his sleeve. He hit 3. The doors closed silently. The elevator swooshed upward. He checked his phone. The red button was beating slowly and steadily.

The doors slid open. Straight ahead was a blackjack table. It was crowded with "respectable" people from the right side of town.

Past the table was a red-carpeted stairway without a sign. Motz clomped over to it. Halfway up the cushy steps, he felt somebody coming down fast. He got ready to put his weight into the punch, but the guy just hugged the brass rail. He looked scared. Poor bastard probably got a finger or two broken. Hasani was big on discipline.

Motz was greeted at the top of the stairs by a huge bodyguard in a bulging suit. Without a word, Motz lifted his arms. He bunched his fists to keep his hands from shaking.

The giant had a light touch. Motz barely felt the P6 leave his holster. The giant pointed to the door, which seemed to open on its own.

Motz lowered his fists and crossed the threshold. This was it.

"Herr Kommissar," a nasal voice said from across the room. "To what do we owe the honor?"

Hasani was sitting at a wide desk, flanked by two more bodyguards. Family members, no doubt. Behind him was a window-framed view of the blackjack table below. Probably one-way glass. Hasani pressed a handkerchief to his nose.

"Murder," Motz said, squinting at the two simmering coals behind the handkerchief.

"That *was* a tragedy, wasn't it?" It wasn't entirely clear who

Hasani was talking about.

Motz felt a jolt of anger. The shakes were gone. "You got hay fever?" he said. "Or just sampling your own product?"

"Old war wound," Hasani said. "But you already knew that."

"Right." Motz had heard something about Serbs and a power drill.

"What do you want, Herr Kommissar?" Hasani said. "I am a busy man."

"You can tell me what's arriving on the *Antonov*," Motz said.

There was a flicker behind the coals.

Good, Motz thought. "Heroin?"

"I run a casino," Hasani said. "I do not touch drugs. That would be illegal."

Motz flicked his own nose. "You may not touch them, but your Taliban buddy does."

Hasani sneered at him. "The Taliban are Sunnis. We are Shia. And you are an infidel." He seemed pleased with his summary. Even his bodyguards were smiling.

"Right," Motz said. "It's all so complicated, isn't it, Sulejman?"

Hasani didn't like that.

"But money makes the world go 'round," Motz continued cheerfully. "And your casino isn't *that* successful, is it?"

Hasani glanced at his handkerchief again.

Yeah, play it down, Motz thought.

"Is this an official visit, Herr Kommissar?" Hasani said.

"No, this is a friendly heads-up, Sulejman," Motz said. "You're my new favorite hobby." He looked at three sets of very unfriendly eyes.

Well, now you've done it, he thought. They won't shoot a cop, at least not in their own casino, but they will do something. That's the problem with these hot-blooded Balkan types. No self-control.

"That doesn't sound very professional," Hasani said.

Motz felt another jolt. "You should have thought about that before you threatened the Hanson family!" He spit out the last few words.

Hasani acted confused. "I sent flowers to the grave."

Motherfucker, Motz thought. This guy has got some balls. "You just threatened his widow in her own home!"

Hasani sniffed.

Motz took a step toward the desk. "You left a Black Hand on her front door!" His head was pounding again.

Hasani waived a bodyguard back. "A black what?"

"Your terror organization," Motz said. "The one you brought from Bosnia." His own words sunk in. *Terror organization*. He didn't feel the jitters anymore. Just electric terror jolting through his veins. He wondered if Lars had felt the same way.

"Oh, you speak of *that* Black Hand," Hasani said offhandedly. "That is a myth, meant to discredit my people. It does not exist."

"It does in Wandsbek," Motz said. Fuck fear.

Hasani affected confusion again. "Wandsbek? Is that not a suburb of Hamburg?"

Motz wanted to slam Hasani's dripping nose onto the desk. The cocksucker was too sure of himself. "It's where you sent your men this evening, Sulejman."

Hasani looked at his fingernails. "Why would I do that?"

Loni's trembling voice reminded Motz to be careful. "Good question," he said. "You got your fifty thousand."

Hasani didn't look confused anymore. "My fifty thousand?"

Fuck you, dirtbag, Motz thought. "The money Willi gave you today."

"Willi?" Hasani said. "Is that what you call Wilhelm Kaiser?"

Motz slammed the gunmetal desktop with the fleshy part of his fist. The desk didn't budge. "You got your fucking money."

Both bodyguards moved into position.

Hasani's eyes didn't flicker. "You mean this?" He threw a

lumpy brown envelope onto the desk. Two stacks of fifties spilled out—along with some dirt.

Motz stared at the dirt in disbelief. It was damp, just like it had been at the cemetery that morning. A freight train was crashing through his skull. So it was Lars all along. He must've gotten it from the property room. And his stupid partner dug it up and delivered it for him.

"Herr Kommissar?" Hasani said.

Motz didn't hear him. He was back at the cemetery, loading bricks into his bag. Why, Lars? We were like brothers.

Hasani misinterpreted his silence. "Next time, tell your good friend Willi to deliver real money, not this—how do you infidels call it?—oh, yes, Monopoly money."

"Jesus Christ, Lars," Motz muttered.

Hasani's eyebrows went up. "Herr Hanson cheated you too?" He didn't seem entirely pleased. "Maybe you should choose your good friends a little more carefully, Herr Kommissar."

Motz snorted. "This isn't over," he said. The fuck it isn't, he thought. They've won, you've lost. And Loni is in deep shit.

Hasani seemed satisfied. "You will excuse me," he said. "I am a busy man."

"Not for long," Motz said. He didn't have a clue what that meant, but it sounded good. The main thing was to maintain attitude. That was the only thing that would get him out of here alive.

At the door, Motz turned back, just to prove he wasn't scared. "Be seeing you," he said in a friendly tone. Then he was gone.

The door slammed behind him. At least it sounded that way. Then came the blinding light. Motz tasted carpet—and plunged into a swirling pool of darkness.

FORTY-TWO

Camp Marmal

After Laura Wesselmann signed her statement, the guard led her back to her cell.

"Well, that's that," Ritter said. Of all the people he had met in Hamburg, Laura seemed the most straight up. Yes, she was serious trailer trash with an impressive rap sheet, but she was motivated by love, not greed.

"Who would have thought it?" Meike said. "A crime of passion in St. Pauli."

Ritter didn't like her sarcasm. Politics was egotism on steroids. Everybody up here was too busy playing political games to see the obvious.

At the other end of the hall, a guard opened a gate. POK Pohl walked through.

"Where's your witness?" Ritter said.

"We've got Silbereisen in the men's section," Pohl said without stopping. He led Ritter and Meike through a labyrinth of barred doors and buzzers.

Two minutes later, another guard opened the lock to the gofer's cell.

Ritter walked in and stopped. The gofer's face had ugly green bruises. There was tape over his nose. This was a lot worse than the lingerie salesman. "What happened to him?" Ritter demanded.

Pohl laughed. "He fell down the stairs, twice."

Ritter didn't laugh with him. "What did you say, Pohl? We're officers of the law. We don't abuse prisoners." Until we do, he thought.

"It wasn't anything like *that*," Pohl said. He acted scared for a second, but his tone immediately went back to flippant. He obviously felt secure on his own turf. "Our little friend here just had a lovers' squabble with his big transvestite girlfriend."

"She's just my roommate," Frederic said.

Pohl ignored the gofer. "He told us quite a story."

"Get to the point," Ritter said. "We don't have all night."

Pohl took his time. "He"—Pohl butted his head at the gofer—"saw a bearded old Afghani go up to Hasani's office."

Meike whipped out her phone.

Ritter directed his anger at the gofer. "How do you know he was Afghani?"

"He had a funny hat on," Frederic said.

Ritter forgot his anger. "A funny hat?" The size and shape would indicate the region and tribe—if the gofer wasn't making this up. He didn't exactly look reliable.

Frederic nodded. "It was flat on top, like a beret. But the sides were higher."

A pakol cap, Ritter thought. So the Afghani was Pashtun.

"Like that president on TV," Frederic said.

There went the pakol theory. The president of Afghanistan might be Pashtun, but he wore a karakul hat with a pointy top to appease the Tajiks and Uzbeks. The gofer was living down to his reputation.

Pohl intervened. "He said he saw diplomatic plates on the car."

Ritter kept his eyes on the gofer. "What makes you think they were diplomatic plates?"

"They started with zero," Frederic said without hesitation.

That didn't even take a second, Ritter thought. The gofer was a natural-born liar. "So do a lot of government cars."

Frederic shook his head. "It said zero dash one five."

Ritter stopped. That sounded right. "How can you be so sure?"

"I'm good with numbers," Frederic said, pride in his voice.

"You have to be in my business."

My business. Like buying enemas for the White Room, Ritter thought.

"One five is the code for Afghanistan," Pohl said. "I already checked it with the federal transport ministry."

Ritter put his hands on Frederic's narrow shoulders, holding him in place. The gofer had a sickly sweet odor that reminded him of kiddie rapist Mathias Lemke's twisted "nursery" in Frankfurt. Even the crusty old toilet stall in the basement of the Polizeipräsidium had smelled better than that. "Where did you see the car?" he said.

Frederic looked up at Ritter with feral eyes. "Outside the Casino Esplanade."

That made sense too. "How do you know he went up to the office?"

Frederic had to think about that.

"You didn't see him go up to the office, did you?" Ritter said.

"What else would he be doing there?" Frederic said. "*They* don't gamble."

"They?" Ritter released his hold on the gofer's shoulders. The little sleazeball was saying whatever he thought they wanted to hear.

"Muslims," Frederic explained. "They don't gamble or drink alcohol."

Or bugger little boys chained to beds, Ritter thought. Like that warlord on Bagram who got "spayed" with copper wire by that special op from Texas. "You hear that on TV too?" Ritter said.

"Yes. HHTV ran a three-part series on—"

Ritter grabbed his shoulders again. "When did the Afghani arrive?"

"What?" Frederic looked confused.

"When did the Afghani arrive?" Ritter emphasized each word.

"Oh, that," Frederic said. "This morning."

Now we're getting somewhere, Ritter thought. Assuming the gofer wasn't lying. "When exactly?"

Frederic had to think some more. "About two o'clock."

An hour and a half after the killing. "What were you doing there?" Ritter said.

"Losing at roulette." Frederic looked down. "I'm not proud of it. I know I have a problem."

The gofer was unreliable, but there was a twisted logic to his story. "Did this Afghani say anything?" Ritter said.

"Antonov," Frederic said.

Ritter's grip on his shoulders tightened. "Say that again."

"Antonov," Frederic said. "The other detective said it's a Russian ship."

"What other detective?" And why a ship?

"Motz," Pohl said. "KOK Beck."

Meike made a funny sound.

Ritter let go of the gofer and looked over his shoulder. Meike was staring hard at nothing. "Beck interrogated him?"

"Yes, sir," Pohl said. "He said the Taliban uses the *Antonov* to ship heroin out of Afghanistan."

"No," Ritter said. "He's wrong about the ship. Afghanistan is land locked. Smugglers use Pakistan or Iran to get to Turkey."

Pohl dug in his heels. "Motz said the *Antonov* ships to Istanbul."

Ritter shook his head impatiently. "There's a Russian transport plane named *Antonov*, the AN-124."

"So the Russians *are* involved," Pohl said.

"No," Ritter said. "If it's the AN-124, the Bundeswehr is involved. They use it to transport troops and matériel."

"Our troops are smuggling heroin?" Meike said. "Really?" She looked shocked.

"Not knowingly," Ritter said. "But they're using AN-124s to transport to Turkey."

Meike didn't seem convinced. "Why Turkey?"

Good question, Ritter thought. At least somebody knew how to think. "It's the nearest NATO base. They ship from there."

"They're using this *Antonov* plane to fly everything to Turkey?" Meike looked scared now.

"Everything but weapons and computers. They use C-160s for that."

"You mean Motz was on the right track," Meike said. "He just thought the *Antonov* was a container ship."

"That's what it sounds like." Ritter wondered briefly why she hadn't been put in charge of the squad. Then he remembered. Ebeling seemed to view competence as a threat. No wonder everybody did whatever they wanted around here. Maybe they weren't supposed to succeed. "Where *is* Beck, anyway?" he said finally.

Pohl looked away. "He said he wanted to talk to Hasani."

"What!" Ritter yelled. He couldn't think of a worse idea. If Hasani was even half as bad as his reputation—

"We spotted some Albanians following Silbereisen," Pohl said.

"What!" Ritter yelled again. That was one piece of withheld information too many. "Why the hell didn't you call it in, Pohl?"

"Motz said not to ruin the surprise."

"What surprise?" Ritter wanted to kick the shit out of him.

"He said he wanted to surprise Hasani." Fear was creeping back into Pohl's eyes.

"Alone?" Ritter yelled. "Without backup? Just like that?" Ritter realized he had the Davidwache cop by the collar. When he let go, Pohl dropped to his normal height.

"He said nobody would back him up," Pohl said, rubbing his neck.

Meike made a hurt noise.

It occurred to Ritter that Motz didn't trust Meike either. That meant Motz was completely off the reservation. And Ebeling was using Motz's well-justified paranoia against him. That couldn't end well. In a cat-and-mouse game, the cat always won.

"If Hasani really is using AN-124s," Ritter said, "he *will* kill Beck." There was no question about that.

Meike gasped loudly.

Pohl's hand stopped. "He would kill a cop?"

"He already killed one," Ritter said grimly. "Call Ebeling! Get MEK to Casino Esplanade, now! A detective's life is in acute danger!" He brushed past Pohl and headed for the door.

Footsteps followed him down the hallway. As Meike ran up, Ritter stopped hammering the elevator button and hit the stairwell door. Her steps echoed his all the way down to the garage. The Eldorado was not in its spot.

"My car is over there!" Meike yelled.

Ritter followed her finger to a red Fiat. "Keys!" he yelled.

Without hesitating, she threw him an oversized ring.

Ritter caught it one-handed and found the right key without trouble. By the time Meike knocked on the passenger window, he had figured out that reverse was down. He popped open her door and ground the gearshift. She barely made it in before the tires smoked. After squealing up the curving ramp, Ritter badged the side window and floored it through the rising barrier.

As they hit the street, Meike put the blue light on the roof.

Ritter blocked her from hitting the siren. "We're going dark."

Meike pulled the light back in.

As Ritter's eyes adjusted to the darkness, he said, "You navigate."

"Take the next right," Meike said.

The Fiat accelerated into the turn.

FORTY-THREE

Red Light

Up ahead was Bahnhof Dammtor. Ritter realized they were retracing the drive he and Motz made earlier in the day. At the train bridge, Ritter made a sharp right that threw Meike into his right shoulder.

"There it is!" she said.

On the other side of the street, white tailfins stood up under a Cinemaxx sign. No unmarked van in sight. Where was Organized Crime when you needed them?

After checking the bus lane, Ritter turned the wheel hard to the left, throwing Meike against the passenger door, and then punched it across opposing traffic, barely missing the front bumper of a silver Audi. He slammed the brakes, bouncing them over the curb to a skidding stop on the wide plaza. Late-night revelers scattered. Behind them was a symphony of horns. Somebody yelled. Probably the Audi driver.

Meike rolled down her window and touched the hood of the Eldorado. "It's cold!" she said.

"Check the glove compartment!" Ritter said, edging the Fiat to the left to give her room.

"For what?" Meike said, squeezing out the door.

"His throw-down gun." Ritter hoped it wasn't still under the eight-tracks.

Meike stopped. "His what?"

"Just do it!" Ritter said.

Meike tried the passenger door of the Eldorado. It was locked. She ran around to the other side. She did a thumbs-up.

The driver's door was open.

Not a good sign, Ritter thought.

Meike leaned past the big steering wheel and out of view. A few seconds later, she reappeared, shaking her head.

Good, Ritter thought. Then Motz had a fighting chance.

Meike jumped back into the Fiat.

Ritter put it in gear and cleared more pedestrians from the sidewalk. Half a block later, he screeched to a halt outside Casino Esplanade. They both jumped out with guns drawn. The smokers loitering outside shrank back.

At the door, a beefy guard brought a cuff to his mouth. Before he could speak into it, Ritter's SFP9 hit the side of his chin, snapping his head to the right. Ritter leaned into him, letting him down onto the sidewalk.

Meike covered the scared civilians.

Running inside, Ritter hopped the turnstile and rushed the stairs. No one tried to stop him. Meike was right behind him.

From the roulette table, the croupier watched the armed couple. "Place your bets, ladies and gentlemen!" he said loudly. "Place your bets!"

Ritter hit the emergency exit and sprinted up the cement steps through musty air, bouncing off the walls at each turn. At the third landing, he yanked open a door. He heard Meike crash into it a few seconds later. He scanned the room and spotted a red-carpeted staircase just beyond the blackjack table. That must lead to Hasani's office. He raced over to it and bound up the plush stairs two at a time.

No one waiting at the top, just a dark stain outside the door. Ritter crouched down, touched the carpet, and sniffed. "Blood," he said.

A dozen steps below, Meike nodded but continued to cover their rear as she crept up backwards, panting heavily, both hands on her P6.

Ritter put his full weight behind the kick. The deadbolt splintered the doorframe. Nobody shot at him as he rolled across the threshold. He cleared the office. The big desk by the window had nothing on it but what appeared to be some dirt.

Meike was at the door now, still covering the stairs, still breathing hard.

Ritter spotted something under the desk. He went down on one knee. He came back up with a phone. A red light was blinking. "It's recording!" he said.

Meike nodded but kept her position.

Ritter hit Stop and Rewind.

So tell me, what's arriving on the Antonov. Heroin?

"That's Motz!" Meike said from the doorway.

I run a casino. I do not touch drugs. That would be illegal.

"That must be Hasani," Ritter said. He hit Fast Forward and then Play.

This isn't over.

You will excuse me. I am a busy man.

Not for long. Be seeing you.

There was a grunt, followed by a rush of air and a heavy thud. Then:

Where should we take him?

Progeco.

Ritter hit Stop. "Progeco? What's that?"

Meike had a bad look on her face. "An empty depot on Steinwerder. They repair old ship cargo containers."

Ritter didn't like what he was hearing. "Steinwerder? Isn't that where the forklift driver was killed?"

"Yes," Meike said. "He worked for Progeco." She looked sick.

Ritter checked the time on the recording. Twenty-three fifty-five hours. Five minutes to midnight, he thought grimly. "They left here almost an hour ago."

Meike's hand went to her mouth.

An empty container depot in the middle of the night would be the perfect spot to interrogate a cop, Ritter thought. He handed Meike the phone. "Let's go."

They flew down all four sets of stairs, riding the railings. When they hit the ground floor and ran past the roulette table again, they were greeted by more open mouths. The croupier calmly told the gawkers to place their bets.

Outside, the guard was leaning against the wall, nursing his swollen jaw.

Ritter ran up and grabbed him by the balls. "Where did they take him?"

The guard screamed. His voice was surprisingly high.

"Where?" Ritter said.

"Con–tain–er," the guard said.

Not good enough. Ritter's grip tightened.

"Pro–ge–co," the guard gasped.

"Which container?" Ritter said.

"Öz–türk." The guards swarthy face was glistening with sweat.

A Turkish container. That sounded right. Ritter wondered how many containers they would find at the depot. "Number," he snapped.

"Last–one–can't–miss." The guard said.

Ritter let go, flipped him around, slammed his face into the stone wall, and frisked him. He pocketed the gun, switchblade, and phone. Then he wrenched the guard's left arm into a half Nelson and frog-marched him to the Eldorado, where he handcuffed him to a door handle and kicked his legs out from under him. The guard ended up on his side, his face toward the rear tire.

Meike was backing toward them, her P6 covering the perimeter. She was wheezing loudly.

The smokers were gone.

Ritter and Meike ran to the Fiat and jumped in. Meike motioned to the wide intersection with her pigtails. "The harbor is on the left!"

Ritter bounced the Fiat onto Stephansplatz and used the intersection to make a wide U-turn through cross traffic, ending up on the right side of Esplanade, where they were met by more outraged horns.

Meike pulled out her phone and hit a number. "Herr Inspektionsleiter!" she yelled in a raspy voice. "They've got Motz—"

Ebeling must have interrupted.

"Change of address!" Meike said. "They've got him at a container depot on Steinwerder!"

Ritter weaved in and out of cars.

"Progeco!" Meike said, rolling with the curves. "A red Öztürk container. Hurry!"

Ritter passed a slow-moving wide load with blinking lights.

"And send a bus for Hasani's guard," Meike said.

Ritter felt her eyes on him.

"He's handcuffed to a white Eldorado in front of the casino," she said.

FORTY-FOUR

Itsy Bitsy Spider

A small spider struggled up the side of the container. At times, it was blocked by steel ribs ten times its height. Despite the obstacles, it soldiered on, over and under and on its way again. Motz admired its determination.

Something bit into his wrists. He struggled to adjust his weight. His wrists screamed. Then he remembered. He was already standing on his steel toes. If only he could reach the .38 in his boot. The thought was laughable now.

He looked up at the meat hook. He barely recognized the bloated paws in the handcuffs. He licked his lips and tasted blood. He wanted to think the worst was behind him, but he knew better.

"Tell us what we want to know, we kill you quickly," Hasani said.

Motz blinked back blood and squinted at the floodlight. It was partially blocked by two shadows, one big, one small. He blinked some more and made out a canister. A steel visor was sitting on top. A blowtorch.

Motz felt hot movement in his bowels. Dear God, please let me die with dignity, he thought. And please make it quick. "I'll tell you whatever you want to know," he said.

"You're more cooperative than your late partner," Hasani said.

"So Lars *was* right!" Motz barely recognized his own voice. His tongue felt like sandpaper. His heart was scraping his throat.

"About what?" Hasani said. He held something to his face.

"Afghan Gold," Motz croaked.

The something went away. "Go on."

"You're smuggling through Turkey."

"How?" Hasani sounded impatient.

The fucker was a regular lie detector, Motz thought. He had to play this straight, stick close to the truth. "*Antonov*. We're tracking it with GPS." At least they would be if he had told anybody but Pohl.

Hasani laughed. "GPS?"

Not a great lie, but Hasani seemed to believe it. "This time, the customs boys have got you," Motz said.

Hasani shook his head. "No, we have got you." His voice had an ugly edge. "What else do you know?"

"That you're an asshole." Motz's laugh caused him to sway painfully. There must be deep gashes in his wrists by now.

The big shadow blocked the light. Motz heard the blow before he felt it in his wrists. He gasped for breath that wasn't there. So much for telling the truth.

The big shadow was replaced by floodlight.

"What else?" Hasani said.

Motz finally got some air into his lungs. "Crates." The word just jumped into his head. He didn't know squat. It would be funny if it weren't for that blowtorch. Please, God, no.

"Crates?" Hasani wanted more.

Motz fought for time. "Yeah. Container." At least he could take shallow breaths again.

"What container?" Hasani sounded mildly concerned.

Good, Motz thought. That was at least something. "For shit."

The big shadow turned to Hasani. "He knows about the toilets."

"He does now," Hasani said.

"What?" Motz said. "You're shitting me." He ventured a laugh. "You're shipping heroin in shitters?"

Hasani stepped forward. "We tried copper pipes for drinking water." His tone was collegial, like they were two engineers discussing a workaround. "But those, how do you say, NGOs, got in the way."

Motz didn't feel the laugh in his wrists this time. "Let me get this right. You're shipping shit in shit?"

Hasani stepped closer. He had a sly look on his face. "Not exactly." He lowered his voice. "In portable toilets. I believe you call them Dixi. In Turkey, the Bundeswehr will load them into a container headed for Germany. That is thoughtful of them, no?"

Motz couldn't believe his luck. Well, under the circumstances. He had uncovered Hasani's real plan. Now all he needed was for Pohl to ignore his advice and call in the cavalry. That meant he had to slow this down. He began to hope again. "Gotta ask my shrink about that one," he said. "I'm sure she's got a name for it."

Hasani looked pained, like he was talking to a slow child. "If you were in Mazar-i Sharif, would you stick your head in a toilet?"

Motz felt a jolt of electricity. *Mar-mal.* "I would now," he said. Camp Marmal was in Mazar-i-Sharif. Lars tried to warn him as he died. He was talking about Hasani's big shipment.

"You're more stubborn than your partner," Hasani said. "The late Herr Hanson."

"Motherfucker!" Motz screamed. He tried to kick Hasani, but he was just out of range. The handcuffs rattled overhead. "You rat fuck bastard! You killed Lars!"

"I do not kill people," Hasani said calmly. "I have it done for me."

"For thirty thousand euros?" Motz said, spitting blood. "Jesus fucking Christ!"

"Debt is debt, interest is interest." Hasani sounded like an accountant with a bad head cold.

Motz couldn't believe it. All that talk about "honor" and "my people" meant nothing. Hasani was just a pencil pusher with heavy artillery and a cruel streak.

"The debt was naturally inherited by his next of kin," Hasani said.

Motz exploded. "You bastard! His wife had nothing to do with that!"

"Do not be so sure. Like you people say, a wife always knows."

"You touch her, I'll kill you!" Motz yelled, spitting more blood.

Hasani nodded to the big shadow. The floodlight went away.

Motz felt cold metal against his pounding temple.

"Any last words, Herr Kommissar?" Hasani said.

"Herr Kriminaloberkommissar to you, scumbag!" Motz screamed.

"Fine words for a headstone."

"Go to hell!"

"That is even better." Hasani nodded to his bodyguard.

The pressure disappeared from Motz's temple. The bodyguard holstered his gun.

Motz didn't know if that was good or bad.

"You make this too easy," Hasani said. He handed his bodyguard something with tape on the handle. Motz's backup gun.

"Son of a bitch!" Motz said. Apparently, Hasani's bodyguard was more thorough than Kaiser's.

The pressure was back on Motz's temple. This time, it wasn't so cold. The container was pounding in his ears.

A flicker caught the corner of his eye. It was the little spider, still making its painful way up the wall, its jerky walk keeping time with a familiar melody.

The itsy bitsy spiii-der,
climbed up the water SPOUT!

FORTY-FIVE

Extreme Prejudice

As the Fiat shot across Lombardsbrücke, the lights of the central business district glistened across the Alster River. Another postcard picture. Ritter wanted to puke. While rich shopkeepers slept in their soft beds, a lone terrified cop they would never meet was being worked over—or worse—by narco-terrorists.

When Ritter looked over, Meike just motioned for him to keep driving straight. She didn't even look up. She had a white cord in her ear. She was listening to the recording. He saw her stop and rewind a couple of times.

"Find anything else?" Ritter said.

Meike shook her head, still focused on the screen.

After they passed the central station, black moonlit clouds took over. Each time they crossed a bumpy iron bridge, Meike just motioned straight ahead.

At something called Kleiner Grasbrook, she told him to slow down and directed him through a tight right–left–right–left. The darkness was punctuated by shadowy outlines of cranes and containers. Bright moonlight glistened on oily water. That was all they needed, Ritter thought. Natural night vision goggles for Hasani's men.

Meike was checking a navigation app. "Right here," she said, pointing to the "Do Not Enter" sign. "We're almost there."

Ritter killed the lights. The Fiat crept through silvery darkness over what felt like train tracks. Squat shadows were replaced by bigger shadows stacked like firewood. *Last–one–can't–miss.*

"There!" Meike said, pointing through the windshield.

Ritter eased the car to a silent stop. At the edge of the water, narrow beams of light streamed out of the top container. Down below, Ritter made out two vehicles, with some figures smoking outside. "You stay here and wait for backup," he said.

Meike nodded.

Ritter got out and eased the door shut. After silently cocking his SFP9, he took scissor steps, Indian style, on gritty cement over to the nearest stack of containers. He ducked his head around the corner. On the other side was a glistening van. Next to it was a four-door Mercedes. He counted three red cigarette coals. He turned back to the car and held up one–two–three fingers.

Meike held up her phone. Good girl. She would call it in.

Ritter put his gun in his belt and slipped between two tight rows of containers. Twenty seconds later, he was on the far side of the cars. Hasani's men were talking in low guttural tones.

Ritter took three quick steps and wrenched the neck of the nearest, who dropped like a dead weight. The second reached behind his back. A swift crack to the windpipe stopped him. The third lunged at Ritter, his knife flashing in the moonlight. Ritter grabbed his hand, pivoted, flipped him over his head, and slammed him on the ground hard. He heard a sickening crack.

Ritter looked up at the light outlining the door to the container. A forklift held an empty pallet outside. He made out block letters. ÖZTÜRK.

Ritter began climbing the bottom container. After sacrificing a knuckle and shin on the second container, he pulled himself up to the light. The steel smelled sharp, like pepper. Something was clanging in the distance.

Inside, a weak voice was mumbling a children's song.

Da idsy bidsy spider climb ub da waderspoud

Ritter concentrated on his breathing. A familiar calm took over. Holding onto steel ribs with fingertips and toes, he shot his head into the half-open doorway.

A large target was holding a gun to Motz's head. A smaller one was off to the side.

Ritter reached for his belt and took a deep breath. In one fluid movement, he whipped his body into the doorway. Rolling to his feet, he lined up the soft part of the gunman's skull, just behind the ear, and squeezed. As the guy went down, Ritter shot him twice in the chest.

The other guy tried to run. He looked less arrogant than his file photo. Hasani.

"Give me an excuse, asshole," Ritter said. The clanging was getting louder.

Hasani stopped dead in his tracks. He looked at Ritter like a cornered animal.

"That's right," Ritter said. "You are fucked."

A laugh behind Ritter turned into a cough. Motz. Good. He was conscious and alert.

Hasani held up a white handkerchief.

Ritter took a step forward and side-kicked his knee, slamming him into rusty steel. Hasani howled in pain. The handkerchief floated to the ground.

Ritter looked down at Hasani's damaged face. The bright mark would soon be an ugly bruise. Blood and mucus dripped from his nose. His knee would never be the same.

"Law–yer," Hasani said, gasping. "It–is–law."

"You're looking at the law, asshole," Ritter said and casually kicked the bad side of his face.

Hasani screamed into the wall.

There was more coughing behind them.

"Game time's over, towel-head," Ritter said. He looked with disgust at the pink fluid on his boot. "How are you transporting? Dingos? Generators?"

"Shitters!" Motz yelled.

Ritter looked over his shoulder. "What?"

"Dixis!" Motz was panting with effort. "Headed–for–here!"

Ritter turned back. Hasani was trying to wipe his face with a soiled sleeve. "Toilets?" Ritter said. "Are you fucking kidding?"

"What–I–said!" Motz yelled.

Ritter heard vehicles skid to a stop outside and doors slide open. MEK was here. He knew the masked team leader was already giving hand signals. *Go, go, go!*

Ritter had to wrap this up *now*. He grabbed Hasani by the collar. "What's the serial number of the container?"

Hasani stared at him with hatred.

"Okay, asshole," Ritter said, stepping quickly to the blowtorch canister. "Been a while since I did this." The walls of the container were banging, but he had never felt calmer. That was probably a bad sign, but fuck it. He'd come this far on the low road, he might as well take it all the way.

Hasani pulled his legs up and tried to press himself into the wall.

Ritter adjusted the head strap and put on the faceguard. He picked up the welding gun and fired it up. White flame shot out.

Hasani struggled to his feet, a desperate look on his face.

Holding the flame away from his own body, Ritter wheeled the canister over to Hasani, kicked him onto his back, and slammed an Iron Ranger onto his neck. "Last chance, asshole."

Hasani panted like a dog, eyes wide with terror as the flame approached his face. He screamed out an eleven-digit ISO code, twice. Pink spittle splattered the faceguard.

Ritter committed the code to memory. "That wasn't so hard, was it?" he said and cut the gas.

He was rewarded with more coughing from the meat hook.

FORTY-SIX

Rat Squad

Rudi crouched down and examined the chest wounds. Two tight shots to the heart. Very professional. He rolled the heavy body with a grunt. Two clean exit wounds. "You find the bullets?"

"Three," the Forensics guy said. "All 9 mm." He held up three tagged bags.

Rudi grunted and let the body down to reexamine the first exit wound. There was a gaping hole where the left eye should have been. He turned the still-pliable head to the left. He stopped at the hole just behind the hairy ear and whistled. This was more than professional. He eased the head back to its previous position.

"The shots to the chest were superfluous," he said. "The head shot cut his motor control. Looks like an execution."

"A detective's life was in danger," the Forensics guy said. "There was no other way."

"I see," Rudi said. He took out a small tube of antacid tablets and shook two into his mouth. "Who fired the shots?"

"KHK Ritter."

Rudi stopped chewing. He would have sworn it was the special ops from MEK.

"Hasani had just ordered this guy"—the Forensics guy motioned to the body—"to execute Motz. Ritter took him out."

Somebody laughed outside.

Rudi looked down to the first ambulance. Ritter and Meike were talking quietly like old partners. "You're right, young man," he said finally. "It does look like self-defense."

■ ■ ■

After Meike went back to her car to "make some calls," Ritter watched Ebeling tell the flashing cameras to get behind the red-and-white tape. "That includes HHTV."

The HHTV reporter kept her eyes on Ebeling while she said something to her cameraman.

The cameraman nodded.

Nearby, paramedics were treating Hasani's bodyguards under the watchful eye of MEK. The wrists and ankles of each were plastic-cuffed to a gurney. All three had neck braces. One had an oxygen mask.

Ritter sincerely hoped the guy with the mask made it. The crack he heard must have been the guy's skull. Best case, the guy would be playing paraplegic basketball in prison. Better that than Ritter facing the rat squad for manslaughter.

Speaking of rats, MEK was leading Hasani to a blue-and-white van, his hands cuffed tightly behind his back. Ritter noted with grim satisfaction that Hasani's face was bleeding and badly bruised.

When Hasani tried to turn his damaged face from the cameras, an MEK glove held it in place. Lights flashed.

The HTTV cameraman gave his colleague a thumbs-up.

■ ■ ■

Ritter reached for the passenger door of the Fiat. He could see Meike fiddling with Motz's phone. Again. The one that should long be in an evidence bag.

"KHK Ritter?" a voice said. It wasn't friendly.

Ritter let go of the door handle. "Yes?"

Two gray suits were staring at him coldly. "We need to talk to you. Internal Affairs."

Well, that didn't take long, Ritter thought. "Yeah, I know, police-involved shooting."

"Among other things," the second suit said.

A door slammed. "What's going on?" Meike said.

The second suit continued staring at Ritter.

Hard shoes crunched gritty cement up to them. Ebeling. "Don't you have anything better to do that harass my detectives?" he said, glaring at the suits.

My detectives. Ebeling was nothing if not territorial, Ritter thought. Sometimes that came in handy.

"We need to talk to KHK Ritter," the first suit said. He seemed to be in charge.

Ebeling shook his head. "Not now."

The suit didn't argue. "Then tomorrow morning, eight o'clock sharp."

"Ten o'clock," Ebeling said. "With union representation."

"We need to talk to Beck and Voss as well," the suit said. "Especially Voss. She seems to have a special interest in secure federal databases."

Ritter saw Meike's pupils dilate. Apparently, all of them had secrets. Nobody on the squad seemed to color inside the lines.

"Tomorrow," Ebeling repeated. "Right now, real police officers have real police work to do."

"Ten o'clock." The suit turned on his heel. His assistant followed.

Ebeling patted Ritter on the arm. "Good job, Herr Kriminalhauptkommissar." He did the same with Meike. "See you both in about"—he pulled up his sleeve—"twenty-eight hours. You can brief me and your union reps before they arrive. Now get some rest. I'll take it from here."

Ritter nodded and got into the passenger side of the Fiat.

Meike climbed behind the wheel. As she maneuvered the car between MEK vans, she tooted the horn at Motz, who was being lifted into an ambulance.

Motz made a circular movement with his forefinger.

If Ritter wasn't mistaken, that meant rendezvous.

FORTY-SEVEN

Welcome to Hamburg

At the old Fischmarkt on the edge of the Elbe River, Motz, Meike, and Ritter greeted the morning sun on the wide hood of the Eldorado. Motz had checked himself out of the hospital—against the doctor's strict orders.

Like all homicide detectives, Meike knew it was important to celebrate victories immediately, before some bleeding-heart judge threw them away on a technicality. Still, the doctor was right. Motz looked like something the cat had dragged in.

His left eye was one big ugly mass of red and green and brown and blue and yellow. His lower lip had half a dozen stitches. White surgical tape showed at the wrists of his leather jacket. He was wheezing like Meike's emphysema-ridden *Opa*. They said he had three broken ribs. The damp harbor air couldn't be good for that. And alcohol probably didn't mix too well with the pain pills in his pocket. But that was the price of victory.

The three of them were holding small brown bottles of Flensburger and watching a container ship work its way up the harbor. The steel monster was being pulled by a small tugboat with a Hamburg flag in front of Dock 11.

Meike knew the hammering in the background was deafening up close. What sounded like distant gunshots were huge cargo containers slamming onto each other. Most of the cranes were now robots operated by computer. Her dad and uncles were the last of their breed at Blohm and Voss. Meike was the first Voss to work on the mainland.

Motz flipped the ceramic cap of his bottle back and forth on its aluminum leash. It clattered against the brown glass. "How did Hasani get the heroin into the toilets?" he said.

"The toilets are loaded by trusted Afghanis in Mazar-i-Sharif," Ritter said.

"Bribery?"

"No, the Taliban holds their families hostage."

Meike remembered the graphic footage she'd seen in a TV documentary awhile back. Wild dogs picking at mutilated bodies. Yuck.

"So what happens in Turkey?" Motz said.

"The Bundeswehr loads the containers onto commercial cargo ships to Germany," Ritter said.

"How did Hasani manage that?"

"A truck drives the container to a subcontractor for cleaning and storage," Ritter said.

Yummy, Meike thought. Another great image to greet the day.

"But they never get there," Motz said.

"Exactly," Ritter said. "Hasani arranged to have them hijacked and rerouted to Steinwerder."

"When?" Motz said.

"In two weeks," Ritter said and took a swig of beer.

"How do you know all this?"

"Used to be in the Bundeswehr," Ritter said behind his bottle.

Motz gave him a hard look. "So was I. That's pretty thin."

"I've got a good contact with Air Traffic Control in Frankfurt."

Meike smiled. Ritter must have called Brigadier General Daddy this morning.

Ritter took another swig.

"Your contact told you all that?" Motz said.

"Yeah, we're like *this*." Ritter held up two crossed fingers.

Meike decided it was time to spring her first surprise. "You'll never guess what Forensics found in Hasani's safe."

"I give," Motz said. "Heroin?"

Meike enjoyed the drumroll in her head. "Documents from Senator Althaus."

"No shit?" Motz said, the bottle halfway to the stitches on his puffy lip.

"No shit," Meike said. "We wondered why he gave a work permit to the widow's tennis instructor."

"We did?" Motz said.

"Part of my alibi check," Meike said. "Anyway, Ebeling just tipped off Organized Crime. They've putting Althaus under observation."

Motz put down the bottle and pulled a small plastic bottle out of his pocket. "That mean Althaus won't be the new boss?"

"I wouldn't be too sure about that," Meike said, watching him dry-swallow a couple more pills. "Ebeling seems to like the idea."

"Because he would have something over his new boss," Motz said.

"*Exactamundo.*"

"Isn't that called extortion?"

"Ebeling calls it managing your manager," Meike said.

"He would know."

■ ■ ■

Meike nudged Ritter playfully. "We know what you did last night."

The two of them were finishing their second beer. Motz seemed to have given up on his first. The bottle was sunning itself on the hood next to his beefy leg. Dry blood had crusted on the worn black leather.

Ritter's face went blank.

"That your girlfriend?" Meike had spotted the blonde on the pedestrian bridge a few minutes before. Her eyes had jumped to the turquoise moped for no reason. That meant the girl had been looking at her. Now she was pretending to look at her phone.

"What?" Ritter said.

Meike pointed to the bridge.

Ritter glanced up and grimaced. "Neighbor girl. Long story."

"We've got time." Meike jumped down, put away the empties, and grabbed two more. This was going to be fun.

Two bottle caps popped in succession.

Ritter took a short drink. "Physical therapist."

"Uh-huh." As in full body massage, Meike thought. "Would you like to talk about it?"

"Not really," Ritter said. "Need to know."

Meike giggled extravagantly, putting on a good show for the blonde up on the bridge.

"Oh, that reminds me," Motz said. He pulled a crumpled piece of paper from his pocket with a grunt of pain and handed it to Ritter. "Excuse the blood."

"More evidence?" Ritter said.

"Optometrist bill," Motz said. "Ray-Bans don't pay for themselves."

Meike laughed. She had forgotten all about Ritter breaking Motz's shades. That felt like a lifetime ago.

"Oh that," Ritter said sheepishly. "You take a check?"

"Nope, just cash or casino chips," Motz said.

Meike sighed. After all the trouble she had taken to clean Motz's phone. *You just got your fifty thousand.* Internal Affairs would have had a field day with that one. And here he was, a few hours later, all cocky. It was like he wanted Ritter to know.

Meike's phone rang. "Ebeling" was flashing on the screen. She jumped down off the hood again. "Herr Inspektionsleiter," she said.

"The office of the accountant for Kaiser Enterprises burned down last night," Ebeling said. "Arson. Organized Crime is investigating."

Meike nodded. "This the same accountant Hasani uses?"

Motz and Ritter stopped talking.

"Yes," Ebeling said. "You knew about that?"

"Yes," Meike said. "You told us at the strategy meeting last night." Not for the first time, she wondered about Ebeling's bad memory. That was the problem with his endless mind games. They tied his brain in knots.

"Well, then you both know more than Organized Crime." Ebeling sounded miffed.

So much for all that "good job" talk on Steinwerder. Good thing Miss Meike knew how to manage her manager. "I'm sure they'll be grateful to hear that from you, sir."

"Inform Ritter when you see him," Ebeling said and hung up. Meike did the same.

"Our fearless leader?" Motz said.

"*Correctamundo*," Meike said. She pocketed the phone and jumped back on the hood. "Kaiser's tax guy got firebombed last night."

"Good move," Motz said, looking at the hood like he was worried about a dent. "Hit Hasani while he's down. Guess Willi's been taking his iron tablets."

Ritter thought that was funny.

Meike didn't. She wasn't *that* heavy. Besides, Motz was *way* too comfortable with the gangster. "Why would Kaiser firebomb his own accountant?" she said.

"Because he was feeding information to Hasani," Motz said, like it was the most obvious thing in the world.

"That would be a reason," Ritter said.

"Willi's the impulsive type," Motz said. Then he sat bolt upright, almost knocking over his beer. "No, he's not. He knew Organized Crime was watching the accountant, not his office." Motz was holding his side, like his taped ribs regretted the quick movement.

Meike completed his thought. "Which means Kaiser is

watching Organized Crime."

Ritter started laughing again.

"What?" Meike said, annoyed. Arson wasn't a joke. Someone could have been seriously hurt or killed.

"You fish-heads sure know how to have a good time," Ritter said, holding up his bottle.

Meike stared at him for a moment and then broke into a big grin. She grabbed her bottle and clinked it against his. "Welcome to Hamburg!" she said.

Motz did the same. "Partner."

While Meike and Ritter drank deeply, Motz rinsed his molars with beer.

The foghorn of a container ship filled the air. "ASIA DAWN" was stenciled on the maroon hull steaming out of the harbor. Half a dozen seagulls circled something in the water. It smelled like rain.

Epilogue

With one quick movement, POK Pohl cut through the red seal on the door to Haus 7b. He clapped his knife shut.

"Thank you, sir!" Anita said. "I appreciate it." She really meant it. Seven long days they had been shut down. In that time, the flood of gawkers had become a trickle. The worst moment in their history was also their best advertisement. Murder sells. Everybody wanted to see the "torture chamber" where the "top cop" was killed.

"Anytime," Pohl said to her breasts. "So what are you going to do now?"

"Like I always say, make it go away with work." Anita gave Pohl a winning smile and turned the lock over twice. The door sprung open. She pushed it to the wall and kicked the rubber wedge into place.

"You'll knock 'em dead," Pohl said. "The rubbernecks will be lining up any minute."

"Thanks again for the siren," Anita said. "That woke up half of St. Pauli." She breathed in stale ashtray fumes. The place really needed an airing out.

"Just doing my job," Pohl said with a grin.

Maybe he was, Anita thought. In St. Pauli, everybody was running a scam, even the cops. Pohl was her new best friend. She'd have to keep an eye on that.

"Well, I'll let you get to it," Pohl said, tipping his duty cap.

"Maybe I'll put on my old latex," Anita said with a wink. "Lead tours of the Black Room."

Pohl grinned again. "You're always at your best in a crisis."

Anita jutted her hip at him. "Who asked you, slave?"

Pohl's laugh was deep and dirty.

. . .

A few hours later, they were ready for their grand reopening. The girls were punctual. Magda was first. Her customary black was especially fitting. She was followed by Tanja, who was *wearing* prayer beads. Chantal and Angelique appeared hand in hand. All of them knew their jobs were on the line. A whole week without work concentrated the mind.

Tanja was in Cage 1, signing autographs for a line of eager customers. Christal and Angelique were doing mother–daughter in Cage 3, like always. Magda's uncle was repairing the window to Cage 4. They had turned Cage 2 into a memorial, with framed portraits of Veronica and Mertens on chairs. Both were draped with black sashes that said: "We Will Never Forget."

With the others settled in, Anita took Magda up to the Black Room. "There's a first time for everything," she said. "My first time was the day Dominica, God rest her soul, went into early retirement and started doing social work."

At the mention of the legendary domina, Magda crossed herself.

Anita liked that. She had already decided to keep Magda in her black veil, impossibly small black velvet dress, black fishnet stocking, and black over-knee boots. Magda had even put Tanja's prayer beads between her own silky breasts. The Polish girl was a natural-born talent.

Anita walked her over to the cross. "This is what everybody is here to see." She marveled at the thoroughness of Magda's aunt. She had Lysoled down the room twice and then placed incense from St. Theresien's in one of those red-glass eternal light things hanging from three brass chains. The whole place smelled like frankincense. The johns were going to go crazy over that. Like Veronica use to say: *It's all about details.* Anita was surprised to hear herself sob.

Magda put her hand on the *Puffmutter's* shoulder. "We're all in this together," she said. The black rings under her eyes looked like deep sorrow. Anita figured charcoal, smudged with her finger. The girl was a marketing genius. Two thousand years of wisdom in a twenty-seven-year-old body that could raise the dead. Still, there was only one way to find out for sure.

"I want you to strap me in," Anita said.

Without hesitation, Magda grabbed Anita's right wrist firmly. She closed the velvet-lined shackle before Anita knew what was happening. Then she did the same to Anita's left wrist, brushing her breasts against Anita's. Her breath was peppermint, her hair Ivory soap. She was whispering the whole time in Polish.

Anita found herself strangely aroused.

"This will be our little secret," Magda said, this time in German. She looked sad but understanding.

Anita remembered her intimate encounter with a young nun in reform school. *The spirit is willing, but the flesh is weak.* It had been decades since she had thought about that.

Magda's thick black hair was now brushing Anita's inner thighs as she shackled one ankle, then the other. She all but licked Anita's nipples on the way back up. "Just relax," Magda said. "Sister Magdalena will take care of everything."

Sister Magdalena. This girl is a goldmine, Anita thought. She decided to call their new service "Polish Inquisition." She wondered if her carpenter could replicate the altar of St. Theresien's. He might have to downsize a bit to stay on budget, but antique church furniture was a must-have.

※　※　※

Clambering onto the blue-and-white Wasserschutzpolizei boat was a piece of cake for Laura, even with the goddamn handcuffs. The uniformed cops "helped" her, making sure to squeeze and pinch her hot ass. The pervs had probably seen her show. Konny said the crowds were lined up around the block these days. Laura cleared a serious loogie over the side.

One guy on board definitely had seen her show. Ritter. The fucker was leaning against a railing like he owned the place, cleaning his fingernails with a goddamn pocketknife.

Laura massaged her temple. The bruise in the mirror was barely visible now, but she'd never forget that sucker punch. Or the kung fu shit behind her knee. She had to try that one out the next time some numb nuts got in her way.

Laura bummed a cigarette off the fat perv. Marlboro Lights. Like that would help the fat fuck's beer gut. Grow some balls, buddy. Be a man—like me. She cackled smoke through her nose and mouth. Shit tasted good after seven days of withdrawals. She could have mooched something real in U-Haft, but they kept her in isolation, and the guards were assholes. She knew they spit in her rations. "Cop killer," they said.

Today was her first shower in a week. And Kaiser's pencil dick lawyer didn't answer her calls. Probably died of old age. She cackled again and threw the butt overboard.

Ritter was staring at her. She stared back. What'cha gonna do, copper? Arrest me for littering?

Hardass probably didn't like her laughing. She *was* supposed to be a black widow and all. Better watch that shit.

The pervs finally pushed off. Their sorry-ass little police boat chugged out of the wannabe harbor. Thing had a wooden dock. Fucking pathetic little backwater. She'd have to tell Konny about that.

Originally, Laura demanded a burial at sea off Ibiza, last wishes, all that shit. But the fuckers said no, like she knew they would. Then she "compromised," as Veronica would say, and said St. Peter Ording, a mainland shithole full of loser breeders. The pervs probably took their ugly wives there. Nothing but hetero nature-freak families with scraggily feet who walked around the mud and dug up shit. The dipwads all had dirty glasses. Just because you were butt ugly didn't mean you got off on butt ugly, did it?

Still, it was a fucking brilliant move, if she did say so her own self. The mud beach was an easy swim—and just this side of the Danish border. Laura started to laugh again but turned it into another loogie. Duck and dive, smoke and mirrors. Now you see me, now you fucking don't.

Ritter was working on his other hand with the knife. Good for him. Get nice and cleaned up for your morning swim, copper.

The boat started rocking. Waves. They were getting close to Dogpatch. Just a final goodbye to the Elbe River—and showtime!

The boat was slapping the water hard now. Laura had to hold on to the railing. "Yahoo!" she yelled into the wind. Oops. That wasn't real black widowy. She looked around quickly.

The guards were in that caboose thing up front. Ritter was crouched down, studying the ash pot. Probably trying to find a secret compartment with a gun inside. Clever fuck thought his shit didn't stink. Laura's cackle was lost in the wet wind. Fuck 'em. This was *her* show.

The wind felt good in her hair. She tried to brush it out of her eyes, but only scraped her nose with the cuffs. Whatever. At least she was outside that U-Haft shithole.

When they were in line with the mud beach, somebody cranked back the engine, sending them into a wide U-turn. Something flashed in the dunes above the beach. Peeking from the tall grass was a glistening green spoiler. Her baby! She knew Konny was watching through binoculars. Yes!

There was something going on outside the caboose. Ritter was on his feet, ash pot under his arm, making his way toward her, one hand on the rail.

Laura turned to meet him, steadying herself against the flagpole. She accepted the pot with both hands. It was lighter than she expected. Veronica in a can. Un-fucking-real. Above her head, a seagull cried out, like it was in pain. Her eyes burned.

"It's time," Ritter said, touching her arm.

Got that right, motherfucker. Laura let him turn her around, toward the water. She looked over her shoulder and raised her wrists. It was a question.

Ritter motioned to the pervs.

The fat fuck appeared at Laura's side with a shitload of keys and a nicotine trail. Insensitive asshole. She really, really needed another hit. It took the dickless wonder a long time to find the right key.

Laura tensed.

The first cuff clicked open. Then the other. Freedom!

Hugging the flagpole with her thighs, Laura moved the pot to her left arm, popped the lid, and handed that to the fat fuck. Then she swung around the pole—and threw the ashes into his face.

The open mouth on his ash face was fucking priceless. She was laughing hard as she let go of the pole and fell backwards into the cold water.

She swam deep and fast, expecting the *ping–ping–ping* of bullets on the surface. That Ritter fucker was dangerous. He might even be in the water behind her right now.

Her lungs burning, Laura broke the surface and swam like a motherfucker. It was only a hundred yards now. Even Ritter couldn't make up for her lead.

Laura stumbled onto the beach and ran for her life, her sneakers sucking up mud with each step. Up ahead was a blur of uglies and umbrellas. In the dunes behind all that, headlights flashed. Laura's jeans made a whipping sound as she sprinted up to the sandy street.

A wide green door with white piping swung open.

Laura dove inside.

The Charger burned rubber.

Out the window, Laura saw the police boat still in place, like nothing had happened. She could have sworn Ritter was waving a phone. Like roadblocks would stop them now.

Something flew into Laura's face. She caught it with a downward slap and turned it over. "My monkey ball!"

"Thought I forgot, didn't cha?" Konny said with a grin.

"You rule!" Laura said, slapping the ball back and forth between her palms.

Konny didn't dick around, just pedal to metal through ugly breeders diving for cover. "Got us a tricked-out Dodge Ram!" she yelled. "V8, one ninety-five PS, and a fucking sunroof!"

"Clean plates?" Laura yelled back.

"Got that right! And no fucking APS!"

"Fuck-n-A!" Laura gave Konny a high five and then went back to slapping her ball happily.

"We got fresh paper waiting for us on the other side," Konny said as they hit the main road.

"Denmark rules!"

"Fuck yeah!" Konny said. "New passports and one-way tickets to Havana!"

The slapping stopped. "How you rig that?" Copenhagen Angels didn't do nothing for free. They were the ones charged Konny top euro for those bulk shipments.

"Sold 'em my business," Konny said. "Well, both of 'em."

Laura's scalp tingled. "Got any?"

"Pope shit in the woods?" Konny slammed on the brakes.

A silver Dodge Ram glistened in the sunlight just ahead.

Laura jumped out and ran up to it. "I'm gonna lose my mind! A tinted fucking sunroof!"

"And your medicine," Konny said. She pulled herself up into the driver's seat and fired up the V8. "Should I Stay or Should I Go" blasted from the door panel.

Laura dove onto Konny's lap, kissed her full on the lips and tongued her tonsils, St. Pauli style. That done, she snuggled into Konny's monster tits, her monkey ball in her fist. Finding a new baby on a desert island would be a snap.

List of characters

Lars Hanson
> Lead homicide detective with gambling problem who has mysterious motorcycle accident while investigating Sulejman Hasani at Casino Esplanade. Close to Motz Beck.

Dietmar ("Motz") Beck
> Bad-tempered homicide detective with deep scars. Born and raised in St. Pauli bar. Drives Harley and vintage Eldorado taken from pimp. Close to Lars Hanson, Ralf Pohl, and Willi Kaiser.

Thomas Ritter
> Too-good-to-be-true homicide detective from Frankfurt with blocked personnel file. Former special operator in Afghanistan who beds girls half his age. Close to Frankfurt police chief.

Heinz Rosenfeld
> Frankfurt police chief. On trial for torturing pedophile kidnapper of young boy. Arranges Thomas Ritter's silent transfer to Hamburg with head of Homicide Division.

Meike Voss
> Voluptuous homicide detective. Daughter of dock worker. Weakness for computer hackers and male coworkers.

Dr. Klaus Ebeling
> Head of Homicide Division. Blue blood from old Hanseatic trading family. Adapts to shifting winds at City Hall. Political animal with convenient memory lapses.

Dr. Dr. Rüdiger ("Rudi") Deichmann
> Cigar-chomping coroner. Cross between grandfather and butcher. First "Dr." is for internal medicine, second for pathology. "Rudi" is for tenure as coach of prison soccer team.

Ralf Pohl
> Rough-and-tumble street cop in St. Pauli who knocks heads. Knows where bodies are buried. Close to Motz Beck.

Vladimir Netsky
> Computer hacker in Frankfurt who does favors for Meike Voss in exchange for sex. Under observation by federal police.

CRIMINALS

Wilhelm ("Willi") Kaiser
> Old-school "King of St. Pauli." Rules red-light district with iron fist. Took over bar from Motz Beck's father in return for "protection." Archenemy of Sulejman Hasani.

Sulejman Hasani
> Albanian mobster who imports heroin from Afghanistan and launders money in casino. Taking over St. Pauli. Allied with Senator Althaus. Archenemy of Willi Kaiser and Motz Beck.

Mustafa Hasani
> Sulejman Hasani's young nephew. Delivers mob packages. Favors gelled hair and sharkskin suits. Terrified of his uncle.

Veronica Lühmeyer
> Ambitious domina who crucifies top politicians for big money in Black Room of Herbertstrasse 7b. Former live sex performer at The Cage. Registered nurse. Pre-med.

Laura Wesselmann
> Veronica Lühmeyer's girlfriend. Adds tattoo every anniversary of their first meeting on Ibiza. Live sex performer at Cage in St. Pauli. Long rap sheet. Close to Konny.

Konny
> Laura Wesselmann's former cellmate. Owns body shop in St. Pauli. Sells crystal meth on side. Close to Hells Angels Copenhagen.

Anita Krenz
> Madame at Herbertstrasse 7b. Works for Willi Kaiser. Takes care of "her" girls.

Frederic Silbereisen
> Anita Krenz's slimy Viennese "gofer." Picks up tax forms from front office. Delivers blackboard chalk and XL enemas to Black Room.

Tanja, Magdalena, Chantel, and Angelique
    Anita's day-shift girls, who give new meaning to "customer service." Standard packages include Daddy's Little Girl, Mommy Dearest, Doc Proc, Yellow Rain, and Polish Inquisition.

Stefan Vollbert
    Sleazy lingerie salesman from Frankfurt. Sells translucent bikinis to Anita's day-shift girls. Witness to fleeing killer in Haus 7b.

POLITICIANS

Carsten Mertens
    Squeaky-clean ruling-party Innensenator. Wants to turn Herbertstrasse into national monument. Good customer in Black Room. Close to Willi Kaiser and Helen Patch.

Charlotte Mertens
    Perfect wife of Carsten Mertens. Former model with weakness for horses, gin, and Italian tennis instructors. Tolerates husband's monthly visits to female "therapist."

Andreas Scherf
    Carsten Mertens' driver. Former underage "film star" with sealed police record. Former page of Senator Althaus. Close to boss of Sex Workers United.

Hans-Dieter Althaus
    Choleric opposition-party senator with ties to Sulejman Hasani. Wants to tear down whorehouses in Herbertstrasse and transform it into high-tech business park named "Silicon Alley."

Helen Patch
    Obese chain-smoking boss of Sex Workers United. Introduced Carsten Mertens to his domina, Veronica Lühmeyer. Close to Mertens' driver, Andreas Scherf.

Norbert Grube
    Manager of HansaBank, private financial institute near City Hall. Straw-man owner of Herbertstrasse 7b for Willi Kaiser. Unwilling business partner of Sulejman Hasani.

List of terms

110

> Emergency number of police across Germany. Analogous to 911 in U.S.

Abitur

> Qualification conferred by university-preparatory schools on students who pass final exams at end of secondary education, usually after twelve or thirteen years of schooling.

Amis

> Plural. German slang (usually friendly) for Americans.

Antonov

> 1. Russian container ship tracked by German law enforcement from Turkey to Hamburg. Suspected of transporting Afghani Gold for Sulejman Hasani. 2. Russian AN-124 transport plane used by Bundeswehr to transport everything but weapons and computers from Afghanistan to Germany.

BKA

> *Bundeskriminalamt.* Federal Criminal Police. German equivalent of FBI. Source of Klaus Ebeling's intelligence on Sulejman Hasani, head of Albanian mob in Hamburg.

BND

> *Bundesnachrichtendienst.* Federal Intelligence Agency. German equivalent of CIA. Database is hacked by Vladimir Netsky at request of Meike Voss, who is investigating Thomas Ritter.

Bundeswehr

> United military force of Germany. Established in 1950. Lars Hanson, Motz Beck, Thomas Ritter, and Sulejman Hasani have deep—and conflicting—ties to Bundeswehr.

Cage, The

> Live-sex theater in St. Pauli. Former machine factory with iron cage for female "combatants." Former workplace of Veronica Lühmeyer. Current workplace of Laura Wesselmann.

Casino Esplanade
: Casino owned by Sulejman Hasani, who launders money from penthouse office overlooking blackjack tables. Scene of confrontations with Lars Hanson and Motz Beck.

ComVor
: Database for tracking police officers. As Meike Voss discovers, Thomas Ritter's record is sealed because of his covert work for GSG-9 in Afghanistan.

Davidwache
: Police Precinct 15. Located on Reeperbahn, main street of red-light district of St. Pauli. Smallest—and busiest—precinct in Hamburg. Home to Ralf Pohl.

Fischmarkt
: Fish market on Elbe River. Where night owls and early birds barter for fresh fish every Sunday morning. Rendezvous point for Thomas Ritter, Motz Beck, and Meike Voss.

fish-head
: *Fischkopp.* Slang for person from Northern Germany in general and Hamburg in particular.

Grundschule
: Grammar school. Motz Beck's former third-grade teacher at Grundschule St. Pauli catches him in act of robbing grave in Hanson family plot in Diebsteich Cemetery.

GSG-9
: *Grenzschutzgruppe 9.* Border Protection Group 9 of Federal Police for hostage rescue operations. Conducted joint operations with FBI in Afghanistan in 2001.

Hahnöfersand
: Women's prison on island outside Hamburg. Where Laura Wesselmann met Konny.

HAM-Int
: Psychology test for medical school applicants at UKE who have passed HAM-Nat. Veronica Lühmeyer is invited to take HAM-Int as final step toward acceptance in medical school.

HAM-Nat
: Test of medically relevant aspects of math, physics, chemistry, and biology for medical school applicants at UKE. Test scores are found by police in Black Room.

Herbertstrasse
> Legendary gated street in St. Pauli with wall-to-wall whore-houses. If declared national monument, as proposed by Innen-senator Mertens, houses cannot be torn down. Main crime scene.

HH
> *Hansestadt Hamburg.* Hanseatic city-state of Hamburg. Former member of Hanseatic League, formed by merchant guilds, or *Hanse*, in Northern Europe between twelfth and seventeenth centuries.

HHTV
> Local TV station in Hamburg that follows killing in Herbertstrasse closely. Thorn in side of Klaus Ebeling, head of Homicide Division.

Innensenator
> Senator for Interior. Analogous to interior minister. Ultimate boss of police. Carsten Mertens is Innensenator of Hamburg.

Inspektionsleiter
> Chief of Detectives. Rank held by Klaus Ebeling, who heads Homicide Division.

Justiz
> Judicial authority. Guards at pre-detention facility where Veronica Lühmeyer, Laura Wesselmann, and Frederic Silbereisen are held have "JUSTIZ" stenciled on uniforms.

KDD
> *Kriminaldauerdienst.* On-Call Services. Normally first responder to emergency 110 police calls.

KHK
> *Kriminalhauptkommissar.* Lead Detective. Rank held by Lars Hanson and Thomas Ritter.

KOK
> *Kriminaloberkommissar.* Detective. Rank held by Motz Beck and Meike Voss.

LKA 411
> Landeskriminalamt 411. Homicide Division of Polizei Hamburg. Contains six squads of five detectives. Includes Klaus Ebeling, Thomas Ritter, Motz Beck, and Meike Voss.

Luftwaffe
> German Air Force. Reestablished in 1956 as part of Bundeswehr.

MEK

Mobileinsatzkommando. Mobile deployment command. German equivalent of SWAT. Commandos from this unit storm container on Steinwerder.

moin

Low German greeting common in Northern Germany, particularly in working-class districts like St. Pauli. Can be used any time of day.

MOPO

Hamburger Morgenpost. Local tabloid with screaming headlines that are usually accurate. Secondary source of news for residents of St. Pauli. Primary source is extensive rumor mill.

Mordkommission

Homicide Division. Sometimes used to designate homicide squads, like that formed by Thomas Ritter, Motz Beck, Meike Voss, and two other detectives. Hamburg has six such squads.

Motz

Nickname for Dietmar Beck derived from "*motzen*," which means to complain. On seeing nickname, Thomas Ritter knows his new partner is complainer.

P6

SIG Sauer P6. Standard handgun used by Hamburg police officers like Motz Beck and Meike Voss. Variant of P225, which has tighter trigger pull.

POK

Polizeioberkommissar. Police Sergeant. Rank of Ralf Pohl from Davidwache in St. Pauli.

POLAS

Police Information System. Police database used to track criminals. Meike Voss uses database to connect Sulejman Hasani and Willi Kaiser with known associates.

Polizeipräsident

Chief of Police. Rank of Rosenfeld, Thomas Ritter's former boss, on trial in Frankfurt for torturing twice-convicted pedophilic kidnapper to find young boy before he suffocates to death.

Polizeipräsidium

Police headquarters. Footprint of mammoth building in Alsterdorf matches twelve-point star on Hamburg street cops' caps. Home to ten thousand cops.

Polizeischule

Police academy. Two-and-a-half-year police training program completed by Motz Beck and Meike Voss.

Puffmutter

Slang for whorehouse madame. *Puff* is whorehouse. *Mutter* is mother.

Reeperbahn

Main street of red-light district of St. Pauli. In eighteenth century, thousand-meter-long street was used to stretch and weave rope for ship masts. Today, street is called "sinful mile."

Santa Fu

JVA Fühlsbüttel. Maximum security prison. After wartime tenure as concentration camp, went back to housing Hamburg's hardest criminals. Coroner Rudi Deichmann is former coach of inmate soccer team.

SERE

Survival, Evasion, Resistance, and Escape program for U.S. military personnel considered to be at high risk of capture. As GSG-9 commando, Thomas Ritter had SERE training at Bagram Air Base in Afghanistan.

SFP9-SF

Heckler & Koch Striker-Fired Pistol 9 – Special Forces. Short trigger reset favored by special ops, like GSG-9 veteran Thomas Ritter.

St. Pauli

Red-light district at edge of Hamburg Harbor. Services foreign sailors and "respectable" citizens.

Steinwerder

Island on Elbe River opposite St. Pauli. Built on rubble from Great Fire of 1842. Today, used to refurbish ship containers. Where Sulejman Hasani conducts hands-on interrogations.

U-Haft

Untersuchungshaft. Pre-trial detention facility. Where Veronica Lühmeyer, Laura Wesselmann, and Frederic Silbereisen are held.

VERTRAUEN

"TRUST." Word tattooed across Laura Wesselmann's hard pecs.

Wäsche-Engel
>Angel Cleaners. Old shop in St. Pauli that cleans sheets and towels for whorehouses in Herbertstrasse. Former owner is in rest home with Motz Beck's mother.

Wehrmacht
>Unified armed forces of Nazi Germany from 1935 to 1945. Like members of motorcycle gangs, Motz Beck wears Wehrmacht helmet as protest against motorcycle helmet law.

Acknowledgements

Many thanks to Kriminalhauptkommissar (KHK) Holger Vehren of the Polizei Hamburg for showing me around the Präsidium and patiently answering too many questions about police procedures, technologies, vehicles, and weapons.

Special thanks to KHK Ralf Evers, KHK Gundi Evers, "Balu" (RIP), and the crew of the Polizei Minden-Lübbecke for their hospitality, fingerprinting, interrogation, and target practice.

Finally, a big thank you to my editor, Chris Rhatigan, for holding my feet to the fire until I got my story straight.

Made in United States
North Haven, CT
11 September 2022

23990335R00168